RETURN TO BERMONDSEY

CHRIS WARD

RETURN TO BERMONDSEY

CHRIS WARD

2016 Chris Ward

All rights reserved

The right of Chris Ward to be identified as the author of the work has been asserted by him in accordance with the Copyright, Designs and Patents act 1988.

No part of this publication may be reproduced, stored in a retrieval system, or transmitted, in any form or by any means without the prior written permission of the publisher, nor be otherwise circulated in any form of binding or cover other than that in which it is published and without a similar condition being imposed on the subsequent purchaser.

ISBN – 10: 1519273614

ISBN – 13: 978 – 1519273611

This book is a work of fiction. Any similarity between the characters and situations within its pages and places or persons, living or dead, is unintentional and coincidental.

My love and thanks go to my dear wife Helen who spent many hours editing the book.

CHAPTER 1

Saturday the fifth of June was a magnificent evening at the Bolton mansion. The stars were shining and the entire marquee was brilliantly lit with beautiful shimmering coloured lights; the birthday cake was an exquisite four-tier, white and pink affair with hundreds of multi-coloured miniature flowers decorating it. It was huge as it had to feed the two hundred odd well-dressed party guests. Fifty-four year old Paul Bolton had pushed the boat out to celebrate his only daughter's eighteenth birthday. Katie Bolton was a stunner; she was tall, five feet eight, slim with bright blue eyes, full bosomed and long blonde hair. She was dressed in a sensational flowing white chiffon dress and was standing behind the massive cake, her right hand wrapped daintily around a lengthy elaborate presentation silver knife protruding out of the cake, pretending to cut it.

There must have been thirty guests vying for the best vantage point to get the perfect photograph. Flashbulbs were exploding which added even more razzmatazz to the almost Hollywood atmosphere. The music was blaring from a live band, and there was a mighty roar as Paul grabbed Katie's other hand and proudly put an arm around her shoulders. He looked around the vast almost magical marquee decorated in cream and beige and held his hand up; a hush descended on the crowd and the band.

"Welcome everybody!"

There was another huge cheer accompanied by clapping and whooping. Katie was laughing, curtseying and bowing and was in her element, the star of the show.

"Thank you for joining us tonight and helping us to celebrate our daughter's eighteenth birthday. Katie can already drive, she can now vote, AND legally, she can now enter a licensed premises, better known as a pub."

One of Katie's friends shouted from the front, "She's been going to pubs for years!"

Cue more laughter and whistles.

Paul had to wait while the noise abated. "No doubt Katie expects even more freedom than she enjoys now."

Katie nodded her head vigorously shouting, "Yes! Yes! Yes!"

"But I have to warn her that while she's still under my roof, and even though she is eighteen, I am still the boss, and will be taking a VERY keen interest in any young men I see hanging around, so be warned." He looked down at Katie with mock sternness. He adjusted and loosened his TM Lewin red and white striped tie. "Now, on a more serious note..." There was now complete quiet in the marquee.

"Nobody could have a lovelier, more caring, sweet, intelligent daughter than us." There were shouts of approval from the guests and Katie became a little emotional.

For a brief moment, Paul allowed his mind to wander to happy memories: Little Katie dressed as a princess with her magic wand and rushing up to him happily and shouting "Daddy!" "Daddy!" "Daddy!" whenever he came in the front door from work; tears filled his eyes and then he got a grip of himself.

"And although I would like to take all the credit for that, I cannot," Paul continued. "Lexi, come up here please!" He beckoned his wife forward to join him. Lexi was looking amazing in a pink figure hugging dress. Paul kissed her and put his other arm around her shoulder.

"My wife Lexi, the love of my life and the person responsible for our children turning out so well." Paul scanned the crowd and saw the two boys.

"Oliver and George, come here please!" The two boys joined the rest of the family and Paul beamed. He had never been so happy in his life and a tear rolled down his cheek. Lexi wiped it with her finger, smiled lovingly at him and kissed him passionately on the mouth. The guests murmured and laughed approvingly.

Paul raised his hand once more for quiet. "Speeches are officially now over so have a great time and let's PARTY."

The music thundered to life and guests headed either to the laden buffet tables or for more drinks, followed by visits to the laser-lit wooden dance floor.

"Thanks Dad! It's wonderful!" Katie gushed happily. "It's been one of my best days, EVER!" She hugged her father tight and then pulled away. "And now I'm going to have a good time," she shouted excitedly as she rushed off to join her friends.

Oliver and George strolled off to find some girls to chat up, leaving Paul and Lexi holding hands. Paul was feeling very emotional.

"I couldn't have done it without you, they've all turned out so well."

"Paul, it was a joint effort, you did your share."

"No Lexi, I've been enjoying myself at work, it's you who deserves all the plaudits." And he took her in his arms and kissed her long and hard on the lips.

"Keep that up and we'll have to sneak off somewhere quiet."

"Well, it wouldn't be the first time would it?" he said with a glint in his eyes.

Paul remembered making love to Lexi on his hard wooden desk at the den nightclub all those years ago; he laughed loudly.

She looked at him and laughed as well. "I know what you're thinking; you're so predictable Mr. Paul Bolton."

He grabbed her by the waist and they moved off to mingle with the happy and boisterous crowd. Soon, the older guests started leaving around one o'clock in the morning, by 3am, even the band had stopped but it didn't stop the diehards from continuing the party. Katie, Oliver and George were right in the middle of things, pouring drinks, arranging music and passing round the joints. It had been one hell of a party and it didn't finish until five in the morning as worn-out family and friends collapsed, and the marquee became littered with sleeping bodies.

Oliver was twenty and the eldest son by a year; he was also the spitting image of his father - six foot four, broad shouldered, short jet black hair, blue-eyed, and drop-dead handsome. He had told his dad he was not attracted to anything other than following him into the family night club business. Funny then that after numerous dialogues with both parents, he ended up at Nottingham University, taking a Business Studies degree. Paul was single-minded that all his children would have a rounded education before they choose which career they would follow. Oliver had a year to go and from what he said when he was at home, nothing had happened to change his mind about enrolling in the family business. Although Paul had not said as much, he was hoping and praying that Oliver would one day take over the business; Oliver was sharp, shrewd and had all the attributes necessary to be successful.

Nineteen year old George was a very different kettle of fish, taking his good looks and temperament from Lexi. He was a very thoughtful young man who was concerned about the environment, about peoples' working conditions and about children around the world who had no food to eat. He was already a volunteer worker for Oxfam and had persuaded his dad to contribute a vast donation to the cause. George was taking a year off prior to going to Exeter University to study Humanities. Paul was immensely proud of George and knew he would lead a fulfilling and worthwhile life, but almost certainly, not in the family business.

And then there was Katie. Paul had no favourites but his daughter was very special to him. Sons were one thing but his precious daughter was the light of his life. She was so damn bright and also wanted to join the family business as soon as she was able. She had just completed her A' levels at Camberley College and her next move was up for discussion. Paul wanted her to go straight to University but she wasn't too keen, and wanted to get out into the big wide world.

The rock for all of them was the ageless Lexi. She had met Paul after the death of his first wife Emma. Lexi was the glue that held the family all together, and she loved her husband and children more than life itself. She had been firm with the children but it had all been worthwhile. They were all respectful good kids who had bright futures ahead of them. It had been hard though. Paul had been through terrible and depressing times after losing Emma and the baby, and then his brother Tony dying by many hands in a victim's court. The nightclub business was as good as legitimate except for some tax fiddles with the cash that disappeared to Switzerland on a regular basis. Paul had built the business and there were now seventeen London clubs and restaurants that turned over millions. Paul and his family were wealthy beyond their dreams but he still refused to spoil the kids who had always had to work hard for their pocket money.

Paul and Lexi woke late on the Sunday morning after the birthday party. The house was so quiet, and they didn't actually get out of bed until 11 am which was a real change as they were both early birds. Lexi had been reasonably sensible with the booze, so felt okay, while Paul had one hell of a hangover. Neither got dressed as they descended and walked down the sky-blue, thick carpeted stairs to the kitchen. Lexi loved her Aga inspired kitchen, newly installed when they bought the six bedroomed house in Virginia Water near Camberley in Surrey. The fridges and freezers were all hidden and it looked like one of those kitchens in the glossy Homes magazine. It had been one of the joys of her life to completely redecorate the huge country house and at the same time, landscape the massive gardens. They still had the flat in Chelsea Harbour but used it far less these days, whilst the children used it more because of its handy location for central London.

This Sunday afternoon was going to be demanding; Paul and Lexi had invited close friends and family for lunch, which would be late at 3 o clock; visitors would start arriving at 2pm. Lexi hoped all would go according to plan. Paul had made the decision regarding Katie's future and he knew she would be over the moon with what he was going to tell her during the meal. Paul was looking forward to seeing his most trusted advisor and friend Duke, with his wife Carole and their kids Bonny and James. Other guests were Ted Farrow who had been chief financial officer for the company since the death of Roddy; Dave Bristow, who was one of Paul's most trusted lieutenants and Harry Green, who Paul had poached from KPMG to work on club acquisitions and the legal processes. Lexi had her usual green herb tea while Paul had strong coffee; neither could face anything to eat and would gladly wait till lunchtime. They knew they would not see any of the children until at least one or two o' clock.

Paul heard noises outside and looked out the window. A team had arrived from the catering company and were busy dismantling the marquee. Pretty young girls in black trousers and white shirts were packing cutlery and plates into crates and others were touring the gardens picking up the seemingly endless number of beer and wine bottles, cigarette ends and disgustingly, a few used condoms.

Paul and Lexi finished their hot drinks and disappeared back upstairs to shower and dress. Lexi had installed a double sized shower cubicle. They showered together, soaping each other whilst laughing and giggling like kids.

Paul dressed in his usual smart Sunday clothes: cream coloured chinos, a blue Armani shirt teamed with a blue cashmere cardigan. Lexi was cooking so was casual in expensive designer red jeans with a see-through chiffon blouse which showed off her still pert breasts encased in a sexy black bra. Lexi went straight to the kitchen, she put on her favourite full-length white pinnie with HEAD CHEF emblazoned across the front, took a huge leg of lamb out of one of the battery of tall solid American fridges and started to season it ready for the oven. When it came to

Sunday lunch, Lexi was very traditional: it was a roast joint, roast potatoes and three veg, followed by homemade trifle or pie, and to finish, a heaving tray of delicious cheeses. Lexi was a great cook, so wonderful food coupled with copious amounts of good quality red and white wine, port and brandy ensured Sunday lunches were very much looked forward to.

Paul disappeared to his favourite room in the house - his upstairs office. He sat at his modern oak black desk and looked out the huge floor to ceiling window. He had a glorious view of the huge landscaped, manicured back garden. It was a hot June day; he thought they might eat outside. He would see what Lexi thought. He looked at his watch, it was one o' clock. He heard noises and knew one of the kids was awake. One thing was guaranteed: come Sunday lunch, they would all be sat round the table piling Lexis famous paprika roast potatoes onto their plates.

Oliver and George came down first, dressed very casually in jeans and shirts. It didn't seem to matter how much they drank, they were always ready for their mother's Sunday lunch. Katie had been in her en-suite bathroom for at least an hour doing what eighteen year-olds do, then followed the two boys down to the dining room. She looked stunning in black tights, black mini-skirt and a black blouse.

The family and guests were all on the south-facing patio, drinking chilled Laurant Perrier champagne and San Miguel beers. As it was such a beautiful day, Lexi had agreed with Paul that they should eat outside, where the big table was laid out. Wine had already been opened to breathe and soon the food was ready. Everybody sat at the long oak table while Lexi, Katie and her friend Bonny, carried serving dishes of steaming hot paprika roast potatoes, buttered roasted carrots, Broccoli cheese, parsnip puree, gravy and Yorkshire puddings to the table. As the food was placed on the table, a loud burst of applause came from those already seated. A South African red and a Pinot Grigio were passed round as glasses were filled, and everybody sipped and gave their approval.

Lexi brought in the Piece de Resistance, which was the huge leg of succulent English Lamb; it was on a tray with spikes that held it in place. Lexi carved massive slices, piling them onto plates as they were passed up the table. Fresh homemade mint sauce finished the meal off as everybody tucked in with gusto. Conversation was muted until plates were becoming empty, only then did conversation begin to flow. Soon afterwards, the empty plates were collected and two large dishes of desserts were placed on the table: delicious looking sherry trifle and a homemade apple and blackberry pie. Lashings of double cream was served with both and everybody had their fill. Again, the bowls were cleared and the platter of cheese arrived - Brie, mature Cheddar, Stilton, Camembert and others which nobody quite knew the names of. Afterwards, Taylors Vintage Port was served in wine glasses, this finished the meal off nicely.

Paul looked at Lexi and raised his eyebrows; it was time. He lifted a clean spoon and banged the table. "I'm sure everyone will join me in congratulating Lexi on a superb lunch."

Everyone lifted their glasses in a toast.

"To Lexi!" and Paul smiled at her knowing she hated the limelight.

"So, in a moment, some of us will be going into the house for a quick business meeting. Yes, I know it's Sunday but work doesn't stop. So now, to Katie's future." He paused, looked at her and smiled. "Katie will not go to University like Oliver and George," he paused briefly again and added, "from this second, Katie is now a member of the family business."

Whoops erupted and everybody clapped loudly. It had been her dream and Paul had decided she had the character to learn the business and hopefully, eventually run it with Oliver. Paul held up his hands and everyone was quiet.

"So, members of the business - Oliver and Katie, lets retire into the house."

Katie was so excited; this was her first meeting and she couldn't wait.

The group left the table and went back into the house, the old children's playroom had been turned into a meeting room with all the technology a FTSE 100 company would have, a large oval table and twelve chairs. They all sat down and Paul opened a book and looked at his notes.

"So let's get through the points quickly. First, Ted, I want you to take Katie under your wings for six months and show her the financial side of the business."

"Sure thing, Paul."

"Harry, what's happening with the proposed new club in Camden?" Paul asked.

"Council are being a pain in the arse, it's not worth going ahead unless we get the planning permission."

"Okay, it's a good site; find someone who can help us, you understand?"

"Of course."

Paul looked at Dave. "Dave, the trouble at the Mayfair, those bouncers were well out of order. What's happening?"

"Sacked them all, the punter's still in hospital. We need to look after him so it goes away quickly."

"I couldn't agree more. Give him whatever you think is necessary, be generous. Okay Duke, anything from you?"

"The manager at the frog and whistle has been on the take; he's been with us for ten years, what do you want to do?"

"Philip Brown! What the fuck's wrong with him? Go and see him, find out if he's got problems, remind him we are a family; any shit, get rid and break his fucking legs."

Paul suddenly remembered Katie and looked over at her expecting her to be horrified at his language and threats of violence. He gave her a weak smile.

"I would break his fucking arms as well," Katie said very seriously.

Duke shouted, "A real Bolton!" and there was uproar as everybody burst out laughing.

Katie was sitting at the back and was already thinking about one day being the boss; such power was so exhilarating.

"Oliver will be working with me soon," Paul said, looking at everyone in turn and back to Duke. "Let all the managers know that when he says something, it's the same as me speaking because soon, another two years and I'll be semi-retired. Oliver and Katie, stay behind. Meeting's over; go and get yourselves a drink and relax."

"So you two, look; you're the future," Paul said as soon as they were alone, looking seriously at his children. "Nothing is more important than the money. Ted will show you how it all works. Remember, everything is confidential; you don't discuss finance with anybody in the organization other than Ted, me and Oliver."

"Okay dad," Katie said, nodding.

"Oliver, one day, in the not too distant future, you'll run this business with Katie. We add one or two clubs a year and that is what we will continue to do. Nobody knows except Harry Green that we are also looking to move into casinos and our first one could be in Victoria; I'll keep you in the loop. Now go and enjoy the rest of the day."

CHAPTER 2

The British Airways 747 jumbo jet from Ontario, Canada, landed on time at Heathrow terminal five. It was 10 am Friday 11th June. The six foot three, well-built, very handsome, blue eyed young man was sitting at the front of the plane in the extra leg room seats. All the aged and young BA trolley dollies had been very attentive to his needs over the whole of the flight and were all smiling as he stood to disembark.

"Thank you ladies. It was a very pleasant flight." The young handsome man beamed at the trolley dollies and strode through the door into the extended landing corridor. He was travelling light with just a small black case containing a few essentials. He hoped to be out of the airport very quickly, on his way into central London. As usual, passport control was slow and he joined the queue snaking towards the checking desks. He relaxed and he was soon showing his British passport to a border guard. Once he was through, he marched down the Nothing to Declare exit and was soon pushing the doors into the main terminal. It was his first visit to London and he was very excited. He looked around at the vast cavern-like terminal; it was so huge it felt like he was entering another world. He followed the signs to the tube station and was soon on the especially steep escalators descending into the bowels of the earth. He bought his ticket from a machine and two minutes later, was sitting on a Piccadilly line train heading towards central London.

Return to Bermondsey

Sixteen stops later, he got off at Green Park and strode through the tunnels to get a connection on the Jubilee line. He waited three minutes and then jumped onto the brand new looking train, a vast improvement on the Piccadilly line that was a noisy old banger. It was only four stops and he got off at Swiss Cottage, his destination. He stood outside the station and looked at the notes his mother had given him, telling him to make his way to the Renaissance hotel. He asked directions from the scruffy old man at the paper kiosk and was soon striding to the hotel that was very near-by. He was surprised at how swanky the hotel looked. He booked in at reception and reminded himself to thank his mother for spending so much money on such a lovely double room. He was soon sitting at the small expensive desk in room 126; he spent an hour studying his tube map and a list of locations given to him by his mother. He had not slept well on the plane and decided to lie down on the huge double bed for an hour. He woke up four hours later at ten past four in the afternoon. He showered and dressed and then felt very hungry. He was on a limited budget so decided to leave the hotel and look for somewhere cheaper to eat. He walked down the noisy Swiss Cottage hill and then saw manna from heaven, his favourite eatery of all time, McDonalds. He quickened his pace and was soon standing at the counter ordering two big macs, large fries, apple pie and white coffee. He found a table near the window and was soon devouring the food hungrily. As he ate, his face lit up as he noticed two pretty French girls sitting directly opposite him a table away; he was pleasantly surprised but what he didn't know was that Swiss Cottage had always been a magnet for foreigners, particularly gorgeous girls from countries all over the world.

He was tempted to chat up the two girls but had a very important and emotional day tomorrow so decided against it and went back to the hotel. He had a pint of Guinness at the Garrick bar and went back to his room for an early night. He was lying naked in bed, flicking through the TV Channels when he noticed a selection of pay per view films. He clicked under the heading Adult and was soon watching a film entitled *Fuck me tonight*. There was a very brief story line but plenty of fucking and cum flying all over the place. He ended up jerking off on the bed and decided he would need some female company while he was in London. He finally crashed and fell asleep at midnight.

The following morning was bright and sunny with blue skies. The young man was up at seven am. He went for a walk outside the hotel; he enjoyed the fresh air so much he strolled around for about twenty minutes. It was going to be an important Saturday and he was looking forward to it; but he also knew it would be very emotional. He heard his stomach growl with hunger. The stroll and fresh air must have triggered his hunger pangs. He looked at his watch, it was eight thirty am and he walked back to the hotel for breakfast. At nine o clock he was filling his plate for the second time, sausages, bacon, eggs, mushrooms and baked beans. Within a few minutes, he polished that off too. He pushed the cleaned plate away, feeling stuffed as he sat back and belched. He thought he had eaten too much, but he didn't care, he had enjoyed the breakfast

Return to Bermondsey

very much. He went back to his room, sat on the bed and looked at a list. He read it twice and a tear rolled down his cheek. If only he had met him just once, he thought. If only he'd held him only for a second, even hearing him say he loved him, he'd have been very happy. The tears turned into a torrent. Eventually he pulled himself together, packed a small rucksack with some Lucozade energy drinks and McCoy Salt and Vinegar crisps and left his room.

He strolled up to Swiss Cottage tube station, bought his day pass ticket and was quickly on the escalators, looking at the underwear adverts as he descended down to the platforms. The train pulled in three minutes later and he stepped on. The train was very noisy but still gave him time to think about Bermondsey, London and life in general. He nearly missed his stop because of daydreaming. He jumped onto the platform at Bermondsey Tube station at eleven am; it was the first of many landmarks. He made his way to the well-lit exit sign. The station was clean, large and airy. He looked around as he climbed the short stairs to the ticket barrier; he was walking in *his* footsteps and could feel the power. He looked around threateningly, ready to challenge anybody to a fight.

Suddenly, he screamed. "Who wants to fight me?" he clenched his fists as a small number of commuters gave him quizzical looks. He took a deep breath and calmed down. He went through the ticket barrier and then turned right out of the station then stopped and looked both ways down the busy road. He took the piece of paper out of his pocket and read the names: The Ship, The Angel, The Mayflower and The Blue Anchor down Southwark Park Road which his mum had said was always one of his favourites. He visited and had a pint in the three pubs, and finally arrived at the Blue Anchor on Southwark Park Road. He entered through the front entrance and immediately saw the large Millwall sign over the bar. He was a Millwall fanatic although he had never been to a game. He hoped to see a couple of matches while he was in London.

He ordered a pint of Guinness and spoke to the obviously Irish man who served him. "You must be Pat?"

"That's right and who might you be?" said Pat giving him a quizzical look.

"David Forest. I saw your name on the Millwall sign and put two and two together."

"You must be brighter than most round here then, that's for sure!" and Pat roared with laughter.

"I haven't seen you in here before." Pat knew everybody and never forgot a face.

"First time. I'm from the States; writing a book about London gangsters. Thought I might base some of it in Bermondsey; so I'm doing some research." he took a sip of his Guinness, looking at Pat over the pint.

"Research you call it; it's alright for some," and Pat laughed again.

"You must have seen some really hard types in here over the years," prompted David.

"You're not kidding either! Some real mean bastards! But ya know what, they was very friendly unless you upset them. So the trick was to keep on their right side."

"Did you know the Boltons?"

"Jesus! Those two, chalk and cheese they was. I knew them both - Paul and Tony Bolton. No, haven't seen either of them for years but understand Tony died a long time ago."

"So I read. Paul's doing very well, I hear."

"Yea, a thriving nightclub business in London."

"How did you find Tony?"

Pat looked thoughtful for a second then said, "He was good fun and would do anything for you if you were a mate but..." and he shook his head.

"Go on."

"He was a madman who could turn into the devil in a second," and he clicked his fingers. "He had a police record as long as the channel tunnel and by all accounts, did some terrible things locally around here; people were terrified of him. He was a regular in here for years."

David said nothing, he just looked at Pat; he felt a chilling calmness. After a few seconds, he smiled. "I don't suppose he would have liked being called a madman?"

"Never would have said it to his face, he would have killed me for sure; or I'd have spent months in Hospital. Another pint?"

It all happened very quickly. Pat was getting old and slow and never stood a chance. He put a new pint glass under the Guinness tap and slowly pulled it to release the black nectar. Suddenly, the young man smashed his empty glass on the counter, and in one sweeping movement, he leaped over the bar and smashed a large jagged piece of glass into Pat's face. Pat howled with the searing pain as he dropped his own full pint he was holding onto the floor as he put his hands to his face, and he stumbled and fell heavily to the floor. David was on him, slashing his face with the jagged sharp glass. Pat's face soon resembled a piece of raw bloody meat. He stood up and started to kick his head which now resembled a deflated bloodied football, sinking his heavy shoes into the back and sides of Pat's head.

"Madman was it, Pat? You fucking Irish cunt!"

The young man stepped back and surveyed the damage. Pat was writhing slowly and whimpering with the searing pain, still feebly trying to protect his face. His demented assailant jumped up into the air and landed on Pat's legs, he heard the snap and crack of bones and Pat moaned loudly with pain. He kicked him in the back a few more times and stopped. People were entering the bar and David didn't want to get involved in anything else. He picked up the new pint of Guinness, gulped down half of it and tipped the rest over the back of Pat's head. As he did that, he noticed a gold signet ring on Pat's left hand, he liked the look of it and bent down to remove it. He didn't think it would come off easily but was surprised as it slid from his finger.

"I enjoyed the drink Pat, thanks cunt," and he gave him one more massive kick in the back of the head and then calmly walked to the side door and left.

***

He looked up and read the blue sign on the front of the stand.

Welcome to Millwall Football Club

He entered the stadium. It had been one of his dreams from an early age to visit this place, the Den, home of Millwall Football Club, and it lived up to his expectations and more. Even though it was empty with just a few people wandering about, he could feel the history. He imagined what it would be like on a match day, fifteen thousand die-hard fans singing their hearts out for the boys in blue. It was cold and windy, with dust flying up off the concrete ground in front of the main stand. He was soaking up the atmosphere as he headed to the club shop. Thirty minutes later, he came out wearing the latest home shirt: blue with white trim. He was proud of his new shirt; just let anyone say something out of place about it and he would teach them a lesson they would never forget. He looked around and started sauntering back to south Bermondsey tube station. He was walking at a leisurely pace and imagining *he* was holding his hand having been to the game together; he was sad for that moment that never took place.

***

The young man had thoroughly enjoyed the day and was back in his room at the hotel at seven pm, and the first thing he did was phone his mummy.

"Hello mummy, how are you?"

"Fine. More importantly, how are you?"

"Very good. The room is so lovely, thank you. All in all, couldn't be better."

"Glad to hear it. What have you been up to then?"

"You know, the usual tourist locations, Madame Tussauds, Houses of Parliament, that sort of thing," he lied.

"That's nice. What are you doing tonight?"

"I'm exhausted, so just a quick beer in the bar and an early night."

"Don't get in any trouble, will you."

"Don't worry, I'm taking the medication; everything's cool."

"Thank goodness, it's a long way for me to come and hold your hand."

"Those days are over mummy, I'm a very responsible citizen now," he laughed. "I'll call you again tomorrow to report in."

"Okay darling, make sure you do. Take care, love you."

"Love you too mummy. Bye."

He put the phone down and was happy he had done his duty. He instantly left the room and made his way to the gym on the first floor. He attacked the machines and had soon worked up a real sweat. He spent an hour performing his customary tough exercise routine before heading back up to his room. He showered and dressed in his best and only pair of decent dark trousers and a crisp white shirt. The shirt was one size too small and flaunted his muscles. He looked at his watch, it was eight thirty. He went to the bar and had a lasagne snack and a glass of water. He wanted to be absolutely fit for the evening ahead so kept off the alcohol. He left the hotel at nine fifteen and walked slowly up to the tube station. He was edgy but very excited; he thought it could be one of the most fascinating evenings of his life. He took the Jubilee line train to Baker Street. The train was packed with young people of all nationalities, going out to enjoy themselves. He changed onto the Bakerloo line and one stop later, he left the train at Oxford Circus. He strode down Regent Street and was soon turning into Kingly

Street. He slowed down a little, sucking in the night life atmosphere. Then he saw what he was after, a small discreet club entrance with the name above it: THE DEN.

He walked past the first two big security men on the pavement and pushed the small door open to be met by two more burley men. They frisked him thoroughly and declared him clean and he was ushered through to the ticket office.

He smiled at the attractive young red head behind the counter. "One ticket please."

The girl laughed. "I bet you don't leave on your own," and winked at him.

The young man passed through another door with two more security men standing guard. The fact they were so huge undoubtedly made them formidable opponents, but the young man was not concerned; he knew exactly how to bring a large opponent down, ten years of Karate had honed his skills to black belt level. The second door was opened for him and he strolled into the main bar and dance area. He stopped and looked around, it was a superb club. There was a dance area in front of the white DJ's box, a long bar and lots of small alcoves for those who wanted some privacy. He also noticed doors leading to other areas, dining rooms and a door marked smoking area, which he expected led outside. He made his way to the bar and ordered a long glass of Pernod and orange juice with ice. The club was filling up and he immediately noticed the girls were all young and gorgeous and dressed in dangerously short skirts and dresses. He checked the whole area and counted four more security men. They were tight on protection and security, he thought. Suddenly, he noticed an older man come out of a door marked staff only; he recognised him from a photo his mom had shown him. Two seconds later, the man was joined by a young couple who he thought, by their looks, were his children. He sipped his drink and watched them; he could feel the hate creeping over him, he took deep breaths; he had to control himself, and he calmed down.

They walked towards him, chatting. The tall, sexy girl in very short blue skirt was on his side, and as she passed, he smiled at her and winked. Katie had noticed the tall good looking young man as soon as she had entered the main floor. She was electrified and now as she walked past him, he had the bloody nerve to wink at her; she loved the attention. The three of them disappeared up a swanky chrome staircase marked private. As they got to the top, Katie turned, ran her hand through her long blonde hair and smiled, but the man at the bar had his back to her. Dam, she said to herself; maybe later, she thought. The man had seen her turn in the mirror behind the bar and smiled to himself; his charm rarely failed. He ordered another drink. He had come with a plan but he couldn't decide whether to go ahead with it or not; there now seemed to be so many options. He sipped his new drink as he thought, and then it was clear in his mind.

His thoughts were interrupted as the three people reappeared, coming back down the stairs. He lifted his glass and finished the drink. He placed the glass gently back onto the bar, turned and strode purposefully towards Paul, Oliver and Katie. Paul caught sight of the young man and instantly knew he was coming straight towards him. He glanced sideways and raised his eyebrows at one of the security guards who immediately rushed to see what he wanted. The young man was so close, Paul held back Oliver and Katie and stopped. Katie saw the man approaching and recognised him as the person who had winked at her. The security man arrived and noticed the man moving towards the group; he stood still and as the young man got very close, he held up his hand in a don't-come-any closer motion. The security man had also spoken into his radio and more guards were rushing to see what the problem was.

The young man stopped and stood right in front of the guard, "Excuse me, I'd like a word with Mr. Paul Bolton." The guard stared hard at him and turned to Paul who had heard every word.

Paul took one step forward as more guards arrived and took hold of the young man. Paul was looking closely at him; there was something familiar about him but he just couldn't put his finger on it. "I'm Paul Bolton. What can I do for you?"

"First, tell these gorillas to let go of me or they'll be sorry."

"Listen, whoever you are, I don't like trouble in the club, gives us a bad reputation. Now, what do you want? And I won't ask again."

"I'm looking for a job, Mr. Bolton."

Paul didn't like the situation. He looked at one of the guards and then back at the young man.

"There are no vacancies. I think you should leave." He nodded at one of the guards and began to walk away.

"You must be Oliver, and I heard you're very beautiful so you must be Katie."

Paul, Oliver and Katie all stopped and stared at him.

"Paul, you don't recognise me?"

Paul was confused, he looked closer; there was something about him, the size of him, the square jaw, the broad chest…

Then the young man smiled and held out his hand. "My name's Callum," he paused. "Callum Bolton, Tony's son and you're my uncle Paul."

Paul could not move or speak; he was paralyzed with shock as he continued to stare at Callum. Now, he could see the powerful build, the confidence, the swagger, the resemblance. He was just like his father Tony!

Callum turned to a dumbfounded Oliver and Katie. "And you two, plus George of course, are my cousins. It's so exciting! I've been looking forward to meeting you for years."

Oliver and Katie knew all the stories about their father's mad brother Tony; they were also in shock, not sure what to say or do. Paul had now gathered his thoughts and wanted to find out more.

"So Callum, who is your mother?"

"Sharon Travis. We live in Ontario Canada."

Paul muttered, "Sharon Travis, I know that name."

"Mummy was a junior doctor working at Broadmoor Hospital when dad was sent there. They fell in love, and she helped him to escape."

"So, you know everything about your father?"

"Just about, I'm hoping you'll fill in the blank spaces."

Paul's mind flashed back to the stabbing frenzy as Tony screamed for mercy and died at the hands of his victim's relatives. He rubbed his face, he was at a loss at what to do but then pulled himself together. He told the guards to disappear and to fetch Duke; he always felt better when Duke was with him.

"So, Callum, lets go and get a drink," he smiled at him for the first time. "You look just like your father. How is your mother?"

Oliver and Katie trailed behind them, still in complete shock. They could not believe what was happening and for no particular reason, were already worried for their father.

The four of them got some drinks and went upstairs to one of the luxurious private rooms. George arrived ten minutes later and he too was in shock. The conversation was stilted with Paul and Callum doing most of the talking. There was a knock at the door and Duke entered. He scanned the room and he held Callum in eye contact for a few seconds.

"So, what are you doing here?" Duke asked Callum suspiciously.

The room went silent, Duke was a massive presence and didn't mince words.

"I live in Canada but mum said I should come over for a year or two for the experience and then go back a more rounded person. She said Uncle Paul would look after me," and he smiled at Duke.

"Why the fuck didn't you contact us before coming over? That would have been the normal way of doing things."

"It was a surprise for Uncle Paul and all my cousins," Callum smiled disarmingly.

"This family don't like fucking surprises!" Duke barked then turned to Paul. "A word please, boss." He opened the door and left; Paul followed him. They walked down the corridor and then Duke stepped into an empty room, Paul followed him in and shut the door.

Duke was the first to speak. "Paul, I'm telling you, nothing good will come of this! I don't like it one bit! Why the fuck has he suddenly decided to get on a plane and visit his Uncle Paul? He looks mad like his demented father! Get rid of him Paul! Give him some money, put him on a plane and tell him not to bother ever coming back!" Duke was getting agitated and couldn't stand still. He remembered Tony well enough: the killings, the torture, and the rivers of blood.

"I'm begging you Paul, get rid of him. Do you want me to take care of him?" He looked at Paul hopefully.

Paul was shocked. "Duke calm down for Christ's sake! You'll have a bloody heart attack."

Paul could understand Duke's reasoning, the boy just turning up was extraordinary and very worrying. "Duke, he could be a perfectly normal young guy. Who wouldn't want to come over to London for a year of fun at his age? He'll get to know the kids, and just because his father was mad doesn't mean he is as well!"

Duke was still agitated and his face etched with worry and alarm. "I've been with you for years Paul, if you trust my judgement, listen to me now. I don't trust him already and he's only been here two fucking minutes. All this Uncle fucking Paul shit! He's laughing at us Paul! As for the kids, I wouldn't let him near them." He paused then added, "And before you say anything, I'll tell you why he's here. He's here for you Paul, and maybe even the kids. He wants revenge, Paul; that's why he's here!"

"Duke! Are you feeling alright? For God's sake! Give the kid a break! He's family."

Duke looked at Paul, and that said it all for him: he was family.

Duke spoke slowly and quietly. "You know I will support whatever you decide but if he stays, then we will go back to the old days when your security was tighter than a duck's ass. That will also apply to the three kids and Lexi."

"Where the hell is he going to stay? I'm not having him at my house with Lexi."

"Give him the flat at Chelsea Harbour."

"Yea, good idea. Tell Oliver to move out. Callum can start work here."

"Doing what exactly, Paul?"

"Learning the trade Duke, all areas from the bottom up; put him behind the bar first. You take charge of him but remember, he still comes to family dos. Let's see if he's after anything other than a year of fun."

It was agreed Callum would move into the flat at Chelsea Harbour on the Monday morning and Oliver would move into his father's private suite at the club. George was travelling but when in the UK, always stayed at the house in Virginia Water with Katie and Lexi. It was all settled and when Callum moved into the Chelsea Harbour flat on the Monday, he was ecstatic and couldn't believe his luck; he fell in love with it immediately.

CHAPTER 3

"Sir, I cannot believe you have agreed with this without speaking to me first; truly I am shocked to the core."

"Shocked to the core! Please Karen speak as you normally do for God's sake."

Detective Inspector Karen Foster was at Surrey Police Headquarters in Guildford.

"Well, in that case Sir, I am well fucking cheesed off that you had the fucking audacity to agree with something like that without first fucking well speaking to me."

"Ah, music to my ears; good that's better and that's one of the reasons you are going back. You are a natural, you know the manor, you know the people and most important, you fit in, and after all, it's only for six months and then you'll be back. Look, you know I can't force you to go although a request has been made through channels; you can say no."

"Well it could be an interesting six months, the time will fly by and I'll be working with my ex-partner Jeff Swan; you know damn well I'm going to say yes, the lure of Bermondsey and Rotherhithe - it's not St Tropez but it's home."

"I knew you would come round. Surrey Police will survive without you for a few months. So, apparently, there are some new gangs in Bermondsey and they need every experienced officer they can get their hands on to sort it; you'll have a ball."

Detective Inspector Karen Foster was on her way back to Bermondsey. She left Surrey Police Headquarters in Guildford and drove back to Epsom police station, her home for the past few years. On the journey, she had flash backs to the blood and deaths in Bermondsey. Although she was now probably one of the most experienced officers in the country, she still had worries and concerns about her performance. The stabbing in Leatherhead had left her near death's door and she had a large scar across her chest to prove it. Although she had completely recovered, she had not been seriously tested again since that horrific incident.

As usual, Karen's private life was a disaster. She hadn't seen Esme Delon or Chau since they had been part of the celebration when she resumed work following the stabbing. She'd had a couple of one night stands when she'd ended up in some bar drunk but she always regretted them afterwards. The giant dildo she used at home was getting far more use than ever, and at the rate she was using it, could break down any day. As always, she immersed herself in work and going back to Bermondsey was thrilling. She couldn't wait to see Jeff again.

***

Karen cleared her desk at Epsom, said an almost tearful farewell to her team and was driving out of the car park in her blue ageing Ford Focus on the way back to her flat. It was Friday eleventh June and Karen was wondering what to do at the weekend. She was due at Rotherhithe nick on Monday morning and would be living at an ex-police safe house in Bermondsey for the duration of her stay. She decided to spring clean the flat, put everything in its correct place and leave it in tip top condition for when she returned. A Friday night and she was planning to clean! Long gone were the evenings when she would be putting on the slap and glad rags for a night on the lash; she didn't miss it. She poured a full glass of some Spanish plonk and sipped at it. She went into the kitchen, emptying cupboards and checking items' use by dates. Some of them were a year out of date and she quickly threw them into a black bag. She put on her large yellow plastic gloves and scrubbed the shelves clean. She was in the kitchen for two hours and decided to have a break. Soon she was sitting in the old comfy brown sofa with another glass of red, contemplating what it would be like to be back in Bermondsey.

The remainder of the evening was spent vacuuming, cleaning and generally tidying up. She finally finished at ten pm, looked around her and was delighted with what she had done. All she had to do now was pack a case and she was ready to go. Another glass of red and she started to think about Esme in Cannes. They had spoken a couple of times on the phone and the last time, Esme said she was seeing a Spanish Flamenco dancer; Karen had laughed at first but after she had put the phone down, cried for hours as she knew their relationship was over forever. Karen had nightmares that she would be left abandoned on her own in old age; it perpetually worried her. She loved company and was a social person who didn't like to spend too long on her own. The rest of the weekend was quiet and Karen spent most of it in her flat.

The drive back to Bermondsey on the Monday morning was a journey of anticipation and excitement albeit with apprehension. Karen had left especially early to miss the traffic and to ensure she arrived on time. The closer she got to Bermondsey, the greyer and darker everything seemed to become. The tower blocks dominated the skyline and the streets were full of take-away food packaging and empty cigarette packets. Soon, she was pulling into the car park at the back of Rotherhithe police station; it was six minutes to nine. She took a deep breath, looked in the mirror and messed with her hair for a second and then jumped out the car. She strode to the back door and keyed in the code.

"Jeff, why did I know you would be waiting for me to turn up!" Keren exclaimed when she opened the door and found Jeff standing there, as if he had been waiting for her. He was in his usual shabby grey suit, white shirt and a red tie hanging at an awkward angle from his neck.

"Its five to nine and I knew you wouldn't be late," said Jeff with a smile.

"So what's first on the agenda?"

Jeff laughed. "Are you serious? We go and get some coffee first, of course."

"Of course, nothing changes, eh?"

Jeff went all serious for a moment.

"It's been quiet, Karen, but now, we've got problems; young guns charging around shooting people! It's out of hand; that's one of the reasons I suggested you should be asked to come back."

Karen stopped. "So it was you then, you bugger! Don't worry, I'm pleased to be back and if I can help, so be it."

Jeff took her arm. "Coffee's waiting," and they sauntered off towards the canteen.

Coffees were grabbed and they sat at a table by the window with a view of the car park.

"So, what's going on Jeff? And don't give me a load of shit! We've known each other far too long."

"That's true. Well, firstly, do you remember Pat, the Irish guy who runs or I should say, ran the Blue Anchor in Southwark Bridge Road?"

"Yea, vaguely. Been there years, hasn't he?"

"Yea, a very long time." Jeff paused. "Got beaten to death on Saturday; he was alive when they found him but died later on in the night."

"Is that connected to why I'm here?"

"Truthful answer, I don't think so; seems to have been a random killing. One thing's for certain: people won't like it. He was popular and knew everybody; AND I mean, everybody."

"Any leads?"

"Some young muscle was seen coming out the pub, that's about it."

"So, what else is happening?"

"Seven shootings in the past month alone, four dead and two injured, plus, one of my men took a bullet in the leg."

"Who are they?"

"Young bloods attempting to take over the area, drugs is the key to it all; the money is just astounding; we're talking millions. Kevin and Graham Philips, couple of hard nuts, moved over from Romford; there, taking on the locals and it would seem at the moment, getting the upper hand."

"Haul them in, tell them they'll end up in Belmarsh for thirty years and see what happens."

"Karen, these people are so fucking clever now; nothing, and I mean absolutely nothing leads back to them. They even have a legitimate estate agent business which satisfies HMRC that they are earning a living and paying for their big cars and mansions."

"So changing the subject, have you seen Paul Bolton recently?"

"No, he has nothing to do with Bermondsey now although he does pop back for the odd celebration or funeral."

"He knew Pat at the Blue Anchor, he won't like hearing that piece of news."

"That's for sure. So look, lets go and introduce you to the team, not sure there are many you'll remember; loads of young graduate go-getters all over the place though."

"Great! That's just what we need when dealing with shooters."

Karen was introduced to everybody in the station and then it was time for lunch.

"How's the food, Jeff?"

Jeff laughed. "It's still pretty good; I'm hoping there'll be lasagne on the menu; I just fancy some."

It wasn't; he had shepherd's pie and Karen had a tuna salad.

Later, Karen was given a desk in the CID office and worked from two to four pm. - no less than seven officers came into the CID office to shake hands and say hello to her.

Karen was slightly mystified. "Jeff, how come I'm so popular?"

"You know why."

Karen thought for a second then said, "I don't know, so humour me."

"Well, if you must know, you're a legend around here; people can't believe you're actually here!"

"A living legend eh?" and Karen broke into fits of laughter. "Me! A fucking legend!" and she continued to laugh.

Jeff just sat there, smiling affably.

CHAPTER 4

Paul and Lexi were sitting in the warm and snug family lounge as opposed to the opulent entertaining guests' lounge.

"I still can't believe it!" Lexi was shaking her head. "Are you sure he's for real? Tony's son? It's just a complete shock."

"Believe me, it's a shock to all of us and Duke's worried to death!"

Lexi looked even more concerned. "Why is Duke so worried?" She trusted Duke with her life as did all the family.

"He's got it into his head that the boy's here for revenge."

Katie came in and sat close to Lexi and took her hand. "I can guess what the topic of conversation is."

Lexi was still looking worried as she smiled at Katie.

"God! Does he look like his father, or Sharon?" asked Katie.

"I don't know, what do you think, Katie?"

"Judging from the photos, he looks like Tony, he's certainly a hunk; I bet he has to fight the girls off."

"Anyway, let's be serious for a minute," said Paul. "Extra security all round and here at the house; and nobody goes out unless accompanied by a minder."

"But dad, is that…"

"No arguing, it's already arranged."

Katie was dying to know. "Who exactly is looking after me then?"

"Mark Heenen"

"Bloody hell dad! He's ancient! Couldn't I have someone a bit younger?"

"He's a young forty for God's sake and one of the best! You're damn lucky."

Paul's mobile rang, he needed to take it. He stood up and began pacing the room with the mobile glued to his ear. He didn't say anything but he looked shocked.

"If there's anything we can do for the family, anything at all, if they need financial help, anything; and let me know when the funeral is. Okay, thanks for the call." He sat back down slightly shaken.

"What's happened dad?"

"Pat at the Blue Anchor beaten to death by some lowlife yob in the pub." Paul had a far-away look in his eyes as he thought about Tony, Callum, and now this.

He quickly allayed his thoughts and fears, smiled and looked at the two women in his life. "Callum is staying at the Chelsea Harbour flat; he's not to come to this house unless I say so, is that understood?" Lexi and Katie nodded. "Now, we treat him like family but we watch him like a hawk."

"How much does he know?" asked Lexi.

"I'm sure Sharon's told him a lot." Paul paused; he wasn't sure how much to say in front of Katie. "Katie give me and mum five minutes."

Katie didn't look very happy but jumped up and left, leaving the door open an inch.

Paul looked at Lexi and said thoughtfully, "I was told by DI Karen Foster that Sharon was the one that shopped him; I'll bet Callum doesn't know that. Sharon also doesn't know how Tony died and I would prefer it if Callum didn't find out either." He rubbed his face; the knives, the blood the screaming for mercy, it all came flooding back.

"That man was responsible for so many deaths and so much misery; I just pray Callum doesn't take after him. Christ! Let's go for a stroll in the garden, I need some fresh air."

He stood up and put his hand out for Lexi, she took it and smiled at him. "Don't worry, you'll sort it, you always do."

Katie tip-toed away from the door towards the kitchen.

***

Callum Bolton turned up for work on Tuesday morning at eight forty five; he was due to start at nine and he reported straight to Duke. Duke had been praying he was going to be late so he could start the day off by giving him a right bollocking. Callum knew from the second he met Duke he didn't like him. In fact, he could feel the hate emanating from Duke, almost physically. Duke didn't say good morning, he didn't say have you had a cup of tea; he just told him to work with a young girl and help her clean the bar area, tables and floors. It was relatively easy work but the bar area was huge as was the floor, which had thirty tables. The girl was called Mandy, she was twenty and dreamed of one day working as a hostess. She had the looks but couldn't add up a round of drinks to save her life. Mandy and Callum finished at one o'clock and had a lunch break together in the staff canteen. He was on the look-out for an easy lay and decided Mandy would do for the time being. As soon as Mandy heard he was a Bolton, she would have done anything for him as she thought he could be her ticket to a hostess job. The next job was to clean all the spirit, mixers and wine bottles behind the bar. There must have been a couple of hundred and it was soul destroying work but Callum had told himself he would do anything asked of him and not complain. Eventually it was five o'clock and they had finished. A nightclub was a twenty four hour operation with staff arriving and leaving throughout the day and night. Callum wanted to work at night when the club was at its busiest and really came to life, in time he would ask Paul. He decided that Mandy liked to be impressed so he told her he had a luxury multi million pound apartment in Chelsea Harbour and that she could come over any time. She was suitably impressed and said she'd love to visit for a drink. She knew why he had invited her, he wanted to fuck her and she didn't mind that at all. In fact, she was planning on giving him the best fuck he'd ever had in his life. There was no pretense; they hardly spoke on the journey to the apartment. All Callum did was to continually stare at Mandy's long legs, her firm rounded arse, nice sized breasts and lick his lips in anticipation of getting his hands on them all.

They eventually arrived at the apartment and it was all Callum could do to stop himself jumping on Mandy as soon as he shut the front door. Mandy said she needed to take a shower and if Callum liked, he could join her. Two minutes later they were naked and Mandy had his huge erection as far down her throat as she could swallow it. He was over excited and filled her mouth quicker than he had wanted to. They soaped each other and went into the lounge. Mandy was gobsmacked by the apartment; she had never seen anything like it. Over the next two hours, they fucked three times. Later Callum opened one of the huge fridges, it was stocked with Champagne and beer. A bottle of bubbly was soon opened and they were knocking it back whilst recovering and getting ready for the next session. There was something so relaxing about wandering about naked and drinking champagne and soon they were both tipsy. The doorbell rang and he jumped up as he laughed loudly and looked at Mandy.

"Somebody's going to get a big surprise!" he said as he went to open the front door. He was semi erect and because of the drinking, had lost all inhibitions. He pulled open the door.

"Oh shit! Sorry about that!" He tried to cover his cock as best he could. "Come in! Join the party!"

Katie didn't answer or smile but just looked at him with disgust. After a few seconds she said coldly, "Oliver asked me to pick up his last bits and pieces. I hope it's not inconvenient?"

"Katie, lighten up! Come in! Of course it's alright. Do you want some champagne?" He gave her the once over. She looked good in tight skinny jeans and a white tee shirt.

"No." She brushed past him and stalked towards the bedroom; she heard a noise in the lounge and stuck her head round the door. Mandy was laying on the sofa naked, legs wide apart, drinking champagne. She immediately recognised Katie Bolton and covered between her legs with her free hand as she gave her a weak smile.

Katie spent a couple of minutes in the bedroom packing items from a list Oliver had given her, she finally picked up the two small bags and walked out the room. She strode down the short hall and then stopped, she heard heavy breathing and moaning, she couldn't believe it, surely not while she was in the apartment, She took two further steps and glanced around the door into the lounge, Callum was thrusting hard in between Mandy's upturned spread legs with his erect cock. They were like animals on heat. Callum turned and smiled at her as he thrust again and Mandy moaned in ecstasy. Katie marched to the front door, opened it, went out and slammed it shut behind her. She was breathing hard; she was sexually inexperienced although not a virgin. She couldn't help it, she knew it was wrong but she wanted it, no not just wanted it she had to have it, she wanted that huge cock in her mouth and between her legs. She couldn't wait to get home and use her dildo; she knew she would be thinking of Callum as she masturbated to orgasm. Callum laughed to himself, he knew, she had slammed the door because she had wanted to be where Mandy was, well he would make sure she was very soon. He went back to the business in hand and started slamming into Mandy, imagining it was Katie moaning in ecstasy.

For Callum, the rest of the week was just like the Tuesday, boring as hell. Duke was totally indifferent to him and the only saving grace was the wonderful sex with Mandy. She had told him she wanted to be a hostess and he had promised her she would have the job within six months. He wasn't sure how he was going to swing it but if he could he would; it was the least she deserved. They had been through the Karma Sutra and Mandy was giving him so much pleasure. They were now having sex in the toilets at the club and she had even given him a blow job behind the bar. Mandy and Callum got paid weekly on Fridays; he was surprised to receive three hundred pounds and a wage slip in a brown envelope. He had no rent and no bills to pay so it was a tidy sum of money. He took Mandy out for a Chinese dinner and then back to the apartment where they fucked for hours until finally collapsing at three in the morning.

Katie was more than cheesed off for her every living thought was the image of Callum fucking that ignorant bitch Mandy on the sofa in the Chelsea Harbour apartment. She'd been using Fred, the nickname for her black six inch dildo more than ever, but she wanted the real thing and sooner or later, she would get what she wanted, she always did.

***

"How's he getting on?"

Paul had asked Duke to join him in his office after Callum had done his first week.

"What do you expect? He does the job, no more no less, does the job."

Paul didn't say anything and just looked at Duke.

"What do you want me to say? Well, bit of gossip, I hear he's shagging the cleaner Mandy Groves."

"The cleaner," Paul was shaking his head. "Can't he do better than that?"

"She's not a bad looker actually, wants to be a hostess."

"What's the problem?"

"It was Duke's turn to shake his head. "Thick as shit, seriously missing upstairs."

"Well, move him around. Where are you putting him next?"

"Toilet cleaning."

Paul wasn't sure whether Duke was winding him up or not. "Is that really necessary?"

"Someone has to clean them, and don't forget Oliver, George and Katie have all done it," replied Duke sharply.

Paul held his hands up, "Okay, Okay! You do what you think best, I'm not interfering."

"Good, plenty of time before we make him managing director. Now, I've got work to do."

Paul took the telling off. "See you later."

Duke was determined to put Callum through the mill and make his life a fucking misery; Paul was going soft.

The next morning Duke told Callum he was on toilet cleaning. It might not have been such a terrible job if there had not been so many. The whole building had no less than ten toilets of varying sizes. Callum just smiled at Duke and thought to himself that one day he would pay and pay dearly.

Callum was cleaning the executive toilets on the first floor and had jammed the men's door open for some fresh air. He was sitting on the floor scrubbing at a stubborn stain when he heard someone laughing by the door. He turned to see Katie standing in the corridor.

"Cleaning toilets suits you Callum, make sure you do a good job," and she laughed again.

"I know you Katie, you can't hide it."

Katie's smile disappeared. "What exactly are you talking about?"

"You want me, I can tell; you want what Mandy's getting three or four times a day."

"You are a disgusting person, you bastard! I wouldn't touch you if you were the last man on earth!" Katie was angry. "Remember, we're cousins, first cousins!" she added.

Callum laughed and nodded "Yea, okay we'll see."

Katie took it one step further, she looked around no one was about. She lifted her skirt to reveal sexy black knickers.

"This is what you want isn't it?" she rubbed her crutch suggestively.

Callum wasn't smiling or laughing. Yes, that was exactly what he wanted.

Katie pushed her skirt back down. "As long as I have breath in my body, you will never fucking get it, never."

She smiled; she could see he was uptight and thought she had won the round. She laughed once more then turned and strode away.

CHAPTER 5

The funeral was well attended. There must have been about a hundred and fifty odd people in the City Hope church, around the corner from the Blue Anchor in Drummond Road. Paul Bolton had arrived with Duke, Dave Bristow and a couple of guards ten minutes before the service was due to start. They were immaculately dressed in black suits, white shirts and black ties. They entered the church and looked around, it was packed. Paul then noticed Mary O'Connor Pat's wife, striding up the aisle towards him, her long black skirt swishing from side to side like a whirlwind. She looked concerned and Paul took a couple of steps towards her.

"I'm so sorry Mary I..."

"I told them not to sit there Paul, two seats were reserved for you, I told them but they just sat down and ignored me, I'm so sorry Paul..."

"Calm down Mary don't worry." Paul took her hand and smiled. "Show me the two seats and I'll take care of it." He turned to Duke who had been listening.

"You come with me." He turned to Dave. "If I put my hand up you, all come over, okay?"

Paul, Duke and Mary strode down the aisle to the front of the seating and turned to the seats on the left side. Mary was nervous as she walked half way down the row, she was praying there wouldn't be any trouble. She whispered to Paul the two giant men in long black Crombie coats.

Return to Bermondsey

Paul looked, yes they were huge; he told Mary to go back to her family. Meanwhile, the two men were looking at Paul and Duke and wondering what was going on. Paul took two more steps and bent down and whispered into the first man's ear.

"Name's Paul Bolton. You two are sitting in my seats."

The man looked up; he had heard of Paul Bolton but he was old news.

"Name's Kevin Philips. Fuck off out of it."

Duke took a menacing step towards the two seated men but Paul grabbed his arm to stop him. Paul turned and pulled Duke with him, they walked back down the aisle to the rear of the church and stood watching as the service commenced. It was ten minutes into the service when Paul felt a tap on his shoulder, he turned to see a smiling Detective Inspector Karen Foster and Detective Sargent Jeff Swan.

Karen whispered in Paul's ear, "How are you?"

Paul nodded as he learned forward and kissed Karen on the cheek. "Very well, good to see you. Chat in a minute."

They watched the ceremony with due reverence and forty minutes later it was all over. Paul and his team were first out the door and were talking thirty yards down the new, beautiful, natural fossil paving stone path from the front door. Karen and Jeff had been grabbed by someone they knew and were still chatting inside the church.

Kevin and Graham Philips strolled out of the church as though they owned it and the surrounding area. They were joined by two thugs who acted as personal guards and they began the walk down the path to their car. Paul saw them coming and was ready. As they got close, he stood in their way on the path.

"That was very rude: you were told by Pat's widow that those two seats were reserved for me; I want an apology."

The Philips brothers noted Duke, Dave and the guards were to the side of Paul. Kevin said, "Paul Bolton isn't it? This isn't your patch anymore best you leave."

Duke had heard enough; he moved forward. "You heard Mr. Bolton, apologise."

"Or what, mutton head?" chimed in Graham, the other brother.

Duke could see the confrontation ending in a fight. "Believe me, you're making a very big mistake. This is the last time I'm asking, apologise."

The two guards flanking the brothers moved forward. The other mourners had stopped walking down the path, they could see trouble was brewing.

One of the guards unwisely went to put his hand on Duke's shoulder to shove him out the way. Duke was ready; his hand moved from his pocket holding a small steel baton. He swung it and smashed the man in the face, he heard and felt the jaw bone crack and the man stumbled away in agony. The two brothers stepped forward menacingly and it was all about to kick off.

"Paul, are these friends of yours?" Karen Foster asked as she and Jeff Swan appeared from the crowd.

"Not exactly."

Karen turned towards the two brothers. "I'm Detective Inspector Foster, this is Sargent Jeff Swan. I've been meaning to look you two up. What's happening here?"

Dave Bristow and the guards melted away, leaving Paul and Duke.

"That man just attacked us; he should be arrested for assault."

Karen looked at Duke. "Did you attack this man?"

Duke kept it short and sweet. "Self-defense, officer."

"There, you see Mr. Philips, self-defense." Karen turned to Paul. "Mr. Bolton, if you would like to press charges, I'll arrest these two yobs."

The two brothers couldn't believe what was happening, it seemed Bolton and the copper were best buddies, and being called yobs was unforgivable.

"They owe me an apology officer; if they don't give it to me then yes, they should be arrested."

Karen turned and smiled at the two brothers, they looked at her with pure loathing.

Karen finally spoke, "Your choice gentleman."

Kevin Philips was the older brother. "Sorry about that; a mix up in the seating arrangements. Won't happen again."

Karen moved very close to him. "Listen, you fuck face. Go back to Romford, we don't want you here; if you stay you'll end up doing hard time in Belmarsh. Now, you and your brother, fuck off."

The two brothers strolled sheepishly past Paul. Duke smiled triumphantly at them as they continued up the path towards the exit.

Paul smiled at Karen. "Thanks Karen, good timing otherwise it could have gotten very unpleasant."

"Those two are the new drug barons around here; real scum."

Paul was against drugs and had never had anything to do with them. "Put them away and if you need any help you know where I am."

The Philips brothers were enraged, they had been made to look like complete prats; and they swore vengeance on Paul Bolton, the one called Duke and the coppers DI Karen Foster and her Sargent Jeff Swan.

CHAPTER 6

Callum had hold of her hips and was pulling Mandy backwards onto his cock; they had been fucking for hours and Callum was getting bored. He pulled away and collapsed onto the bed.

"Callum, what's wrong?"

"Nothing I'm just tired."

"You should have said," and Mandy went down on his erect cock sucking and licking. It didn't take long; Mandy was an expert and soon Callum was shooting his load into her mouth, grunting with pleasure.

He turned over and stretched his long body. Mandy ran her hands across his arse, she licked her middle finger and rubbed his hole, he moaned in pleasure.

"No more, Mandy, I've got things on my mind." He felt her hand reaching for his cock. He jerked away from her.

"Fucking hell Mandy! Enough before I really lose my temper!"

She looked at him; his eyes were shining. She backed away knowing he could turn very nasty in a second.

"Get dressed and fuck off. I'll see you tomorrow."

Mandy did exactly as she was told; she pulled a blue dress over her head, slipped on a pair of red knickers and walked out of the bedroom with a sour look on her face. A minute later Callum heard the door open and shut with a bang. He relaxed back on the bed, he had thinking to do and that was not possible while Mandy was sucking his cock.

Work was okay even though Duke gave him the shittiest jobs in the club. He loved the flat and even though Mandy was a pain in the arse, she let him do whatever he wanted to her which was exciting and pleasurable. On the other hand, He was annoyed whenever he saw Katie at the club because she blanked him every time as though he didn't exist. He swore to himself one way or the other he would have her.

He jumped up, went into the ultra-modern kitchen and made himself a coffee; he took it to the lounge and sat on the black leather sofa and relaxed. He was looking forward to Saturday; he had been invited to Paul and Lexis' house in Virginia Water for dinner. He was looking forward to meeting Lexi; he had heard so much about her from his mother. It was going to be a small intimate dinner with immediate family. The rest of the week was as boring as usual; Duke made sure he was working hard and getting the shittiest jobs possible. Duke's latest idea was for Callum to sand down some of the internal window frames and repaint them, a complete waste of time as they didn't even need doing.

Saturday came round quickly enough. Callum had bought himself a new pair of tight fitting jeans with **a** leather belt and an expensive Paul Smith multi-coloured designer shirt. He showered, put on his new gear and looked in the mirror. He was happy with what he saw. Let's see what Katie thinks of his new look, he said to himself.

Getting to Virginia Water was a pain. He took the tube to Waterloo Station and got the six thirty South West Train to Virginia Water. The train was almost empty and he sat in the third carriage. The train seemed to stop at every micky mouse station in Surrey, and finally arrived at Virginia Water at seven forty. It was in fact good timing as dinner was at eight. Callum exited the station and got a taxi from the aptly named station cabs. It was a short journey as Callum took in views of the huge beautiful houses in the wealthy area. The cab finally turned down a wide tree lined road and proceeded right to the end.

The imposing solid black gate reeked of money and affluence. Callum could see vast houses with massive grounds and knew this was where Paul and Lexi lived. The cab stopped and a burly black man in uniform approached the driver, he asked who was in the cab and where he was going. Callum announced himself and that he was visiting the Bolton residence. The guard disappeared; Callum tried to see where he had gone but could not locate him. He reappeared two minutes later opening the gate and telling the driver he could proceed. The guard had actually rang the residence and confirmed they were indeed expecting Callum. Callum was in awe that people lived in such opulence. The cab pulled into the massive driveway and was directed by a huge bodyguard to park in front of the triple garages.

Callum paid the cabbie and got out; he began to walk towards the front door but was called back by the guard.

"Go round the side to the back." He pointed to a path leading around the side of the house.

Callum turned and walked around the corner towards the back of the property. He was shocked as he nearly fell over another bodyguard who stared at him as he headed towards the direction of laughter he heard. He finally saw a patio and recognised who was there: Paul and a very striking slim woman who had to be Lexi. He also noted Oliver, George and then the stunning but very aggravating Katie. The last person was Duke who was sipping a beer from the bottle and chatting to another bodyguard who then wandered off. He approached the group with a smile on his face. Duke, on seeing Callum walked straight towards him. Callum stopped. Duke reached him and proceeded to search him from head to toe; Callum had never been so embarrassed and humiliated in his life. He glanced at the others and noticed Katie with a sardonic smile on her face. He closed his eyes for a second to control his rising anger and then he heard a gentle but strong voice.

"Duke, please! This is a family dinner," said Lexi, laughing.

Lexi took hold of Callum's arm, smiled at him and led him onto the patio. "Don't pay any attention to Duke; he's over protective when it comes to the family. So Callum, Paul was right, you look just like your father, very tall, broad shouldered and handsome." Lexi kept hold of Callum's arm; he was mesmerised by her.

Return to Bermondsey

Paul stepped forward. "Welcome to the family home, Callum."

"It's a pleasure to be here Paul," he replied, with his eyes glued on Lexi, unable to take his eyes off her.

Oliver and George came forward and shook hands while Katie headed towards the kitchen. "I'm going to check on dinner."

Lexi had finally let go of Callum's hand. "So, Callum, how are you finding London?"

"Well, I haven't seen too much of it as yet but I am planning on doing some regular sightseeing soon."

"Katie could show you the sights, she knows London better than anyone, isn't that so, Paul?"

"I guess but I hear Callum has a young lady so he might prefer it just to be the two of them," he laughed, looking at Callum.

Callum cursed under his breath, he should have been more discreet where Mandy was concerned; of course everybody in the club knew so the whole family would as well.

"It's nothing serious but Mandy is a nice girl." Then he decided to say it, "She's after a job as a hostess and personally, I think she would do a very good job."

Duke butted in, "I run the clubs and I'm not interested in what you think."

63

Return to Bermondsey

There followed a deafening silence, you could have cut the atmosphere with a knife until Katie breezed out from the back door, "Food's looking good!"

Paul said quickly, "More drinks everyone! Come on, let's get stuck into the champagne!"

Katie had noticed Callum's new look and she approved; even though she hated him, she still wanted him. Lexi disappeared to the kitchen and five minutes later announced dinner was served. The family and Duke rushed in, laughing and being playful. Lexi was standing by the table telling people where to sit. Callum was told to sit next to Katie which he couldn't decide was a blessing or a nightmare. Katie could smell Callum's aftershave and she sucked it into her nose and mouth. She had decided not to speak to him and spent the early part of the dinner talking to George who was on her other side.

The avocado and king prawn starter went down a treat and soon the main course of Coq au Vin was served. The wine was flowing and everybody was becoming tipsy. Jokes were being told as Eton mess dessert was served followed by the vintage port being passed round. Callum had downed far too much of everything due to his nervousness and was well on the way to being drunk. Katie was talking to George when she felt it, a hand on her thigh. She knew it was Callum; she was just about to jump up and shout but decided she liked it. He squeezed her thigh and moved his hand down pulling up her short skirt. He slipped his hand down her purple knickers and was about to touch her most intimate place. Katie had let him go far enough, she moved her legs and he whipped his hand out and back onto his lap.

"Are you having a good time Callum?" Lexi asked.

"Wonderful, thank you Lexi." Callum knew it wouldn't be long before he was fucking Katie.

The dinner had ended well; the only sober person was Duke. The group then retired to the very impressive lounge and sipped at their final drinks. Conversation flowed and it was soon gone midnight.

Lexi was feeling sorry for Callum and without looking at Paul she said, "Callum, it's far too late for you to be going back to Chelsea Harbour; you must stay the night." And she gave him one of her lovely smiles. Callum glanced at Katie, telling her with his eyes that tonight was the night.

Duke had quickly left the room and returned five minutes later. "Callum, your mini-cab is here."

The room went quiet for a moment then Paul said cheerily, "Thanks for coming Callum, we must do it again soon."

Callum smiled but underneath was seething. He would have to deal with Duke and the sooner the better.

Forty minutes later Callum arrived back at Chelsea Harbour. He had been nodding off in the back and woke with a start as the cab pulled to a stop. He reached for his wallet.

"How much?"

"Eighty quid gov," replied the Pakistani driver.

Callum stopped dead. "How much?"

"Eighty pounds please, gov."

"You've been round the houses mate, that's a bloody fortune."

"It is very late that is why it's expensive."

"You're a lying bastard! Here, take thirty; that's all you're getting."

The cab driver opened the driver's door and got out, he was a big man.

"I want my money or I call police," and he held his mobile up as though to call.

The red mist rose and Callum was beginning to lose his temper. He climbed out the back of the cab and met the driver at the front by the bonnet.

"Look mate, you have one chance and one chance only. Take the thirty quid and consider yourself lucky to walk away."

The cab driver lifted the mobile and started to press 999.

Callum leaped forward and delivered a karate kick to the man's left knee; the man screamed and his leg buckled and he fell heavily to the floor. He dropped the mobile as Callum followed that up with a massive punch to the man's jaw as he went down. He heard the crunch and snap of the jaw breaking. The man was moaning as Callum threw him into the back of the cab. He jumped into the driver's seat and accelerated away at speed. Six minutes later he pulled into a dirty unlit industrial estate five miles from the flat. He dragged the man out of the back of the cab and threw him onto the concrete.

"You cunt, clever fucker eh! Well, see where being a clever cunt has got you!"

Callum's eyes were shining bright as he started to kick the man. After a frenzied three minutes he stopped. The man's face was smashed to pieces, a massive puddle of blood had formed under his head. His legs and arms were at irregular angles as Callum had stamped repeatedly on the joints. Callum was now feeling happy as he didn't like being taken for a ride; the bastard got exactly what he deserved. He spat on the man's face and with some difficulty, lifted him into what looked like a disused old skip, covered him with rubbish and jumped back into the cab. He drove the cab for a couple of miles, looking for a suitable spot. Then he saw an old grotty warehouse at the end of a cull de sac and drove the car straight round to the back and left it. He pulled the collar up on his jacket and set off back to the flat.

CHAPTER 7

Detective Inspector Karen Foster was staying in a big old house in Surrey Quays. It had been used as a safe house by the Metropolitan Police so hadn't been properly decorated for years. She felt a bit intimidated by it and would have preferred one of the much smaller modern properties just around the corner. It wasn't great going back to a huge old house on your own. The heating took an hour to warm all the rooms and when you put the hot tap on in the kitchen, there were clanging noises throughout the piping system. Karen had stocked the cupboards and filled the wine rack with mostly red wine, which cheered her up.

Karen and Jeff had been given a brief and it was simple enough, crack down on organised crime that had somehow started flourishing once again in Bermondsey and Rotherhithe. Jeff had already explained that Kevin and Graham Philips were the new drug barons and needed to be taken down. Matt Craven, the officer in charge of the Pat O'Connor murder at the Blue Anchor, had gone sick with serious depression; Karen and Jeff had been asked to assess the progress and if needs be, take over the investigation. They found out that the whole investigation from start to finish had been badly conducted, and there wasn't a hope in hell of finding out who committed the murder unless they started from the beginning again, which they chose to do. Karen took a couple of days to settle back in, but very soon she felt as though she hadn't been away for long. Karen was determined to lay down a marker that she was back, and the way to do that was to sort the Philips brothers and find out who killed Pat at the Blue Anchor.

***

Kevin and Graham Philips had both left Pat's funeral in a filthy mood. It had been a very long time since anyone had made a public joke of them and they swore an oath of vengeance to sort Paul Bolton, the one called Duke, Detective Inspector Foster and her sidekick Jeff Swan. Kevin and Graham were big, hard, ugly men. They had built their criminal drugs business with violence, intimidation and money from drugs. Nothing brought in profits like drugs and anything or anybody who got in the way were ruthlessly dealt with, usually with severe violence. Kevin was the boss and that suited the two of them; he was the brains while Graham enjoyed dishing out torture and cutting people. They had returned to their favourite pub the Anchor Tap in Tower Bridge Road. It was one of those traditional pubs with no loud music, gaming machines or large screen TV's. Graham got the beers in and they sat in their seats near the bar, with a good view of the door.

"Well, Kevin, what's the plan?"

Kevin gave Graham a withering look. "Give me a fucking chance! We've just left the funeral." After a long pause he said, "One thing's for certain, they're all going to pay."

Graham's lips curled into an evil smile. "Lovely! I'm looking forward to it already!" and he sank half his pint.

"Coppers are a tough one, kill a copper and they never stop looking for you," Kevin said thoughtfully. "But accidents happen all the time," he looked at Graham and laughed. They raised their glasses to each other and continued laughing hysterically. Twenty minutes later, they left the pub and got in a black Mercedes that was waiting at the kerb.

***

Karen and Jeff were sitting in her office with the usual lattes, trying to find a way forward in the Pat-Blue Anchor-pub murder. As Karen had done throughout her career, if you were getting nowhere and had hit the proverbial brick wall, she had always advocated going back to the beginning. Pat had been beaten to death in the bar of the Blue Anchor; it was just after opening time and the pub had been empty. A punter had walked in the main entrance to see the back of a young man leaving by the side entrance into Blue Anchor Lane. He could not give any helpful description of the young man. And that was it, nobody outside the pub saw anybody enter or leave. The only clue they had was DNA evidence from shards of the broken glass and there were no matches to it on the police system.

"So, what do we do next?" Jeff asked glumly; he couldn't see a way forward.

"Get word out to all the snitches; I want answers," Karen answered. "You know what Jeff, I have the feeling this was a random killing because of an argument, maybe he didn't like the beer." They both smiled weakly.

"One thing's for sure, if we don't get a lucky break, this could well join the long list of Met unsolved murders."

Jeff nodded his head in agreement. He leaned over and picked up Karen's empty cup. "Another coffee, boss?"

"Thought you'd never ask," said Karen jokingly.

CHAPTER 8

Callum entered the staff entrance of the Den Club, singing to himself, "I don't like Mondays, tell me why?" Rob, the sixty-nine year old doorman laughed.

"Morning Callum! Good weekend?"

Callum just smiled at him and thought back to having had his hand down Katie's knickers. Rob knew he was a Bolton and trod carefully; he loved his job and didn't want to jeopardize it in any way. Callum signed in and walked through the dingy corridors noticing the cobweb infested ceilings; he grimaced, thinking he might be cleaning them off later. He eventually entered what was laughingly labelled the staff canteen, a small room with two vending machines that dispensed coffee and sweets. The room was empty. He helped himself to a free coffee and sat down; he sometimes liked to be on his own and this was one of those moments. Two minutes later, Graham, one of the bar staff, stuck his head round the door.

"Morning Callum, Duke wants to see you in the cocktail bar."

Callum cursed; the coffee was too hot to drink and you could not take food or drinks into the guest areas. He left the plastic cup on the table and followed Graham out. He walked into the guest area and was always impressed; it was huge and was coming to life as it did every morning. He bounded up the impressive staircase towards the VIP area.

"Duke, good morning."

Duke eye-balled Callum, making sure he kept a hard face on.

"You got promoted, from now on your working in the cocktail bar. Go home and be back here at seven o clock; black trousers and white shirt." He strode off leaving Callum standing there in slight shock. He looked around and smiled, it was progress. The cocktail bar was popular with the well-off punters and apparently, loads of the women were supposedly very good looking. He thought it might be time to trade in Mandy and get a new model. Yes, he thought, a bit of posh totty would be exciting and a nice change. He about turned and made his way back to the canteen; the coffee was still hot and he drank it down quickly. Then he opened the door and almost bumped into Mandy.

"Callum, I've been looking for you."

"Well, you found me; we're finished and don't fucking bother me again." And he strode past Mandy towards the exit. If he'd looked back he would have seen her standing holding the door with her mouth agape, unable to speak.

"That was quick, young man." Rob said with a slight surprise on seeing him back so soon.

"Back later Rob." Callum smiled at the old boy. "Have a good day, eh?"

Rob shook his head, thinking he was too old to understand young people anymore.

Return to Bermondsey

Callum walked down Kingly Street and decided to buy some new gear for his first night. He knew a designer clothes shop not far away and increased his stride; he would make sure he looked good for the new woman in his life.

***

Callum entered the cocktail bar at exactly six forty five that evening in his new Church black brogue shoes, black trousers and crisp whiter than white Van Heusen shirt. His fake diamond cuff links glittered in the lights. The whole gear had cost him nearly five hundred pounds but as he stood behind the bar he felt a million dollars.

He smiled at the head barman Tony. "I'm ready to learn the tricks of the trade."

Tony looked surprised and looked at Callum from head to foot.

"Hmm, well you are without a doubt the best dressed glass collector and bottle washer we have ever had in this bar."

Callum's smile disappeared in an instant, he could feel the rage growing in him; collecting fucking glasses! Was he a Bolton or not? He stormed out the bar and headed towards the executive offices. Never had he felt like this. He hated Duke, hated him with a passion. He hurtled through the offices pushing aside the executive secretaries and stormed into Paul's office.

"This is it Uncle Paul, the final fucking straw! Cleaning toilets, washing fucking floors and glasses! I've fucking well had it up to here!" and he put his palm across his neck. "Unless things change I am leaving, not in a minute, not later on! Right fucking now!"

They both looked at each other with no facial expression. After what seemed like an eternity, Paul smiled.

"So you're not happy then?"

Callum didn't answer for a few seconds, then He shrugged, "You could say that; I think I have more to offer than cleaning toilets and washing glasses."

Paul studied him. "Yes, okay I agree. You are now on the management ladder, which means no more cleaning toilets." He paused and added, "I like you Callum, you have put up with everything without complaint; and by all accounts the toilets have never been so clean," and he laughed.

Callum smiled happily and he felt some sort of new relationship had started with Paul.

Paul stood up. "Let's walk round the club and you can tell me where you would really like to work, although I think I can guess."

Paul wanted to show the staff that Callum was a Bolton and had served his time and he was now joining the senior staff and should be treated accordingly. They made their way around the ground floor but Callum felt as if he was dreaming and couldn't speak. Eventually they took the lift to the executive floor and entered into the premier club facility. It was beautifully decorated with expensive carpets and wallpaper, the dining facilities were five star and it reeked of money.

Callum looked around and decided very quickly. "This is where I want to work."

"I thought you might say that, it's a very important part of the business, less footfall but huge margins and that equals good profits. You'll start behind the bar." He paused. "And try," he looked imploringly at Callum. "To not chat up the women. It's actually against club rules. And remember, Duke will be keeping an eye on you."

Callum had forgotten about Duke but he was happy; in fact he was over the fucking moon.

"Thank you Uncle Paul, I won't let you down."

"And I don't want to hear any more of that Uncle shit, Paul is fine."

"Okay, when do I start?"

"Well, you're dressed for the occasion; so what's wrong with right now?"

"I'm ready."

Paul called over the premier club manager Barry Gunn.

"Barry, Callum is starting behind the bar tonight. Break him in gently, okay?"

"Of course Mr. Bolton."

"Oh, and come and see me when it's all set up, and you have five minutes."

Barry nodded and he and Callum disappeared off towards the bar.

Paul didn't like plonking a new member of staff onto a manager and particularly a Bolton. He would explain why he had done it and what he expected from Barry and Callum.

Paul went back to his office and called Duke. He explained what he had done and although Duke was seething inside, he didn't show that to Paul. Duke still didn't trust Callum and was watching him closely. The club opened as usual and the rich and not so rich turned up in their hundreds, splashing cash or mostly, gold and black credit cards. Callum was helping behind the bar, doing odd jobs and serving the occasional customer. He was in his element; loud music, beautiful woman and he felt he belonged. Nightclubs were intoxicating and the women! Oh God, the women! He had even seen a woman pick up her purse she had dropped and got a clear flash of no-knickers. The men varied from older and wealthy to young and wealthy. Smart expensive designer clothes were essential, as was the ability to order champagne at three hundred pounds a bottle, without knowing or caring what the price was.

Most of the woman were young and gorgeous and he laughed as he hadn't actually seen a woman buy her own drink for hours. The night went on and a couple of the older female customers had smiled at him and he was sure they were after a good fuck. He would behave for a time until he learnt the ropes and knew what was going on. Finally it was 3 am and the bar shutter was pulled down. Callum was excited and exhausted at the same time; he wasn't sure he would sleep but he had enjoyed the night and was looking forward to the same again. He said goodnight to Barry and left the bar.

As he went out onto the landing to the stairs, he saw Katie. "Hey Katie! How are you?"

Katie turned and was confused, but not for long.

"I hear you got promoted. Congratulations."

"I'm behind the bar but its progress," he smiled at her.

"We have all done the toilets, the bars and every other shit job in the club; you have to understand every element of a club if you are ever going to manage one."

Katie turned and started walking down the stairs.

"You're so right Katie and I want to learn. Paul has given me a huge opportunity and I mean to make the most of it."

Katie stopped and turned again. "I'm pleased to hear that Callum. Why don't you take me for a drink sometime?"

Callum could not believe what he had heard. "How about now?"

Katie shook her head. "I'm too tired. I'll let you know when." She turned and walked quickly down the stairs. Callum stood still and digested what had just happened. Things were certainly looking up and he couldn't wait to get Katie naked in his arms. Callum stood a while, thinking. He knew he was going to be a somebody; he had been given the opportunity and it was now up to him. There were plenty of clubs owned by Paul Bolton and he would make one of them his. He skipped down the stairs and started whistling as he made for the exit and home.

CHAPTER 9

Callum answered his Samsung mobile.

"So, that drink then this Saturday. Meet me at the Pitcher and Piano Dean Street midday, oh and don't tell a soul, you understand?"

"Of course, couldn't agree more. I can't wait." Callum smiled triumphantly and whispered to himself, "Katie, here I come!"

Callum put his mobile on the small coffee table next to the plush sofa. He put his feet on the poof and smiled to himself. It was a start, he put his hand down his trousers and felt his cock; just the thought of Katie was enough to start an erection. He closed his eyes and imagined what she would be like standing naked in front of him, and he started to masturbate...

Friday night was busy; Callum was rushed off his feet and didn't have time to think about his date with Katie the next day. It was the usual three am finish and he collapsed into his bed at four am, setting the alarm for nine. It wouldn't be enough sleep but it would have to do. He slept deeply and cursed when he was woken by the alarm which sounded like an atomic explosion in his ears. He reached over and clicked the alarm off. It was the day, the day he had been waiting for, and he was finally to get Katie on her own. He pushed the duvet back and stretched, he then jumped up and made for the shower; he needed to look the part. He luxuriated in the shower, washing thoroughly. He shaved his face and tidied his pubes and then spent a full five minutes brushing and flossing his teeth. He then sprayed himself liberally with Lynx deodorant and expensive Italian Aqua Di Parma after-shave. He was ready at ten fifteen and looked in the mirror. He smiled; there was no way she would be able to resist him in his tight pair of Levi jeans and a crisp blue Ralph Lauren shirt with glittering fake sapphire cuff-links. He ran his hand through his black shiny hair, pushing it back off his forehead, turned and made for the door.

***

Katie was up early at eight am. She spent her customary hour in the bathroom and went back to her bedroom to dress. She chose a matching set of black knickers and bra, blue jeans and a white shirt. She then went downstairs to the kitchen, and was soon sipping scolding hot instant Maxwell house coffee. Paul and Lexi strolled in at nine thirty to see Katie sitting at the breakfast bar, both were surprised at her unusual early appearance.

"Katie! What on earth are you doing up?" asked Lexi.

"I'm going shopping," she said, smiling from ear to ear. "And I mean serious shopping. I'm meeting some friends later and afterwards, I may go straight to the club; so don't worry if I'm not home later."

"Okay darling, that's fine as long as we know where you are."

Paul was making toast. "And if you're going to Oxford Street, watch out for those bloody Romanian pickpockets, they're after your phone and purse."

"Don't worry daddy, I'm a big girl now," she chuckled.

Paul looked at her with pride. "You may be a big girl now but you're our daughter and always will be. Be careful, alright?"

Katie stood up took a skip to Paul and flung her arms around his neck and gave him a big hug.

"What was that for?"

"Because I love you and mum so much."

"That's nice but still, be careful out there."

***

It was a fresh morning, Callum had intended to take a taxi but he changed his mind and instead he took a leisurely stroll to Fulham Broadway tube station and was soon on a district line train hurtling noisily towards central London. The train was packed and as he looked around at all the various nationalities he wondered if Britain was losing its identity. He thought of home in Canada and although immigration was increasing it was nothing like in the UK. He smiled at two teenage girls sitting opposite him; he thought they looked South American, at any other time he may have chatted them up but it was out of the question this particular day. He was day dreaming and nearly missed his stop as the train ground to a halt; and when he casually glanced up and saw it was South Kensington, he jumped up and was through the door just as it began to close. He followed the signs to the Piccadilly trains and entered the platform. He ambled down the long platform, noticing a gorgeous older woman of about thirty who was dressed to thrill in a short green skirt and matching tight jumper. He suddenly thought he had to stop his obsession with women, but then shook his head; every young normal guy he knew was obsessed and thought of and looked at women constantly.

The train thundered into the station two minutes later and Callum got annoyed as his hair was swept every which way by the powerful gust of wind. It was busy again and he had to stand, it didn't bother him. He sorted his hair as best he could as his mind wandered back to touching Katie; he had to have her. A drink was a start and it was a long day before they had to be at the club for work. Six stops later, he got out at Covent Garden. He could have gone to Tottenham Court Road station which was nearer Dean Street, but he loved Covent Garden and wanted to meander through the small side streets. He walked past a couple of sex shops and then crossed over Shaftesbury Avenue towards his destination.

***

Katie pulled on her short shiny black leather jacket and shouted out to Paul and Lexi. "Bye! See you later!" She heard mumbled byes and take cares, and opened the front door.

The mini cab had been waiting; she jumped in the back and made her-self comfortable. Five minutes later, she

Return to Bermondsey

was at the local station where she bought a South West bound train ticket to Waterloo. It was ten past ten; she climbed onto the ten twenty train and sat at a table. She opened her bag and took out her latest read, Driven to Kill, a crime thriller with lots of violence and sex, which was just what she liked. She read a few pages but couldn't concentrate. She put it on the small table and settled back in the seat. She began to wonder what the hell she was doing; she hated Callum's arrogance, his I-can-have-any-woman-I-want attitude. She thought back to seeing him fucking Mandy at the flat in Chelsea Harbour. God! That had turned her on immensely. She closed her eyes and saw him naked, ramming his massive hard cock into that stupid dumb woman. She wanted it, she couldn't help herself, but not today, that was for certain; he would have to earn it. The train trundled on and she nodded off. She woke with a start as the train stopped; she heard the tannoy announcing Waterloo as the final destination. She looked around, people were rushing towards the doors. She decided to wait until they had all gone, there was no rush. She looked at her watch, it was ten past eleven.

***

Callum was in Dean Street and found the Pitcher and Piano. It was eleven fifteen, he decided to walk on and he found a lovely little coffee bar; he went in and sat on one of the tall wood and red plastic stools at the counter and ordered an Americano. The coffee arrived steaming hot and delicious; he sipped it slowly so as not to burn his mouth. He leaned over as far as he dared and he could see down to the front entrance of the Pitcher and piano.

Return to Bermondsey

He was going to wait till he saw Katie arrive but then thought better of it. Instead, he would leave shortly and be inside waiting for her.

At dead on eleven thirty he left the coffee bar and made his way to the bar and ordered a large whisky and sat facing the door. He downed the whisky and ordered another, he was feeling nervous. He looked at his watch, five to twelve. God, he was excited; he wanted her so much! Attractive women were ten a penny to Callum; t was the sexual power, he liked to control them, be completely in charge. He liked to tell them exactly what to do and if they didn't, he would use his strength to subdue and overpower them; they always enjoyed it in the end. He kept glancing at the door, then another look at his watch, it was ten past twelve.

Then he suddenly remembered he hadn't taken his pills. Shit! He fumbled in his pocket for the loose tablets he put there before he left. He swallowed one thousand milligrams of the anti-psychotic solian medication with a gulp of whisky. He knew he shouldn't drink while taking them, but he had done it before without any problems. He looked at his watch again, it was nearly twelve thirty. He was getting annoyed, he didn't like being kept waiting. He ordered another whisky and began to feel light headed. The bar was filling up and he was becoming agitated; she was taking him for a fool and for a minute, he thought she might not even turn up. God help her if she didn't. Finally, at twelve forty, he saw her walk in and he smiled his warmest greeting as she saw him and walked towards him.

"Callum! Good to see you!"

"Nowhere near as happy as I am to see you! What would you like to drink?"

"Dry white wine, please. Been here long?"

"A bit but I would have waited forever for you."

Katie laughed. "Bloody hell! Bit cheesy but I'll take the compliment."

Callum went to the bar and ordered a large white wine and another whisky for himself; he went back to the table and moved the chair very close to Katie.

"You look fantastic, I mean it; really beautiful," he said with a sincerity that pleased Katie.

"You don't look half bad yourself and you smell lovely."

He learned over and kissed her on the cheek.

She smiled at him, "You can do better than that."

He looked into her eyes and their lips met in a passionate kiss. He eventually pulled away.

"I...I really like you Katie, in fact I...words fail me."

"Words fail you! Never!" Katie laughed and ran her hands sexily through her hair.

She looked deeply into his eyes. "I have a surprise for you."

"Hmm, I like good surprises, not so keen on bad ones."

"Oh, this is a good one, you better believe it. Finish your drink, we're off." She stood up and turned towards the door. Callum knocked back his whisky and dashed after her, wondering where they were going. He caught her up at the door.

"I'm on tenterhooks! Where are we going?"

"Just follow me, it's not far."

Katie strode down Dean Street and quickly entered Carlisle Street, stopped and turned to Callum, "I want you to do exactly as I say, agreed?"

Callum opened his eyes wide and opened his hands in surrender. "Whatever you say!"

"Good. You see that building at the end of the road, with a strange statue over the entrance?"

He looked down the short road and could see an impressive entrance with a silver statue above it that looked like a silver woman with wings; he could just make out the name, The Nadler.

"It's a hotel and I have a room booked there. For reasons you don't need to know, you will enter through the tradesman's entrance and go to room 22 on the second floor. The less people who see you, the better, you understand?"

"Yea okay, but why don't we just walk in together?"

"Because I don't need the world knowing what I'm up to." She was sure of herself as she strode off down the short distance to the boutique Nadler hotel. She swept into the impressive black and white reception and approached the desk.

"Room 22 please."

"Certainly Madame." The suave Italian receptionist handed over the key card and couldn't take his eyes off her arse as she waltzed towards the lift.

Two minutes later she entered her room and shut the door behind her. She had tidied the room before she left but checked again; it all looked neat. She then opened the small fridge and took out a miniature bottle of white wine, she turned the black screwcap top, pulled it off and pored the wine slowly into a glass. She sat on the edge of the bed and began to panic; he could be here any moment. She knew what she wanted to do and would not let him go any further. She wanted to be treasured and her boundaries to be respected. Little did she know Callum was having his own problems trying to avoid delivery drivers, maintenance men and chefs who all seemed to be wandering about at will.

He waited until there was a clear path and made his move. He was sure no one saw him and soon he was striding down a long corridor where the ceiling was criss-crossed with pipes of all sizes. He saw some fire escape stairs and knowing he had to get to the second floor, he took them. He bounded up the stairs two at a time and then thought he must be at the second floor. He gently pushed the door and saw a well decorated hotel corridor. He pushed the door open more and felt the thick carpet as he took a step into the plush corridor to get his bearings. He smiled and was relieved he had been right, he saw room 29 and scanned which way to go. He followed the even numbers and came to room 22. There was deathly quiet; you could have heard a pin drop. He went to the door and knocked. It opened slightly and he heard Katie whisper, "Come in."

He opened the door fully to see Katie walking away from him towards the huge bed in her deliciously looking black knickers and bra; he was mesmerised. She sat on the side of the bed and smiled at him. He pushed the door completely shut and took slow steps towards her; he already had a massive hard on and could barely wait.

"Lie on the bed," Katie commanded.

Callum stopped. "Undressed?"

"Yes."

He slowly undid his shirt followed by his shoes, socks and then trousers. Katie looked at his muscular body and got incredibly excited as she saw the massive erection in his boxer shorts.

"Lie down," she said.

Callum slipped his boxers down and climbed onto the bed and lay down.

Katie stood and took a bottle off the table at the side of the bed; she opened it and poured some oil into her palm. She started on his shoulders, massaging firmly but softly with the oil. She made her way down his stomach and then to his thighs; she was sorely tempted to take hold of his big cock but she wanted him to be dying for it.

"How are we doing so far?" She asked teasingly.

"I'd say it's going very well for a starter," he managed to answer breathlessly

Katie continued downwards, massaging his feet and then sucking his toes. She glanced to see if he was still erect; if anything, he had gotten bigger.

"So, we have some fun and then if you're good, next time you might get it all."

Callum thought he knew what that meant, but if she thought he was leaving this room without having fucked her, she was on a different planet.

Katie moved closer and took his cock in both hands and started masturbating him slowly, his cock was so swollen and she heard him moaning.

"Hmm! That's good Katie, you know I think the world of you, always have from the second I first saw you!" He moaned again loudly.

"And I like you Callum, but we play this slowly okay? There's no need to rush."

Callum suddenly reached out and grabbed her knickers, Katie took her hand off his cock and pushed his hand away. She raised her voice to him.

"Callum! My rules today! I know you're not used to that but that's the way it has to be."

"For fucks sake! What's wrong? At least let me touch you!"

Katie smiled and looked at him sweetly. She took his hand and slipped it down the front of her knickers. "Feel how wet I am?"

Callum explored with his fingers until he found her, he roughly probed and rubbed her, and he was becoming more and more excited. He got on his knees retrieved his hand and grasped Katie round her arse cheeks and pulled her towards him. She tried to move back but he was so strong, and she could see the sharply defined muscle on his torso shining with droplets of sweat.

"No, Callum! Whatever you're thinking, it's not going to happen."

She slapped his arm, "Let go of me!"

In answer, Callum held her very tight and manoeuvred her legs wide apart and pulled her even closed to his erect cock.

Katie thrashed her legs and managed to catch him slightly off balance, then she pulled her leg back and lashed out at his own leg, catching him on the knee. He was getting angry; he couldn't understand what was wrong with the stupid bitch. He slapped her hard on the thigh.

"Look, you fucking idiot! You're not a child! I'm going to fuck you whether you like it or not, so play ball!" He was getting angry.

"Choices, Callum, you miserable fuck! I have choices and I choose no, not today! Do you understand?"

Callum closed his eyes; the red mist was taking over. He wanted her and he was fucking well going to have her. Then it hit him! She must like to be dominated! He laughed to himself; he was good at that. He jumped off the bed and then grabbed her hair tightly and started to pull her round the room.

"You see Katie, I'm in charge! I'm the one with the power!" He tugged her hair even tighter and she cried out.

"You fucking slag! You'll do as I fucking well say or there'll be consequences!" he kept on pulling her hair until she went down on all fours on the carpet.

"You want it doggy style Katie? Up the arse, is that what you want?" Callum was becoming almost uncontrollable. With his other hand he started slapping her arse very hard.

"You bastard you'll pay for this! Oh believe me, you'll pay for this!" Katie was beside herself with fury; hot, angry tears stung her eyes

Callum hadn't heard a word she said; he was shoving his fingers in both her holes and she was yelping in pain. He couldn't wait any longer and let go of her hair and grabbed her hips, he pulled her back so he could penetrate her but as he went to push she suddenly scampered away across the floor towards the door.

"Help! Someone help me please help! Help me!" Katie was yelling as she tried to open the door.

But Callum was on her in a second like a hunting dog on a fox. He slapped her around and then he looked down to see her face and put his hands around her throat and squeezed, but not too tightly, only so she would stop shouting. He dragged her back to the bed and threw her on it. He clambered on top of her, pushed her legs open and thrust into her. She bucked and screamed as he slammed into her. He was in another world, not listening or caring. Katie felt the penetration, it wasn't meant to be like this, she thought. She brought her right hand back and then attacked his arm, tearing at the flesh with her sharp nails. He gasped and swore as the pain hit him. He squeezed her throat again to keep her quiet.

The attack stopped and Callum continued thrusting and holding her throat; he was a god and in control; he thrust and thrust, slapping her breasts with his left hand. He continued to hold her throat tight as he fucked her hard. It seemed to go on for- ever and then he felt it, he bucked and gasped as he finished himself inside her. He stopped and sat up stretching his back and neck, the stupid bitch won't give him any trouble after that, he said to himself. If anyone could have seen him, his eyes were shining very bright and he was covered in sweat. He looked down, expecting to see Katie smiling but was shocked, for she was white as a sheet; he looked closely.

"Katie!" he shouted and frantically shook her shoulder and slapped her gently on the face; then he realised she was dead. He lurched back and disengaged himself. He was suddenly very terrified and started shaking all over.

"Katie! Oh God! Look what you made me do, you fucking stupid cow! I didn't mean... why did you make me do it?" He broke down and started crying, sinking to the thick carpeted floor. His mind was in a whirl; he had to get away, get out of the hotel, get home; create some sort of alibi. Fucking hell! He rubbed his face and glanced over at the lifeless, already greying body; she looked so peaceful. He shook his head, he wished his mummy was there. She wouldn't blame him, it was the medication, and he was just like his father; she would have known what to do. She would have been giving him regular hand jobs to keep the urges at bay; she understood him. He cried some more and then pulled himself together. He stood and looked at the body; should he try and take it out the hotel and bury it somewhere? He shook his head; how the fuck could he carry a body out of a hotel?

Then he remembered some movies he had seen, they always put the body in a laundry trolley. He closed his eyes; that was fucking Hollywood, for Christ's sake! A fire! He could start a fire and burn down the entire hotel! He couldn't think straight, he had to get away. What about DNA evidence? He had come inside her that was a lot of DNA but the good news was that the UK police would have no match for it, he was clean as far as the police were concerned. He knew he had to decide quickly. First he grabbed the DO NOT DISTURB SIGN and opened the door an inch, there was no one in the corridor; he opened it further and stuck the sign on the door. No one would find the body until at least late morning or mid-day on Sunday.

He got dressed then searched the entire floor and bed to make sure nothing had fallen out of any of his pockets; the room was clean. He looked closely at Katie lying there, going greyer and looking colder by the second. Suddenly, Paul Bolton's image appeared in his mind, he shook his head again to get rid of it. There was nothing else to do; he took a tentative step towards the door. He'd never meant it to work out like this; he loved Katie. He turned and opened the door and then quickly shut it again, he looked around and saw Katie's small blue hand bag; he picked it up, opened it and took the mobile out, put it in his pocket and threw the bag on the floor. Then he reopened the door and listened, nothing. He stuck his head out, the corridor was empty; he shut the door behind him and strode quickly down towards the service stairs. He pushed the heavy door and went through. He stopped again to listen, it was all quiet and he bounded down the stairs two at a time to get clear and away from the smell of death. He was soon outside and making his way as fast as he could to the tube station. He was on his phone in seconds.

"I know I was horrible to you, I didn't mean it, I promise. Look, meet me at the flat in an hour, I promise I'll make it up to you." He held the phone listening.

"Brilliant! Can't wait to see you!" He sped up as he began to smile. Katie was only a fucking slapper, for Christ's sake.

***

"How are you enjoying the premier club?"

Callum just stared at Duke, sure that there was a cutting remark to follow.

"Callum, wake up and answer the fucking question!"

"Eh, yes I am enjoying it; thank you for asking." Callum answered without smiling.

Duke smiled, "Keep up the good work or you'll be back washing dishes," and he walked off.

Callum was surprised; it was the first time Duke had ever said a decent word to him. He went behind the bar and started a stock check of the mixers.

***

Paul was sitting in his office, it was seven pm and his extension phone rang.

"Evening Duke, what's new?" His face immediately turned serious. "I haven't heard from her since she left home early this morning, you've tried her mobile?"

"It's ringing but she's not picking up; I've left a couple of messages. Shall I phone Lexi?" Duke was worried.

"No, I'll call her. I'll speak to you soon. When she comes in, let me know straight away." Paul phoned Lexi at home.

"She's probably left her mobile on the tube or in a bar, don't worry," Paul said, trying not to sound worried himself.

He told Lexi not to worry but it was so unlike Katie to be late for work without phoning; and her mobile, what was going on with that?

A few minutes later, Paul looked at his watch, it was seven thirty.

***

Lexi put the phone down, she worried about the kids when they were in the house with her let alone when they didn't turn up for work. She began to fret and decided a coffee was in order. She went into the kitchen, filled the bright red, trendy kettle with water from the tap and switched it on. She put a teaspoon full of Maxwell House instant coffee granules and half a teaspoon of sugar into a tall mug. The kettle boiled and she filled the mug and topped it up with milk. She placed the steaming coffee on the breakfast table, went to a drawer in the French dresser and took out a thick well-thumbed green contact book. She turned to K for Katie and looked at the names. She would finish her coffee and then call one or two of her best friends to see if they had heard from her, she decided.

***

Callum was smiling and chatting with the few customers that had begun to trickle into the club. He was particularly taken with a long legged red head who had been giving him the come on since she arrived. He was definitely going to arrange to meet her outside the club. He had already boxed off Katie as the past and she no longer deserved a thought or care.

***

Duke was snarling around the club talking discreetly to staff to see if anyone knew where Katie had been during the day. He was having no luck and he too kept glancing at his watch; it was now eight pm and he was more than a little worried. He went back into the premier club and spoke to the staff there about Katie. He finally got to Callum.

"Callum, do you have any idea what Katie was doing today?"

He answered confidently, "No idea Duke. Why, is something wrong?"

"She hasn't arrived for work and she's not answering her mobile, very unlike her."

"She'll probably walk in any minute," and he smiled at Duke.

"Yea, well, I hope so." And he walked off.

***

Paul had become more and more frantic; Lexi kept phoning, which made it even worse. He left his office and went to find Duke, it was now eight thirty. He found him in his office.

"Duke, I'm more than worried and Lexi can't stop crying. We need to take action, I can't sit around doing nothing."

"Hospitals, police; call Karen Foster, she can get things done much quicker than us."

"I agree." Paul rushed back to his office and put a call into DI Karen Foster.

"Karen its Paul. Katie's gone missing, I need your help." It was all Paul could do to hold himself together and Karen was aware of that.

"Let's start at the beginning Paul. When did you last see her?"

"This morning, she left the house early to go shopping in town."

"Have you spoken to her at all today?"

"No, she should have been in for work at seven, but no sign of her."

"So, what's wrong with her mobile?"

"It's ringing but she's not picking up; we've left hundreds of messages."

"It's unlike her to go AWOL, isn't it?"

"That's why we're all so worried; Lexi is in pieces. Can you help us?"

"Of course, I'll do everything I can. We'll check all the hospitals and police stations first and then take it from there. Don't worry too much, there could be a simple explanation. I'll call you later."

"Thanks Karen, I appreciate it; you know Katie's...." He held the tears back and put the phone down.

Paul went to his drinks cupboard and took out a bottle of whisky; he poured a generous measure into a crystal cut glass and knocked it back in one. He wondered what to do next, and then he knew.

"Lexi I've just spoken to Karen Foster, she's on the case and will get back to us."

Lexi was sobbing. "Something's happened! Oh God, pray she comes back soon! Please God, bring her home safely."

"I'm on my way home, Duke will look after things here. I think we need each other."

"Hurry Paul, but be careful on the road."

"Don't worry, someone will drive me; I'm not up to it." He couldn't stop thinking about Katie, quietly praying she was safe. "See you soon and try not to worry."

He put the phone down and looked at his watch, ten past nine. He was getting more terrified by the second, he had this terrible feeling something awful had happened to his Katie.

***

DI Karen Foster got straight on the case; the name Katie Bolton was transmitted to all hospitals and Police stations in the South. Karen liked Katie very much and was worried as it was completely out of character for her to just disappear. Once the alert had been put out, there wasn't much she could do. She was at home doing nothing so decided to go into the station. It was ten minutes away and she surprised the officer on duty as she strolled in, in casual civvies.

"Anything happening?" asked Karen.

"Nothing boss, very quiet."

Karen stopped by the officer's desk. "I've put out an alert for a Katie Bolton gone missing since seven pm. Do some digging for me; female, aged eighteen, long blonde hair, very pretty, tallish, probably in London. See if anybody's had an accident, been arrested with that description, no ID."

"Okay boss, I'll get on it." Barry Gunn was more than delighted to have something to do on a very quiet Saturday night. Karen went to the vending machine just inside the staff entrance door and pressed twenty two, white latte with sugar.

Karen shuffled around; there was no news it got later and later. Eventually, it was ten pm and she knew she had to make the call. She tapped the Bolton home number and someone answered the phone.

"Paul Bolton please."

"Paul, its Karen. Are you and Lexi alright? Look, I'll come straight to the point. There are no reports of a Katie Bolton in a hospital or police station in London or the South. I'm checking now for unidentified females who could fit Katie's description. I'm sorry I can't help any more..."

"Karen, you've done all you can. What about reporting a missing person?"

"If she's not back in the morning, we will put out an official missing person's report; unofficially, I already have officers working on it."

"Thank you Karen. From your experience, is there anything else we can do?"

Karen thought. "As long as you have contacted all her friends, what about a boyfriend, did she have anyone special?"

"Not that we know of. Thanks Karen. I'm going to get back on the phone; we'll speak soon."

"Before you go Paul, how's Lexi?"

"In bed traumatised; I've called the doc out to see her."

"Give her my love and keep your pecker up, eh?"

Paul stood, phone in hand, not knowing what to do; the tears flowed down his cheeks as he feared the worst."

The nightmare was on-going; Lexi was given a sedative while Paul paced the lounge, intermittently calling anyone he could think of on his mobile. The club shut at three am and Duke turned up at Paul's house to give support. Duke was a second dad to Katie and he too was a worried wreck. Callum took Mandy home with him and although they were both tired he fucked her brains out for a couple of hours, finally falling asleep at six am. Callum had thought briefly about his women and decided Mandy was perfect, uncomplicated, and not too bright and let him do

Return to Bermondsey

what he wanted to her; it was perfect. Why he had ever gotten involved with that stupid fucking cow Katie, he didn't know.

Paul finally slept for what seemed an hour and woke up with a start in the lounge, on the sofa. He heard breathing and looked over to see Duke asleep in one of the arm chairs. Paul rubbed his eyes and grabbed his phone, there were no messages. He got up and decided to see how Lexi was. He climbed the stairs and opened the bedroom door. Lexi was sitting up staring into space; she looked terrible.

"Paul, I have a terrible feeling that something awful has happened, otherwise, if she was able to, she would have called us; that means for some reason she cannot. Her phone rings but she, and for that matter, no one else, is answering it. I can't help but think the worst, I... I just want to go back in time and stop her leaving the house yesterday." She started to cry.

Paul sat next to her on the bed and hugged her but she suddenly pushed him away.

"You're her dad Paul, you're meant to protect her! She's your little girl! Where were you, Paul? Working as fucking usual while your daughter's out getting raped or God knows what!" She threw herself down crying buckets. Then amid her tear, she started praying, "God, bring her back safely, please, please!" Paul couldn't stand it; he decide he would ask Duke if his wife Carole could come over and help. Then he went back downstairs and smelt coffee brewing; he trudged to the kitchen.

"Morning Duke," Duke was stirring two mugs of coffee.

Duke, his eyes bleary, nodded his head. He noticed Paul looked like shit and he had heard Lexi crying and screaming upstairs.

"I feel so helpless Paul, usually with a problem we take action, but what can we do other than wait by the phone; it's a living hell."

"It is Duke but I'm glad you're here. I'll call Karen again, after that I don't know what else we can do."

Duke looked thoughtful. "We could mobilise everybody to look for her."

"Where are we going to send them? London is a vast city, it's a waste of time."

"It's something Paul, I need to do something."

Paul thought some action might do them all good.

"Okay this is what I want you to do, get people phoning all the nightclubs and bars that we know Katie has ever been in; ask the question, has anybody seen her? Next, get people out on the streets: Soho, Covent Garden, Leicester Square; get photos done and distributed. Tell everybody we know and I mean everybody; we are looking for Katie, and a big reward, Duke don't forget that."

"Last thought, Paul, could it be a kidnapping for money?"

"If it is they'll be in contact; no police, we'll handle it ourselves. Go to it."

Duke felt better he had something to do and he rushed to Paul's upstairs office to start the ball rolling."

***

It was ten thirty and the housekeeping team at the Nadler Hotel had started cleaning rooms. Agraciana Abana was fifty three and had been cleaning rooms at the Nadler for twenty four years; she was five feet three and round. She was on the second floor as usual and had commenced cleaning early check out rooms. She had passed room 22 on several occasions and noted the DO NOT DISTURB SIGN; it was not unusual, and she would normally leave them till last. The hotel policy was for guests to check out of their rooms by midday.

***

Lexi had taken two sleeping tablets and had finally nodded off. Paul and Duke were organizing teams to search for Katie. They both felt better doing something. Paul was becoming increasingly concerned as time went on. There had been no kidnapper's phone call and Paul checked his watch for the umpteenth time, it was eleven thirty. The silence was broken by the phone ringing. Paul and Duke stopped; Paul picked it up slowly.

"Paul Bolton."

"Paul, its Karen, any news?"

"Nothing." Tears flowed down Paul's face. "I should be with her looking after her; if anything has happened, it's my fault."

Karen interrupted him, "Paul pull yourself together! We have no idea what's happened; it can still end well. Keep the faith."

Paul sniffed loudly and deeply and pulled himself together. "Yes, we have to remain positive. What are you doing?"

"Missing person has been notified to the Met and Surrey police. I've pushed as much as I can for action, but it's not easy to find a needle in a haystack."

"I know Karen; thanks for your help. What about the hospitals, can we ask again?"

"I'm getting reports of all Accident and Emergency patients from last night and this morning; if she's in hospital somewhere; we will find her."

"Thanks Karen, I don't know what we would have done without you. Keep in touch and speak soon."

"Keep your chin up Paul."

***

Callum was pouring champagne over Mandy's breasts and licking it off. They were rolling around on the bed as he groped and playfully wrestled with her.

"Mandy, we're going to be together for a long time, and don't worry about a good job at the club, I promise you you'll be up working with me very soon; you're going to get the most incredible tips."

Mandy was very happy. "Hmm, that sounds good! Now, I want you to do something else with that champagne bottle."

Callum burst out laughing. "Now, that sounds like a really good idea." Then he moved the bottle to...

***

It was eleven forty five and Agraciana had finished her allocation, apart from room number 22. She walked purposefully down the thick grey carpeted corridor and arrived in front of room 22. She got very close to the door and put her ear to it. The room doors were made of very thick oak wood, and try as she may, she could not hear any movement or noise at all. She then sniffed the air and took a step back; she had smelt something horrible like rotting meat, and she recoiled in horror and waddled as fast as she could towards the stairs which would take her to the housekeeper's office on the first floor. She sped down the stairs and rushed towards the office. She didn't knock but pushed open the door and started shouting in Mexican and English. Nicola Thorpe the housekeeper, had seen it all; she stood up and lifted her hands.

"Shhh! Calm down Agraciana! Calm down."

Agraciana was shaking. "Room 22! Something terrible! Bad smell! Oh God! Something has happened! Poor lady need help...quickly...!"

Nicola knew something was wrong but didn't want to sound the alarm until she was sure what it was. Better to take all precautions though, she thought. She tapped an extension number on her phone.

"Max, its Nicola. Are you duty manager?"

"Yes."

"Room 22, possible code 5; meet you there in a minute?"

"I'm on my way."

Code 5 was a possible guest death.

Nicola arrived at the room first and sniffed the air, she couldn't really smell anything but trusted Agraciana. She looked at Agraciana and told her to wait outside then she banged on the door, "Housekeeping!" but there was no reply. She banged once more, "Housekeeping!" still no reply. She took her duplicate key-card and swiped the lock; it went green, and she pulled the handle down and pushed very slowly. Then the smell hit her nostrils and she gagged as it overcame her. She turned back just as Max arrived. He held her shoulder and pushed past her into the room. The sight that greeted him was soul destroying. Katie was lying on the bed naked; Max noticed how young and pretty she was. He moved closer and shuddered as he saw the deep red welts and black and yellow bruising around her neck. The smell of excrement, urine and decay was overpowering. He put his hand to his mouth and turned to leave. The door was shut, Max, Nicola and Agraciana moved back down the corridor; Agraciana was making the sign of a cross and sobbing. Max immediately sealed off the second floor to all but residents. Leigh

Grant the hotel manager, was informed, followed by the police and ambulance service.

The police arrived within five minutes and requested that all the rooms on the second floor be vacated at once. Room 22 was now a crime scene and officers were stationed at either end of the corridor. Detective inspector Richard Martin arrived ten minutes later to take charge of the case. Richard and the crime team donned masks and entered room 22 at twelve fifteen; it was a harrowing experience. The smell was extraordinary and it was immediately apparent that the young attractive woman had been strangled to death and that it had probably taken place the night before. Richard stood and looked at the body; he couldn't help but think very soon, some poor couple would be told that their daughter had been found in a hotel room, strangled to death. He wondered for a second if she was a prostitute. He left the room and gave instructions to his experienced Sargent, Nathan David, to instigate the usual procedures.

Richard headed down to the manager's office and was straightaway ushered in. He wanted to know who had booked the room and under what name. Leigh Grant instantly phoned through to reception and asked for the information. Richard Martin was informed that room 22 had been booked in the name of Katie Bolton by telephone. The crime scene boys would look for identification and any contact details. Meanwhile, a room was designated on the first floor to interview staff. The crime team reported that there was Identification in the room, which confirmed the body was that of Katie Bolton;

but there were no contact details for anyone else, and no phone. The murder was reported onto the Metropolitan police system and very soon, the name Katie Bolton was connected to a missing person's report.

***

Detective Inspector Karen Foster was sitting behind her huge oak desk, twiddling her thumbs. It was the Sunday from hell and she should have been at home, or more likely, in a bar somewhere, with a bottle of red. She had racked her brains and could think of nothing else that she could do. The missing person's procedure had been followed, and she had called in a couple of favours to get things moving faster than usual. She took a deep breath and was startled when the phone rang shrilly. She immediately had a very bad feeling; tears filled her eyes and she didn't want to answer it. But she picked it up quickly and snapped.

"Detective Inspector Foster."

"Good afternoon Inspector, this is Scotland Yard admin team."

Karen knew what was coming. "Please don't tell me any bad news; I know the family."

There was silence for two seconds that seemed like minutes.

"Detective Inspector, I'm so very sorry," the caller cleared her throat. "Thirty five minutes ago, a young woman identified as Katie Bolton was found murdered in the

Nadler hotel in central London. No family members have been told as yet."

Karen put the phone on the desk and started wailing.

"Hello detective, hello…"

Karen shakily picked up the phone up and slotted it back onto its cradle.

She had closed her eyes, she was remembering Katie, that sweet lovely girl. She had to phone Paul and Lexi; she didn't know if she could, but better from her than some stranger. The tears wouldn't stop, she tried going into professional work mode but that didn't help either. She got up from her desk and went to the tall grey standard police issue filing cabinet in the corner. She opened the bottom drawer and took out the bottle of whisky; she unscrewed the cap and put it to her lips, it burned her throat as she gulped it down. She went back to her desk and put the bottle next to the phone. She sat there looking at the phone, wondering if she would ever be able to pick it up. She reached for the bottle again and took a gulp then slowly put the bottle back down and picked up the phone.

***

"Tell me you love me then."

"For God's sake! How many times do I have to tell you in one fucking day?"

Mandy was beginning to get a little upset but recovered quickly. "Okay Callum, you've been an angel this weekend I've never been, you know so often in my life."

"Spit it out Mandy! You've never been fucked so often but it's not just quantity, is it?" and he moved his face close to hers in a friendly way.

"Oh God no it's been five star all the way, especially the fun with the champagne bottle. I've never done that before. Thanks Callum, you're being so nice to me and this meal is just great." Callum had taken Mandy out for a Chinese; he wanted her very much on his side if there were any questions as to his whereabouts on Saturday.

He lifted his wine glass, "Here's to you Mandy, now drink up because I need to get you home for a good fucking session."

Mandy squealed and knocked back her glass of white wine.

***

It was exactly half past one. Lexi had woken and donned a thick, fluffy, pink dressing gown. She looked terrible as she slowly staggered down the stairs and eventually joined Paul and Duke who were having a break in the lounge.

"No news, is that good or bad? I can't work it out," she said out loud to the room.

Paul got up from his armchair and helped Lexi to the sofa. As he turned towards his seat, his mobile rang. The room had never been so quiet, the ringing was so loud he prayed silently as he touched the answer button and switched on the loud speaker.

"Paul Bolton," Paul said. There was silence, but Paul knew someone was there.

"Paul Bolton. Who is that?"

Lexi and Duke were tensed, watching Paul, praying for good news.

Paul raised his voice, "Who is it?"

He heard a sob and then a voice. "It's Karen." He knew straight away; his tears started again.

"Tell me quickly," Paul said shakily.

He heard Karen sniff and breath in deeply. "They found her, she's dead, Paul." Paul heard Karen burst into tears as he fell to the floor and then he heard Lexi let out an ear-piercing, blood-cuddling scream.

Duke shot up and grabbed the phone. "It's Duke. What's happened?"

Duke's matter of fact voice brought Karen back to hazy reality.

"Found in a hotel room; raped and strangled to death." Duke heard the phone crash and it went quiet.

At that, Lexi fainted; Paul was lying on the floor unable to move; Duke thought he might have had a stroke. He pressed 999 and requested an ambulance as quickly as possible. He turned to Paul and placed a pillow under his head; he then tried to make Lexi as comfortable as possible. He heard the ambulance siren as he picked up a huge vase and smashed it onto the wall. He stared at the broken pieces and started to cry, hot angry tears cursing down his face.

***

Karen Foster sat at her desk for an hour; she was glued to the chair and could not move. The only movement she could make was to lift the whisky bottle and pour the burning liquid down her throat. She had felt pain before and this was up there with the worst of them. There was a feeling of emptiness about everything, what really mattered in life? She was drunk and decided to go home, but she couldn't possibly drive. She dialed a number.

"Jeff, sorry to bother you on a Sunday; there's been another death, another stinking, rotten, fucking death!" She could hardly continue. "But this time Jeff, it hurts, really hurts." She was sobbing and taking deep breaths. "Do you want to know who's been taken from us this time Jeff?" She sniffed deeply and wiped her nose with her cuff. "Katie Bolton. She's been killed; she was a lovely girl Jeff, just eighteen, fucking eighteen, Jeff. Now I'm drunk and need to go home."

"I'm on my way."

"Oh Jeff don't worry. She was so young, very pretty; had all her life ahead of her. Why Jeff? Why?"

"Because that's life and sometimes it's a bastard; no other reason."

"Yes, you're right Jeff, life is a pile of fucking shit sometimes. Look, don't worry I'll order a cab."

"Are you sure? I can come over."

"No don't bother, I may or may not see you in the morning. If I do come in, I'll be late. Thanks Jeff."

"What for?"

"Just being you and being at the end of the phone."

CHAPTER 10

Kevin and Graham Philips had grown up modelling themselves on the Kray twins; they had the same short haircuts, wore similar dark sharp-cut suits and thought they were as tough. They had started work at fourteen in Romford as runners for drug pushers; someone would do a deal, they would be phoned on a mobile they had been given and they would run to deliver the gear. It was easy money and much better than being at school. They both did that for two years and then decided they were being taken for mugs. The pittance they got was nothing compared to the massive profit the pushers got. It was easily resolved: the pusher Tim was beaten to death in an alley; Kevin and Graham were contacted by Pete Banks the main distributor, and asked if they wanted Tim's patch. They agreed and over the next five years they took over numerous patches until they were the go-to people for drugs in the whole of Essex. It had all happened very quickly and now no-one messed with the Philips brothers.

The business in Essex had eventually reached saturation point and they had been looking out for areas to expand into in London. Bermondsey had been ripe for plucking; gang wars had raged for over two years, drugs could be bought from so many sources it had forced the prices down and that created even more mayhem as pushers fought for the clients. Kevin and Graham had experience, and the only way to deal with gang wars was to take out the leaders and scoop up the soldiers into a new team.

The brothers had murdered three of the key gang leaders and four of their top lieutenants; most of them had been gunned down in hails of bullets as they left their homes, while one had had his throat slit in his local barbers. The area was now tight and completely under their control, even the slightest sign of trouble was answered with extreme violence.

***

The brothers were very traditional; once a week they went to Manze, on Tower Bridge Road. They would have the same meal every time, double pie and mash with lashings of liquor, and then pour on a generous topping of chilli vinegar. They always drank in the same pubs, bought their newspapers from the same shop and had their hair cut every two weeks at the same Barber's. They liked everything to be nicely boxed off and tidy and in its place, with no confusion or change.

CHAPTER 11

Paul and Lexi Bolton had been taken to Frimley Park Hospital in Camberley. Paul had been kept under sedation, having had a minor stroke. He couldn't remember anything. The doctors woke him on Monday lunchtime. His left arm and left leg were weak and he had slight slurring of the speech. He had been devastated by the news of Katie's murder which had brought on the attack. He opened his eyes and looked around; everything was white and grey, he knew instantly he was in hospital. He looked from side to side and saw a large overweight nurse in a dark blue uniform looking at what were presumably his notes on a clipboard; on the other side were Duke, Oliver, George and Callum.

He just managed a weak smile and heard someone shout, "Thank God he's awake!" He felt his hand being squeezed and turned to see Oliver looking into his eyes, smiling.

"Hi dad welcome back; don't worry, the doctors say you will be fine."

It was a huge effort but Paul needed to know; when he spoke, he could tell his speech was very slightly slurred.

"Where is Lexi and how is she?"

Tears came into Oliver's eyes at the mention of his mother. He couldn't speak at first but he knew his father had to be told. "Mum's had a seizure, it's like a brain attack; she's in intensive care here but she's alright."

Paul shut his eyes and tears rolled down his cheeks, he thought of Katie, the best daughter any father could have, and now Lexi. What had he done to deserve it, perhaps it was because of what happened to Tony. He closed his eyes and heard the screaming for mercy again, as the knives sunk and sliced into his flesh. Whatever it was, he was being paid back in spades.

"I want to see her."

Oliver looked at Duke who shook his head.

"Not yet dad, wait till you're a bit stronger."

Paul raised his voice, "I want to see her NOW!"

The nurse, Angela Craven, had heard the conversation and intervened.

"Mr. Bolton you need to rest and…."

Paul shouted, "I want to see my wife!" and he pushed the covers back and started to climb out of the bed.

The nurse looked very worried. "Okay Mr. Bolton, at least let us get you a wheelchair; you're too weak to walk."

Paul collapsed back onto the bed. "Okay but hurry!"

The nurse left quickly.

"Duke." Duke came forward and leaned close to Paul. "Take care of everything till I get back," Then Paul leaned even closer and whispered into Duke's ear. "Find him for me, I want him Duke, alive so I can skin him, promise me?"

Duke whispered back, "Don't worry Paul, nothing will stop me finding him; wherever he is, I will find him and deliver him to you." Duke was crying for the second time in a couple of days, which was unheard of.

"Boys," Paul motioned for the three young men; they stepped close to the bed.

"Duke will run the business while I am away; he is me, do you understand? Do exactly as he tells you, is that clear?"

Oliver and George answered in unison, "Yes dad."

Paul shut his eyes and murmured, "Good, now I must sleep."

The door opened and the nurse appeared with the consultant Harry Fish, who was looking after Paul. He had come to tell Paul there was no way he was visiting anybody as he could very easily have another stroke. But it was now unnecessary as Paul was already fast asleep.

Lexi had been rushed to intensive care and an MRI brain scan showed that she had suffered a massive abnormal surge of brain activity, resulting in a seizure caused by the terrible news of Katie's death. The doctors were one hundred percent certain she would recover but wanted her to rest and gain strength.

Duke had arranged for the three boys to stay in a hotel close to the hospital so that someone was always with Paul and Lexi, twenty four hours a day. He, meanwhile, returned to the business of running the clubs and looking for Katie's killer. He called Karen Foster and requested a meeting to discuss how the investigation was progressing.

CHAPTER 12

"Karen, its DI Richard Martin; I'm on the Katie Bolton case."

Karen had still not got over the murder of Katie and had taken a couple of days off work. Richard had rung Karen at home because of an extraordinary development in the case.

"Hello Richard, sorry if I don't appear at my sharpest; things have got on top of me."

"Been there Karen. You knew the girl?"

"Yes." Karen was about to start crying again but just managed to control herself. "She was the daughter of good friends of mine."

"Look, I'm sorry to bother you but I knew you would want to hear of a serious development in the case."

"Have you found the bastard? God, I hope...?"

"No, but listen to this, we got DNA from the man's sperm, we put it into the system to see if we could get a name, nothing came up but it did match a previous crime."

Karen stiffened, listening intently. "What crime? Go on."

"The murder at the Blue Anchor pub, which I believe is bang in the middle of your patch?"

Karen couldn't take that straight in. "You mean the man who killed Katie Bolton in a central London hotel, also killed Pat O'Connor, the landlord at the Blue Anchor Pub in Bermondsey? Are you sure? Have you had the results checked?"

"Checked and confirmed."

"Richard, are you sure there has been no mix up? It just sounds too incredible!"

"What can I say, except that these are the facts as passed to me by the boffins; I asked them to recheck the results, they did and it was the same."

"You'll have to excuse me Richard but I'm having difficulty getting my head round this."

"I know, but it opens up all sorts of new leads to follow; its progress."

"It's certainly that; let's hope it helps us to catch the bastard who's responsible."

"Okay look, I'll leave you to it; let's keep in regular contact and get well soon, eh?"

And the phone went dead.

Karen was in shock and suddenly, the names flashed into her head. She jumped up and rushed to the bathroom; fifteen minutes later, she was on her way to Rotherhithe nick.

"Jeff, I'm coming in, get an armed response team ready to go; I think I know who killed Pat from the Blue Anchor and Katie Bolton. Find out where those bastard Phillips brothers are, we're going to pick them up."

Karen arrived at the nick ten minutes later; she punched the car park authorisation number into the key pad and drove in. She clocked the armed response team, checking weapons and getting ready to roll. She rushed inside straight to the CID office where she found Jeff Swan.

"Where are they?"

"Apparently, they're in the Lord Nelson on the Old Kent Road, conducting business with some low-life pushers."

"How the hell did you find that out?"

Jeff smiled and tapped his nose, "I couldn't possibly divulge..."

"Yea okay, let's go."

They rushed out through the door and seconds later were jumping into a patrol car. Karen put a thumbs up to the armed response team and they shot out of the nick. It was about four minutes to the Old Kent Road.

Karen decided not to mess about, officers would go straight in the front door. Both cars slowed down and stopped in front of the pub. Officers were out the vehicles in a second and through the door in another. Karen and Jeff followed the armed officers in and Karen saw the two brothers sitting by the window with two other men. She approached them quickly and turned to two officers.

"Hand-cuff them!"

Kevin and Graham Philips just sat there, their mouths agape, not believing what was happening. They were quickly hand-cuffed and Karen got right in their faces.

"I am arresting you for the murders of Patrick O'Connor, landlord at the Blue Anchor public house, and Katie Bolton at the Nadler Hotel, Covent Garden London. Anything you say may be used…"

The two brothers looked at each other and burst out laughing.

And in that instant Karen knew they hadn't done it and that she was well down the road of making a complete prat of herself.

"Take them in!" She said angrily.

She then noticed the two other men trying to slowly disappear.

"Jeff, you see these two 'upstanding' gentlemen here, perhaps you would be kind enough to ask them if they would mind accompanying us to Rotherhithe police station, where they very likely may be able to help us with our enquiries."

"I'd be delighted, Detective Inspector Foster," and he raised his eyebrows.

Karen got back in the patrol car, she was well pissed off.

"You know they didn't do it?"

Jeff made a funny face. "Well I sorta got that idea from their reaction to the charges."

"Arse holes! Jeff, that's what they are, complete fucking arse-holes! Anyway, even if they didn't do it, we can have some fun annoying them for twenty four hours."

Return to Bermondsey

Kevin and Graham Philips were put in separate cars and driven at speed to Rotherhithe nick. They were booked in and then had their DNA taken by mouth swab with a large cotton bud, two samples were taken; this was followed by electronic finger printing and photographic images. The booking-in officer then checked the DNA sample on the Police National Computer data-base, they matched previous entries, but no current crime that was being investigated. Neither were best pleased when shown into what could only be described as very basic police cells.

Karen and Jeff arrived back to the nick and picked up coffees from the canteen; they then went and sat in the CID office, discussing the coming interviews.

"This is going to be very interesting Jeff; we'll find out a lot more about our two friends. By the way, have you checked their criminal records? And before you go, some news you will not find easy to take in. Listen to this, the killers of Katie Bolton and Pat O'Connor are the one and same person. DNA from both locations matched; what do you think of that?"

Jeff said nothing, he was putting that piece of information through his brain and trying to find something to say. Karen understood it was so incredible that his reaction was the same as hers had been.

Jeff was shaking his head slowly, "That is..." he stopped, then continued, "absolutely astounding; we need to sit down and discuss the implications of that over a coffee or two as soon as possible. As for the Philips brothers, I'll check their records now. Shall we let them stew a bit?"

"Definitely!" Karen answered vehemently. "You can't start a good interview unless the baddies are well pissed off. Make sure they get nothing, and if any of those fucking do-gooder prisoner visitors are about, keep them away from our two friends."

Jeff laughed. "With pleasure boss."

Kevin Philips was brought out of his cell and taken to one of the three interview rooms. He was given a cup of tea and some chocolate digestive biscuits. The chairs had been taken out of the room so he was standing, holding his tea in one hand and chomping on a biscuit help in the other. Karen and Jeff joined him and they had cups of coffee and biscuits also.

"Mr. Philips, sorry we've kept you how's the tea?" Karen asked.

Kevin Philips thought Karen Foster had finally come to her senses and that she knew he had had nothing to do with the murders in question. He decided to be as friendly as he could to get out of the place as soon as possible. He laughed as he spoke.

"The tea's good Detective. So, when am I getting out of here?"

The timing was perfect, just as he held the tea up and laughed, Graham Philips was escorted past the room. He glanced in and saw his brother apparently joking and having a laugh with the coppers. He was immediately confused, it was so unlike his brother; he couldn't understand what was going on.

Graham was placed in a separate stark interview room and left to stew.

Chairs were put back in the interview room for Karen, Jeff and Kevin Philips.

"Where were you last Saturday night and the early hours of Sunday?" Karen asked, her voice hard.

Kevin smiled, "I was at home with my family and Graham was there as well, loads of witnesses; I have an airtight alibi."

Karen answered harshly, "A young woman was brutally murdered, there's no such thing as an airtight alibi where family are the only witnesses. Was there anybody there other than family?"

Kevin smiled again and Karen was getting well pissed off.

"Actually there was, my accountant who by the way is a much respected member of the community."

Karen's immediate thought was yes, the fucking criminal community.

Philips continued, "Look, you're wasting my time. I never met Katie Bolton, I have no idea what she looked like and I do not chase young girls."

"Mr. Philips, did you know Patrick O'Connor?"

"I knew him, we weren't best buddies. It wasn't my boozer anyway, and word is he was done by a young thug looking for cash. You can't pin either of these murders on me, you know it, and I know it so why don't you shut the fuck up and let me go." He sat back, eyeballing her.

Karen thought of the drugs, the misery the bastard sold so he could lead the high life.

She leaned forward across the desk and said between gritted teeth, "You cunt Philips, animals like you should be put down."

Jeff was ready to intervene as he saw Karen working up into a fury.

"You sell misery and death for a living!" Karen continued angrily. "You are the fucking scum of the earth and I WILL have you locked up!" She nodded angrily. "You are like all the others, you'll make a mistake; you won't be laughing when the judge gives you twenty years in Belmarsh! Twenty years Philips!" It was her turn to smile and laugh.

Philips jumped to his feet and pushed the chair back onto the floor.

"You fucking bitch! I suggest you take care, even crossing the road can be dangerous! I wouldn't want anything to happen to you!"

Karen stood and put her face an inch from his. "Are you threatening me, you fucking bastard?" She clenched her fists, she wanted to punch his face, wanted to rip his eyes out of their sockets, wanted to hurt him so badly. She leaned very close to his face. "Your time will come; I might even come and visit you to remind you of this conversation." She stepped back.

"Escort this piece of shit to reception so he can be booked out and released."

The two of them stared at each other and made no move. Finally Jeff took Karen's arm and led her to the door. He whispered to her "Get the coffees and I'll see you in CID." He pushed her out the door, and turned back to Kevin.

"Your boss should watch it, her mouth will get her into big trouble."

Jeff wasn't going to take that and said quiet anger, "I'm a bit quieter than Karen but remember this, if anything should happen to her accidentally or not, I will come for you and put a gun in your mouth and pull the trigger."

"I'm scared shitless. Are we going?"

Jeff left Kevin Philips at Reception and headed to CID.

"Karen, what is wrong with you? You need to calm down."

Karen was down in the dumps and just nodded.

"What's wrong?"

Karen chuckled suddenly. "Nothing a good drink and a hard shag wouldn't sort out."

"Well, that's not difficult to find but shall we deal with Graham Philips first?"

"I guess we better, but it's a waste of time."

"This brother is the weak link; eh, perhaps we should keep our tempers in check this time."

"Yes okay," and then she laughed. "As long as he doesn't upset me; I'm a woman, I have mood swings."

It was Jeff's turn to laugh. "Yes and don't we know it, come on lets go."

"Sit down please Mr. Philips," Karen said quietly.

Graham sat down and didn't look very happy; he was always nervous with coppers.

The interview room was quiet, the only noise was the rustle as Jeff turned the pages of a file he was holding.

Jeff finally looked up. "I see you have a long history of criminal activity Mr. Philips."

"I'm a reformed character," Graham answered, trying not to show his nervousness.

It was all both Karen and Jeff could do to keep a straight face.

Jeff continued as Karen grimaced at Philips.

"So stealing cars from an early age, drug delivery boy, GBH, but the latest and most serious would be the distribution of class A drugs; reformed character?"

"I was not guilty."

Jeff looked up and smiled, "So where were you last Saturday night and Sunday morning?"

"I can't remember."

"Can't remember? This was not long ago. A murder was committed on that night, a young girl was strangled to

Return to Bermondsey

death in a hotel room, she shit herself as she was being strangled; it could have been your daughter."

The three of them sat there, it was so quiet you could have heard a pin drop.

Eventually Karen said, "You had better start remembering Mr. Philips or you're going to be enjoying our hospitality for some time. Look, I'll make it easy for you. Kevin said you were both on a pub crawl down the Old Kent Road, is that right?"

"Well, if Kevin said so, then yes, he has a much better memory than me."

Jeff butted in quickly, "Graham your brother said under oath that he was at home that night. I'm confused, where exactly were you?"

Jeff used the under oath comment as it gave it weight, and Graham wouldn't understand anyway.

"Truthfully, I don't remember but I had nothing to do with any murders."

Karen sneered, "Truthfully, you don't know the meaning of the word!"

There was a sudden knock at the door and a constable stuck his head in.

"A quick word please boss."

Karen stood up and went out.

There's a solicitor in reception, says he wants to see Graham Philips. I thought you ought to know."

"Yes, thank you; tell him to wait."

Karen went back into the interview room.

"Kevin's been very helpful and I was hoping we could also have an understanding." She smiled at Graham.

Graham stuttered, "I always like to get on with the..." he was going to say filth. "Local law enforcement officers; if there is anything I can do to assist you in your enquiries, do please let me know."

Karen and Jeff looked at each other, it was hopeless.

Karen stood, "Take this moron and get him booked out." she opened the door and strode out.

Karen and Jeff were soon back in CID sitting at the large meeting table sipping at piping hot coffees.

"Jeff this DNA news is going to help us catch this bastard. We know the man who killed Pat at the Blue Anchor was a young, late twenties lowlife, possibly looking for some cash for drugs."

Jeff looked very thoughtful. "I'm not sure about that. The big question for me is, if that is the case why, how on earth did Katie Bolton end up in bed with him in a four star central London hotel? It just doesn't fit together, I just don't get it."

The phone rang and Karen asked for the visitor to be escorted to CID. She stood up and waited. The door opened and the big man entered. The constable nodded at Karen and left.

"Duke! How are you?"

Duke, looking like your archetypal gangster in black suit and long coat, lumbered to the table and shook hands with Karen and Jeff.

"Fine, but under a lot of pressure."

They all sat down.

"How are Paul and Lexi and the boy's?"

"Paul's much better; he'll be home soon. A nurse will move in to assist his rehabilitation and a housekeeper will look after everything else. Lexi is awake and slowly recovering. They're just so happy that both of them are alive."

"And the boys?"

"Oliver is strong and taking on more responsibility every day, George will do whatever is asked of him, and then we have Callum."

"Tony Bolton's son, what a turn up that was..."

"You said it. He's buckled down though and works hard; he may be useful to Paul in time, we'll see. So Karen, what's the news?"

"Firstly, I have to point out to you that I am not allowed to divulge to you any confidential information on any case, you understand that?"

"Of course Karen, we don't want you getting into any trouble. So, what can you tell me?"

"What's happening at your end, first?"

Duke smiled, "Okay, so we have private investigators on the case but there is no progress as yet. Obviously, we have put the word out through the clubs for information and will pay a huge reward for the right information, that's it."

Karen looked thoughtful for a few seconds; she glanced at Jeff as she decided what and what not to tell Duke.

"Well, Pat's murder, there's no news; all we know is that it could well have been a young man looking for cash which isn't really that helpful. The best hope of progress with that is info from a snitch. The other case, I don't want to say her name; I still get upset, is ongoing and to be truthful, we have made no progress."

It was Duke's turn to be thoughtful. "So, what about Katie's phone?"

"There was no phone at the scene, so presumably, whoever was responsible took it with them."

"Have you investigated the calls made through the phone company?"

"Yes, but they were all coded and could take years to crack."

"Well then, she was speaking to someone on the phone but didn't want anyone to be able to know who it was; maybe a lover?"

"Maybe, who knows? You must have made enquiries too, but it seems she didn't have a boyfriend."

Duke shook his head. "She's never had a serious relationship. What about the DNA?"

As he said the word, he saw Karen flinch.

Karen wanted to tell him but wasn't sure; she made the decision and didn't want to involve Jeff.

"Jeff, do me a favour please, get some more coffees."

"Sure." He got up and left the room.

Duke leaned forward. "Now, we can talk."

"God, I never told you this, alright?"

"What is it?"

Karen took a deep breath. "The DNA found at the hotel room matched the DNA at the Blue Anchor pub."

Duke leaned back, astounded, then leaned forward again, tensed. "Are you saying it was the same killer? That's unbelievable!"

"That's exactly what I'm saying. Can you think of any connection, The Blue Anchor, The Nadler Hotel, Katie and Pat O'Connor?"

Duke scratched an itch above his ear, "I don't get it, I really don't get it."

"Join the club. Could Pat have somehow upset Katie, and the boyfriend? We have to conclude there was one who

Return to Bermondsey

went to see him; things got out of hand there, was a fight and he got killed."

"That's possible," agreed Duke. "Then he meets Katie in a swanky London hotel room, they argue and he kills her. So, we are after a lunatic who likes killing people," he shook his head. "It's all a bit far-fetched but somehow, it has to fit together."

Duke remembered something else. "Presumably, you have tried to trace the physical whereabouts of the phone?"

"Yes, no luck; it could be at the bottom of a canal, been smashed to pieces, who knows?"

Jeff opened the door, holding a brown wooden tray. "Fresh Coffees."

"Thanks Jeff, you're a darling."

"Tell my wife that," and they all laughed.

"Duke, watch out for the Philips brothers. We had them in at the station; a nasty couple of shits."

"Yea, I know. You think they may give us some trouble?"

"I don't know, but if I was you... watch your backs. I presume Paul has protection at the house?"

"Heavy security; it's like fort Knox."

"Good. Send Paul and Lexi my love and tell them I'll pop in to see them soon."

"I will. You'll keep in touch, if anything should..."

"You'll be the first to know."

Duke shook hands again and Jeff escorted him to reception and the exit.

Jeff returned to the CID office. "You told him about the DNA?"

"You can come to your own conclusion on that but you are not involved if anything goes wrong."

"I don't mind being involved, we're a team."

"Thanks for that Jeff, but it's better this way. Come on, let's get something to eat; I'm starving."

***

Paul Bolton returned home in a private ambulance. He was shaky and his left side was weak. He could stumble around but a lot of physiotherapy was needed to build up the strength in his legs and his left arm. He was happy to be home but not happy to be surrounded by a team of security guards, nurses, physiotherapists and Miss McLaren, the new tough as nails Scottish Housekeeper. He was just thankful that he could go to the toilet on his own, as assistance with that would have been unthinkable. He was also over the moon that Lexi would be home in a week's time; she was still unwell and needed more time to recover. There was no point in her being in hospital really, thought Paul; she could recover just as well if not better at home. It was the end of July and Paul prayed for some good weather so that he and Lexi could spend time in the garden she had landscaped so beautifully. He wasn't worried about the clubs; Duke had a firm grip on them and was also getting a lot of help from Oliver who was progressing well.

Katie's death had hit Oliver and George hard. Oliver had been very close to her and was shocked that he had not known about any boyfriends. He was equally as keen as Duke to find the bastard who had done it, and when they found him, my God, he would pay. George had done his stint visiting mum and dad in hospital and had gone off for a few days to get his head together; he chose Dublin for the break.

Lexi arrived home and Paul welcomed her with a huge hug and plenty of kisses. She was smiling but he could see the pain and anguish behind the façade; it would take time, Katie was so special to her. The weather improved and the two of them spent hours sitting outside in the shade, reading books and talking. The subject usually came round to Katie and they would both cry their eyes out in pain.

Paul had physio every morning and afternoon; he was determined to get fit enough to return to the office part time by October. He was in constant contact with Duke plus Oliver asking questions about the business and progress on the murder enquiry. He too had been shocked when Duke visited and told him about the DNA match. Paul racked his brains but could not help with any sensible suggestions. He rang and chatted to Karen Foster, she told him the police were not making any progress with either case. She also wanted Paul to understand it could be a long haul; there were hundreds of cases unsolved every year, some would get solved because of DNA advances but in the end, there would be some that were never solved. She had assured him Katie's murder would not be one of them.

The first week in August brought terrible news. The Pussy Cat club in Soho had burnt down on a Sunday. There was no one present in the club at the time and it was all insured, but it had to close and that hit turnover and profits. The fire Brigade carried out a thorough origin and cause investigation and concluded that the fire had been started by someone using a fire accelerant, and that was probably petrol. Duke alerted all the club managers and introduced two mobile security patrol vehicles who toured the clubs on Sundays. This was okay for the central London area clubs but there were one or two out on a limb, and that was where the perpetrators struck next.

The Angels was a lap dancing club in Islington. Paul had owned the club for ten odd years and because of its beautiful décor, was one of his favourites. He was mortified to hear of its loss and again; it had been arson, by petrol. Paul, Duke and Oliver held a meeting and came to the conclusion the clubs were under systematic attack and that someone was out to ruin their business.

***

Callum Bolton had almost forgotten Katie, and only ever thought of her when someone else brought her name up. He was shagging Mandy with renewed passion; they had gone through the Kama Sutra again and were now working out new methods of sexual deviation, mainly based on erotic asphyxiation, which in simple terms, was restriction of oxygen to the brain. Callum had been reading about it on the internet and laughed as he thought Katie Bolton must have had the best orgasm of her life, just before she died.

Callum had been astonished and happy when Duke had asked him to join Oliver and George at the Cumberland hotel to visit Paul and Lexi on a rota basis. Callum was a brilliant actor and was always suitably distressed when Katie was discussed. He was now running the VIP bar at the Den Club and as he had promised, Mandy was working with him as a hostess. It shocked Callum that she was, on average, making over two hundred pounds a night in tips. It was a good situation as sometimes when he was feeling horny he would take Mandy into the back store room and fuck the living daylights out of her. Life was good; as far as he knew, the police were getting nowhere with the murder enquiries and the body of the cab driver hadn't even been found yet. He spoke to his mother Sharon Travis once a week to keep her happy, and she thought he was doing really well and did nothing but praise him.

CHAPTER 13

"Paul, has it all been worthwhile?"

Paul and Lexi were sitting in their favourite dark brown Rattan high backed chairs on one of the patios at the south facing side of the house. It was shielded from the wind and had beautiful views to some woodlands and was a perfect place to relax.

Paul became very anxious and tearful.

"You mean that if I hadn't pursued the career I chose, Katie would still be alive?" He sniffed deeply.

Time stood still for seconds.

"What would life have been like if you'd had a nine to five job and I was a hairdresser?" she paused, then added, "Have you ever thought about that Paul?"

"I have but it never makes sense, you can't live in the *if only world,* it doesn't exist. We have lived our life as we chose at the time, there can be no regrets; what is the point? I only know one thing, when I find who did it, my God, they will suffer, they will suffer more than anything you can imagine, and I'm going to skin him or them alive."

"Will that solve anything Paul? All that will do is satiate your thirst for vengeance, for retribution."

"She was our daughter Lexi," said Paul crying. "My little girl and I wasn't there when she needed me most; I was her father, her protector and I let her down, I failed her."

He was crying harder now, sobbing and trying to breathe; then he leaned over and fell from the chair onto the tiled patio.

Lexi stood up; she just looked at him, shook her head and then went to the nearest door and entered the house.

She shouted loudly, "Miss McLaren! Please see to Mr. Bolton on the patio!" she walked off towards her room as the housekeeper almost ran past her towards the patio.

Lexi pushed the solid wooden door and entered her room; she shut and locked the door. She took a deep breath and knew it was time again. She went to her bedside cupboard and slowly pulled the top drawer open and took out a small black handled Sabatier kitchen knife. She lay down on the bed and pulled up the sleeve of her blouse on her right arm; she tightened it near to her shoulder so it would not slip back down. She took the knife and ran the very sharp edge lightly across her arm; it stung with pain and pleasure and blood dripped down onto the bed. She repeated it again and worked down her arm…

Strong and dependable Mrs. McLaren almost carried Paul to his room. She helped him onto his bed and he lay there breathing and remembering everything he regretted doing in his whole fucking life.

***

"Oliver, listen to me; Duke is as near to family as you can get but he is not blood, do you understand? It was ten am, Paul and Oliver were in the kitchen having a late full English breakfast.

Return to Bermondsey

Paul shouted out to Miss McLaren who was somewhere in the house, "Miss McLaren breakfast is delicious, thank you!"

He tucked back into his bacon, sausages, grilled tomatoes, fried eggs, mushrooms, black pudding and sauté potatoes.

"How's your breakfast, Oliver?"

"Ten out of ten," said Oliver as he maneuvered his tongue to catch the egg yolk dripping down his chin.

Paul had asked Oliver to drop in to discuss what was happening with the clubs and the investigation.

"Is mum coming down?"

Paul sighed, "Mum's not at all well, and truth is I don't know if she'll come down or not." He paused until he decided what to say next. "Look Oliver, there are things you have to understand; I love your mum more than anything in the world but women are very emotional, I am also very emotional but the time comes when the emotion stops and you have to take control. I have reached that point, so you may say I am now colder than cold, it is the only way." He paused for a few seconds then continued with a shaky voice, "Katie was and will always remain my treasure but I am moving on. The fires at the clubs, two clubs not earning money, employees not working, not earning money and moving onto other clubs, it's all bad news; and no fucking progress on finding the bastard who.." Paul stuttered, stopped, and continued, "I want you to work even more closely with Duke, I've also assigned two bodyguards for you."

"Two bodyguards! Is that really necessary, dad?"

"Yes, and George will have the same until I say otherwise. Duke is loyal like a dog and I love him but you have brains and that is what we need to move forward. The arson attacks we think, no we are sure, are those fucking arsehole Philips brothers. They are the new drug barons of Bermondsey. We had a small set-to with them at Pat O'Connor's funeral. DI Karen Foster didn't help either; you need to meet with her, she is a senior Met officer going places."

Oliver changed the subject. "Why was Katie being so secretive?"

Paul shrugged, "She was with someone who she obviously didn't want anybody to know about, but who that could have been remains a mystery at the moment. Don't be mistaken here Oliver, I will never rest until this person is found, no matter how much money it costs. NOTHING will stop me, us, from finding this animal and when we do, I have already said I will skin him alive and I meant it."

"It could be someone in one of the clubs."

"I like that you are thinking already, do we do lie detectors for all staff?" he laughed.

"You may laugh dad but that's exactly what I was thinking, I'll organise it at once."

Paul was surprised but pleased. "Good, anything else you want to do go ahead, it would be wise to keep Duke on side by mentioning it."

"Of course, I'd like to bring Callum in to help."

Paul didn't say anything for five seconds then said, "Not sure what Duke will say about that, but even he has said Callum is working hard and is reliable. Okay, go for it, he's family and that's what we need at the moment; you can't trust anyone else."

"What has been decided about the Philips brothers?"

"They have a huge drugs business and its all cash; we are going to strangle the life out of those bastards by hitting them where it hurts most, their cash and their drug shipments."

Paul had put the clubs on high alert, as soon as things started happening he expected the Philip's brothers to come out fighting.

CHAPTER 14

The first few days of August had been sweltering and the Friday was no different. Two of Dukes best operatives were parked up in their silver Ford Focus in Cathay Street near Bermondsey Tube Station, the windows were open to let in the little breeze there was. Terry Fitch and Mad Keith Malone were watching house number thirty two. It didn't look any different to the other hundreds of houses in the street or surrounding area. It was four thirty in the afternoon and the last delivery was always made on the dot at four forty, at exactly five o'clock two big bodyguard types would then leave the house with a large brown suitcase get in a black top of the range Mercedes and drive off to Basildon in Essex.

Terry and Keith had done their homework and spent a week watching the house and following the two men. Cash deliveries came in every day of the week and then left in the suitcase on the Friday afternoon, the money was then taken to a counting house in Basildon owned by the Philips brothers. Terry and Keith had done jobs for Duke over the years, they got well paid and on time. They were sitting in the car dressed in matching light weight grey track suits; they had bought them together and they found them comfortable to work in. Underneath the two front seats were cudgels, short wooden weapons that could inflict serious damage when used correctly. They had a well-practiced habit of hitting the head as it immediately incapacitated the victim. They also had two loaded Glock 9mm semi-automatic hand guns in a secret box built into the boot behind the back seat. Terry glanced at his watch, it was four fifty three, not long to go. Three minutes later, they got out of the car and strolled slowly down the road. They stopped across the road from thirty two, behind a white Vauxhall van, making sure they could not be seen from the house.

They heard the heavy, red front door open at exactly five pm. The two men took a quick look around and strode down the path towards the Mercedes. They had done the same thing a hundred times and were perhaps slightly complacent. Terry closed his eyes and was counting the steps and knew exactly when the front man was two paces from the car door. He nudged Keith and they exploded into action one on each side of the van. They hurtled across the road in a second, and that was all it took; the two men were so surprised they didn't even have time to draw the guns they carried. The cudgels were smashed over their heads, cracking their skulls; the two men slumped on the floor, unconscious. Keith was nearest to the suitcase and went to pick it up, he cursed when he saw it handcuffed to the wrist of the man; they had never seen the hand-cuffs before. Keith glanced over at Terry and held the suitcase up so he could see the cuffs. Terry was the boss and was always prepared for any eventuality. He put his hand inside the leg of his tracksuit bottoms and brought out a vicious looking hunting knife. He threw it to Keith who caught it in his right hand. He looked at the knife; he had never cut someone's hand off before. He hesitated for a second and then gripped the man's wrist with his left hand and started cutting. The knife was so sharp it cut through the skin, muscle and tendons like butter. What Keith hadn't expected was the explosion of blood as he cut through the arteries; it shot up and covered his hand and arm. When it was finished, he grabbed the case with the cuffs and hand banging on the side as he ran back across the road to their car, a Focus. He jumped in the passenger seat and put the case on his lap; it was disconcerting to sit there with the hand attached, still dripping blood all over his tracksuit.

***

The cocaine was piled high in one kilo white plastic bags that stretched across the long wooden table. The small business unit 1 in Dagenham had a sign above the front door with the white lettering *Norma's Catering Services* engraved on it. The fact was not even one egg sandwich had ever been produced in the two years that the unit had been open. It was the main warehouse for cutting and storing drugs owned by the Philips brothers. Duke and three of his security team from the clubs were sitting in a dirty old white van three units down. They had been watching the unit and knew there would be five or six men inside at any given time. Duke had taken a personal interest in this gig as it would really hit the Philips business hard.

It was Friday afternoon, three thirty pm; they were waiting for the delivery van from Amsterdam that would arrive at four O'clock. The cocaine would arrive in large bags, which would then be cut-trebled in size and repacked in varying sizes. Duke was more than happy to fuck the Philips brothers after they had messed with him at Pat O'Connor's funeral. It got to three fifty five and Duke tooled up, ready to go. The Amsterdam van pulled into the estate and parked directly in front of no 1. A shutter went up and two men came out; the driver opened the side door on the van and all three started carrying in boxes. Duke nodded at the driver and the van slowly moved forward. They were twenty feet from the unit 1 and all three men were inside. Duke and two of the men jumped from the van and entered through the shutters.

Duke lifted his machine gun and shouted, "Everybody, out NOW!"

The men inside didn't hang about, they galloped for the door and freedom.

The two men with Duke took a side of the unit each and started pouring petrol, dousing everything; one minute later, they had finished. Then the three of them retreated to the shutter and Duke lit a match; he smiled as he threw it to the floor and the petrol erupted into flames. A second later, the whole unit was on fire and the million pounds worth of cocaine was destroyed.

***

Brian Frazer instantly recognized the two men. He had been given their descriptions by Duke and the two men were the ones who had been with the Philips brothers at the funeral. Brian was sitting in the box-like bedroom of a shabby flat opposite the centuries old Greyhound Pub in Station Road, Romford. He had seen the two men enter the pub and he had set up his .338 Winchester Magnum sniper rifle with silencer, ready for when they left. It was all very easy, a short range, big target; it would be the most uncomplicated simplest twenty grand he ever made in his life. He sat still, watching, not many men were capable of the level of concentration required but not everyone had been in the special-forces. It was three hours later when he saw the door open and the two men came out. They were so kind as to even stop outside the pub and start chatting. Brian looked through the telescopic lens and lined up on the first man's forehead; he slowly pulled the trigger. He saw the bullet enter the man's forehead and knew it would be exploding inside his head, and that he would be instantly dead. The man fell to the concrete pavement; the second man bent down and seemed to look up right into Brian's eyes. The subsequent shot was half a second later and hit the man just above the ear, he too died instantly as his brain exploded.

Just as the unit in Dagenham burst into flames, Kevin Philips received a phone call from one of the workers telling him about the attack. It wasn't long before he heard about the killings and the loss of two hundred thousand pounds in cash. He went into a frenzy, screaming that he would kill Bolton, Duke and as many of their family members as possible. Graham arrived fifteen minutes later at Kevin's house, frothing at the mouth, he was so wound up. Kevin had opened a bottle of whisky and had knocked back a quarter of it in about ten minutes. As soon as Graham arrived, he hit the bottle as well.

"Cunts! We've been had, Graham! Done up like fucking kippers!" He knocked back more whisky.

"This could almost put us out of business!" he yelled again with demented anger. "Get the emergency stock and start distributing it, arrange new drop off locations, get all the boys tooled up. They want a war, we'll fucking well give them one!" He finished the glass of whisky and threw the empty glass against the wall, smashing it into pieces. "Cunts! Get bodyguards here and at your place, they could be planning..."

Before he could finish the sentence, a grenade came hurtling through the window and rolled across the carpet. The two men were lucky the grenade ended up behind the expensive well-built solid sofa, they both dived to the floor covering their eyes and faces as far from the grenade as possible. It seemed to take such a long time before they heard and felt the explosion; wood and debris from the sofa, the roof, walls and floor showered the entire room, much of it seeming to rain down on their backs. Kevin opened his eyes, he couldn't see anything; the room was covered in smoke. The one thing he did know was that shooters could be approaching the room now to finish them off.

He reached out to Graham and said, "Have to move, weapons are upstairs."

Graham got the message. If they wanted to live they had to move. Kevin pushed debris off his back and crouching, made for where he thought the door was; he felt Graham grab his jumper and followed him. Kevin was right, he thought as he burst through the open door into the hall. He didn't bother looking about as he hurtled towards the stairs and took them two at a time. He could feel and hear Graham breathing behind him. He got to the top of the stairs and stopped, he shook his head; a second later he was running to the main bedroom. He smashed open the door and rushed to the bedside draws; he frantically pulled open the bottom drawer and took out two pistols, turned and handed one to Graham who was right behind him. They both felt better with the weight of guns in their hands, the guns gave them some confidence.

Kevin rubbed his eyes and strode back to the door. He pushed the door until he could see down the stairs into the hallway. It was a good job they had moved quickly, three men dressed all in black with balaclavas and holding machine guns passed in front of their eyes. Shit, thought Kevin; a lot of firepower. He thought they were safe at the top of the stairs and he expected phone calls had already gone through to the emergency services. Just to make sure, he took his mobile out of his pocket and pressed 999. He ducked back in the room and whispered his address, and that there were armed men coming to kill him. The police were already on their way as were the Fire Brigade and an ambulance. An armed response team was activated, that was also soon heading towards the house at one hundred miles per hour. Armed officers were praying they would get some shooting practice. Kevin and Graham knew that once the killers had cleared downstairs, they would make their way to the stairs. Kevin was watching the bottom of the stairs like a hawk, and then he saw the first gunman look round the corner and up the stairs. The face in the balaclava was frightening, even to a hardened criminal like him; these men looked and acted like professional hit men. The killer took a small step to see clearly and Kevin fired; he knew he couldn't hit him but it would let them know they were waiting. The killer ducked back as the bullet whistled past his head and hit the wall. Kevin was caught unawares as one of the killers rolled across the bottom of the stairs to the other side. Kevin raised his gun, he knew they were coming sooner or later and then they were saved, he heard a police siren approaching. Kevin saw the killer from the other side of the stairs calmly walk back across, staring and shaking his finger at him as he went. Kevin placed his hand on Graham's shoulder and then they hugged, it had been close but they had survived.

***

"That's bad news Duke."

"Yea, I know. They'll come after us."

"Well, in that case, we must be prepared. They'll go to ground, watch the houses, and where the families go. You better get in more protection, I don't care what it costs."

"Okay Paul, I'll get right on it." Duke paused for a second then added, "Sorry it didn't go to plan."

"Duke, forget it, these things happen. Let's hope we're not made to pay for sloppy work though."

"Speak soon," and Duke clicked off his mobile.

Duke was seething. The highly paid hit team had failed to kill the two brothers and now they would be coming after Paul, the family and without question, himself.

***

"You're family Callum, Dad's a great believer in blood ties, says ultimately it's the only people you can really trust in bad times. Even Duke is slightly on the side, he's not blood."

"I really appreciate your confidence, I won't let you down."

"I know you won't. Now listen, it's all started, we hit them where it hurts, their gear, cash and best people. Bloody shame we missed the two brothers; but we'll get them sooner or later, teams are out looking."

"What do you want me to do?" Callum was anxious to please.

"Nothing at the moment but we'll work together," Oliver smiled. "You're now my right hand man, how does that feel?"

Callum smiled back, "It feels good, really good but I want to earn my bones."

"Don't worry, you'll get your opportunity. Now, check all the security, make sure everyone's armed and alert. See you back in Dad's office."

Callum couldn't believe what had happened, he was now really part of the family and was trusted by all. He would be working with Oliver and had been promised a serious job when all the trouble had passed. He walked around the club reminding all the security men to be alert and ready, the Philips brothers would without question retaliate.

CHAPTER 15

Mid-August, another dull grey overcast Monday morning. It was eight thirty am, DI Karen Foster was sitting right in the corner of the staff canteen at Rotherhithe nick, bemoaning her work and personal situation. She'd been fed up when she got dressed that morning and stuck on an old pair of black trousers and a shabby white shirt. She was almost hiding, she didn't want to speak to anyone and that included Detective Sargent Jeff Swan who she had left working in CID. Karen glanced around the canteen, no one looked particularly happy; the drab décor and grotty weather probably didn't help. She sipped at her Americano coffee, she had given up on the normal Lattes as it had become like drinking hot milk. Most officers who came in grabbed a take away coffee and a croissant or Danish. One or two did see her and nodded in recognition.

There was suddenly a flurry of activity at the entrance and three young female officers entered. Karen had been expecting them, they had recently completed their training at Hendon and were on their first three month operational introduction to the Met. She suspected they may have been well pissed of getting Rotherhithe hardly the most glamorous of locations. Karen gave the three officers the once over; they were all very different, one a red head, tall well-built, almost an Amazonian, the second slim, perhaps a bit too slim with short brown hair and then the third, who had caught her eye, medium height, bit curvy with very short blonde hair and a pretty face. There was something about her that attracted Karen. Karen couldn't take her eyes off the three of them, it reminded her of her first station at Croydon where she was swamped by men trying to chat her up. She wondered if any of the three were lesbians or had ever made love with a woman. Karen decided not to introduce herself, she couldn't work up any enthusiasm and tried to act invisible.

The red head was Kathy, the slim one Chloe and the blonde was Alison. They collected coffees and looked round for a table. Alison took the lead and headed towards the corner Karen was sat in, she got to the table next to Karen and placed her coffee down so she was sitting directly opposite Karen. Alison sat down and smiled across at Karen.

"Good Morning Ma'am," which was repeated by the other two officers.

Karen was surprised, someone must have warned them she was in the canteen.

Karen got up and decided to leave; the three new officers immediately stood.

"Whoever told you I was in here should also have informed you that in this station, I am called boss. Enjoy your coffees and see you later today."

Before anybody moved Alison blurted out, "Yes Ma'am" and then compounded that by whispering, "Shit!" and the three new officers all burst out laughing.

Return to Bermondsey

Karen laughed as well and smiled at the three of them as she walked off. She picked up a take away latte, as she got to the door she turned and glanced at the three new officers. Just at that second Alison turned as well and their eyes met for the briefest of moments.

The vitality and exuberance of the three new officers had rubbed off on Karen a little. By the time she reached CID she was feeling considerably more positive about the Police force and life in general. She breezed back into CID and deposited the latte in front of Jeff.

"Thank you, and are we feeling any better then?" Jeff asked.

Karen smiled, "There are three new female officers in the canteen; made me feel a bit old but they cheered me up."

"Good, because we have a catch up meeting scheduled for..." he looked up at the large cheap black and white clock on the wall. "In five minutes time."

"Oh God, back to serious already. I'm ready when you are."

"Okay, let's go for it."

Karen picked up her notebook and sat at the communal meeting table, Jeff joined her.

"First port of call is the Pat O'Connor murder, I haven't got anything new. What about you?" Karen asked. She knew the answer before Jeff replied.

"No."

She picked up the notebook and hurled it across the office. "We don't need that anyway because there's fuck all in it!" Then she picked up her mobile and pressed for contacts and put the phone to her ear and waited.

"Richard, it's Karen Foster at Rotherhithe, how's things?"

"I wish I hadn't answered the phone now," he laughed. "If you want an update on the Katie Bolton case, I'm afraid, I've got nothing for you. We've hit a brick wall, so I'm going back to the beginning," he paused. "Sorry Karen, I know it's personal for you."

"Don't worry Richard, I'm in the same situation with the Pat O'Connor murder. It's bloody frustrating, we need a lucky break."

"Let's hope for one eh? I'm in a meeting, I'll call you as soon as I have anything."

"Thanks Richard," and they both clicked off.

"Fuck! This case is going nowhere." Karen looked seriously at Jeff. "Are we missing something?"

Jeff raised his eyebrows, grimaced and shook his head, "This is a bastard of a case. All we need is just one piece of information, one lucky break and then we can move but until then, I honestly don't know what we can do."

Karen looked miserable. "I want to find this man so badly Jeff. Katie was eighteen, she had her whole life ahead of her; there must be something we can do."

She picked up her phone again and pressed one of the stored speed dials.

"Duke, it's Karen Foster. How are you?"

"Alright." Karen's immediate thought was *another fucking happy soul.*

"Any news from your end, Duke?"

"Starting tomorrow, every member of staff, manager, director, everybody even I will take a lie detector test. We've got professionals in. If nothing else, it will give us all something to do and should exclude people who are positive. After that, we will DNA test everybody and give you the results to put through the Met system."

Karen was pleased. "Well done Duke, at least you're doing something. There's nothing to report from this end, let me know any news."

"Will do Karen."

"You see Jeff, they can do things we cannot. Great idea to polygraph test all the staff and the DNA is even better; that could possibly lead us straight to the killer." Karen sounded more optimistic now than earlier before. "Is it your round?"

"Yes, what do you want?"

"A large glass of red would be nice" she said with a big smile.

"One Americano coming right up," and Jeff left the CID office.

Karen logged into her messages on a shared computer, she was shocked to see as part of the Met news, the reports of killings and arson attacks in Essex. She was even more surprised when she saw that two brothers had been attacked in their home by a professional hit squad throwing grenades. The brothers' names were Kevin and Graham Philips. She looked more closely at the reports, two known thugs and associates of the Philips brothers were shot dead outside a pub in Romford. Her friendship with Paul Bolton, Lexi and Duke could be over. She reached for her phone; and Duke would not do this time.

The phone rang for a full twenty seconds, she was just about to click off when she heard his voice.

"Hallo Karen." Paul Bolton knew why she was phoning and had considered her reaction when making his move against the Philips brothers.

"Paul, are you involved in this Mayhem in Essex?"

He never answered and the phone went dead; but she had gotten his answer from his silence. She was thinking about the future when Jeff returned with the coffees.

"Paul Bolton is off the Christmas card list; take a look at the latest news."

Jeff put the coffees down and leaned over Karen to see the screen.

"That's nice perfume." Karen wasn't sure if Jeff was for real or... "Shall we stick to the job at hand?"

Jeff laughed and kept his eyes on the screen. "I see what you mean; are you speaking to Essex?"

Karen took a deep breath before answering, "I guess so; I'll be in the empty office upstairs."

Karen spent the next hour giving chapter and verse on everything she knew about Paul Bolton and why he was almost certainly the cause of the shooting and arson in Essex. It got to three pm and her PA phoned through to say the three new officers were waiting as instructed.

Karen thought about the short haired blonde again.

"Send them in please."

The three officers trooped in and stood to attention in front of Karen's big desk.

She looked then up and down and liked what she saw, smart, confident officers who, if they worked hard, could have a good career in the force.

"So, one at a time. Name, where you're from and what do you want to do in the Met?"

Alison with the short blonde hair spoke first, "Alison Carter, Purley; I eventually want to work in traffic."

"I started in Croydon nick so I know Purley. Whereabouts?"

"Brancaster Lane, Boss." Karen smiled.

"Nice big houses. Mum and dad pleased you joined the force?"

"No, Boss."

"I'm waiting."

"They wanted me to be a doctor, dentist actually; anything would have been preferable to the force."

"I've heard that before. Why traffic?"

"Seems glamorous, Boss."

Karen couldn't hold back the snigger.

"Someone told you traffic officers have twelve inch cocks or you are completely mad, which is it?"

The three new officers doubled up in hysterics.

"Would you recommend I... eh...." she faltered. "Aim in another direction?"

"No, you all follow your dreams, but I can tell you there is only one place to be in the police force and that is in murder investigation, and to be doing that, you have to be in CID. Next."

The red haired officer stated her name as Kathy Morgan from Dover; she was desperate to work in the investigation of rapes. She didn't tell Karen she had been groomed and raped at the age of fifteen by a fat slime ball, forty year old uncle.

"That's a good area to work in Kathy."

The last to speak was the very slim officer. "My name is Chloe Jones and I am from the Rhonda valley in Wales. I want to make a difference by working in intelligence."

"I have some experience of Intelligence out of Sutton nick, they do some incredible work."

Karen loved all three of them, she remembered her introduction to police life, and some of it was a shock but the overriding commitment to protecting the public kept her sane and together.

Karen showed her teeth again.

"Welcome to Rotherhithe, we may not be glamorous but believe me, you will learn more here in three months than at some stations, in years. All of your aspirations are to be recommended. We are here to protect the good guys from the bad ones; that is put very simply but it is still the value I hold most dear today after years of service. I wish you all the very best and I know you will be a credit to Rotherhithe while you're here, and to the Metropolitan Police in general. That will be all, thank you."

The three new women officers didn't budge. Karen looked at them, they were still standing at attention.

Alison chirped up, "Boss, we were hoping to be able to may be sit with you and talk. You are an inspiration to all female police officers throughout the Metropolitan Police, and please we would really appreciate it."

Karen didn't know what to say but smiled, "You have twenty minutes. Who's getting the coffees?"

Kathy almost ran to the door but stopped, "How do you take your coffee, Boss?"

"Americano, thank you Kathy, now hurry, we haven't got all day."

They all sat closer together.

"So, what do you want to know?" asked Karen.

Chloe was nervous but spoke first. "If the rumours are true and we believe all of them, which is why you are such a legend, sorry boss, but what's it like to kill someone?"

Karen closed her eyes and tried to remember a death and the particular feeling attached to it. It was impossible as there were too many deaths and her feelings were confused. She decided to be truthful.

"The truth is, there have been too many killings and all of them for good reasons," she paused, then added, "I have shot dead quite a few criminals, I've also seen numerous police officers killed in the line of duty, which is very sad. What's it like to kill a bad guy? It's a good feeling because usually, they're trying to kill you or one of your colleagues and believe me, that's not nice."

Alison was next to ask a question. "Can it be fun working in the Police Force?"

Karen held her hands up. "OMG! The fun, yes we do have some fun now and then, and in lots of different ways but most of them involve alcohol."

"Are you married boss?" continued Alison.

"No; the trouble with the police force is you work all sorts of funny hours and understandably, partners can't cope with that. That of course is why there are so many police couple marriages, and then even they don't usually last. Come on last couple of questions."

It was Kathy's turn. "Have you ever regretted joining the Metropolitan Police?"

Karen didn't speak straight away, she had to think about that. "Yes, many times but today, now, I am glad I stuck it out; I love my job more than anything." She paused for a few seconds. "Okay, that's it. Well, enjoy your stay. If you have any issues at all, come and see me, my door is always open."

The three officer's chorused "Thank you, boss."

Karen couldn't take her eyes of Alison, she was wondering what type and colour of knickers she was wearing, she so wanted to find out.

CHAPTER 16

It was three O'clock in the morning, pitch black and there was a slight drizzle. The street lamp lights threw shadows across all the buildings on both sides of Turner Place, the man was standing in the doorway of a women's clothes shop at the southern end of the road. He looked up and down, it was completely deserted and considering what time it was, and being a Monday morning, it was not surprising. He could see his breath as he stood waiting and watching. There were no people about, no funny noises, not even a single car had driven down the road in fully five minutes. He was dressed in black shoes, black trousers and roll neck pullover and a short black jacket. He took a bundle out of his jacket pocket, loosened it and stretched it over his head; now he had his black balaclava on, it was almost impossible to see him. The eye and mouth slits added a sinister look to his appearance. He reached down and picked up the jerry can and walked briskly up the road towards the Bluebird club. It took thirty seconds and then he was in the alley way next to the side of the club. He of course had been here before, he had reconnoitered the club and surrounding area a week before and knew exactly where he was going.

He reached the end of the alley and turned right, stopped and took off his small backpack. He opened it and felt inside; his hand came back out with his extremely sharp fence cutters. He cut a hole in the thin steel fence and passed his backpack through; then he slipped through and straightened, looking up at the back of the club premises. He stood stock still and listened, nothing; he quickly covered the concrete ground to the delivery entrance, cut the padlock on the shutter and slowly pushed it up enough to squeeze under; he was through within a few seconds. He tapped and broke a small side window to the door and reached in and unlocked it. He pushed open the door and went in, stopping for a moment or two to let his eyes get use to the darkness, listening intently. Then he was on his toes, moving quickly through the kitchens and up some stairs. He pushed a door and entered the club with its real, plush carpets, a huge bar and a stage for shows. He looked around, delighted in the knowledge that he was about to destroy another Paul Bolton club.

The flashlight hit him in the eyes and he was blinded for half a second. He ducked down and threw himself to the floor, rolling over and over, trying to hide from the torch's beam.

"Whoever you are, I've already called the police; they're on their way!"

The man was swinging the torch to and fro and sideways, trying to locate the intruder in black.

He didn't feel it much, there was a burning sensation around his neck, and then he swallowed what seemed like a gallon of blood. He couldn't breath and fell onto his knees, dropping the torch. He knew he would be dead in seconds, blood was pouring onto the carpet and then there was nothing. He fell forward, gurgled and he died.

The man cleaned his deadly hunting knife on the night watchman's scruffy old coat and slipped it back into its scabbard at his side. He hadn't wanted to kill some old boy earning a few extra pounds but he had been forced to. Were the police really coming? He thought they could be, so he had to hurry. He ran in a circle the full way round the main club floor, pouring petrol as he went. He got back to his start point and took a packet of matches out of his pocket and lit one; he loved the brightness of it. As he threw it to the floor, there was a loud whoosh sound as fire shot up and swirled around the floor. He couldn't take his eyes off the flames, the yellow and red colour splashing across and lighting the darkness; the crackle and noise was deafening and the smell was a burning stench. The carpet, curtains and furniture were soon burning and thick black smoke was enveloping the room. The man in black disappeared back down the stairs through the kitchens and out the back door. He shot up the alley way and was back out of sight down the road in seconds. He didn't see but heard the police car career into Turner Place towards the club. It had been a good night and another wound in Paul Bolton's business.

CHAPTER 17

The two very ordinary looking men in dark suits and boring old ties arrived in a small clean silver Ford Transit Courier van at the delivery entrance to the Den Club at eight o'clock on Monday morning. As usual, it was a drab grey morning with a little chill in the air. The pre-arranged security guard was there to meet them. They parked up in one of the white marked visitor bays and opened the back of the van and took out two standard looking black briefcases and a large case. They were escorted through the back delivery entrance and taken straight to Duke's office. Duke was happy to see them and couldn't wait for them to get started. Duke had liked Oliver's idea and had decided all staff, regardless of seniority, would take a Polygraph test, or what most people knew as a lie detector test.

The two men would each test individuals for confirmation of innocence. A typical test took two hours; over the whole day and night, they would test about twenty eight people. There were fifty six staff working at various times so the plan was to squeeze all the tests in if possible, over two days. The company employed over a thousand people, and Polygraph testing everyone was a massive task. Duke and Oliver wanted to see how it went at the Den club before rolling it out to the rest of the estate, to do that they would have to hire every Polygraph examiner in the country, and probably more from abroad.

Duke's good mood about the polygraph test soon changed. He was in a foul mood as word came in that the Bluebird Club had been burnt to the ground and that the old night watchman had been killed. He swore vengeance and rang Paul immediately to tell him what had happened.

Duke was to be tested in his office and Oliver in another that had been taken over for that purpose.

The examiner opened one of the briefcases to reveal one of the testing machines. Duke sat in a chair next to the table and relaxed as best he could. Two rubber anemograph tubes were placed round his upper chest and abdomen. The examiner explained these would record breathing and movement. The examiner then attached two small fingerplates to the index and ring finger of Duke's right hand; it was explained they would trace changes in skin resistance during the test. Next, a cuff called Cardiosphygmograph, very similar to what a GP would use to check blood pressure, was placed around his upper arm; this would record the blood pressure and pulse rate.

Duke was ready and it was explained there would be three questions.

- Were you involved in the murder of Katie Bolton?
- Have you set fire to One of Paul Bolton's clubs?
- Have you stolen property from this club?

The questions were asked and Duke answered in a clear and positive voice, and that was that. The examiner put on his glasses, sat over his briefcase machine and studied the results. The examiner told Duke verbally that he had passed the test, all other staff would not be told verbally and a written report of results would be sent to Duke the next morning. Oliver passed his test, and then senior managers started arriving.

The tests were carried out and completed on Tuesday night at midnight. The results were conclusive; one, that nobody was involved in the murder of Katie Bolton, two, that no one had set fire to any of the clubs and three, that probably all the staff had stolen something from the club at one time or another.

On Wednesday morning Oliver and Duke met to discuss the results.

It was Oliver's idea and he spoke first, "I think it's been a good exercise, no one is involved in the murder or fires. As to the theft, it could be a biro, a leg of lamb or a drink."

Duke looked thoughtful, "It's good that everybody passed the two most important questions, BUT I will not have staff stealing drinks or anything else. I'm going to introduce even more CCTV like they have in the casinos, that'll put a stop to it. Are we sure everybody has been tested?"

"Yes, I'll check with Ralph again but he's confirmed everybody has been tested and passed."

"So, do we roll it out?" asked Oliver.

"Yes, definitely, it's costing a fortune but it is money well spent and once we complete the polygraph testing, we will start on the DNA test."

The door opened. "Morning all," said a cheerful Callum. "I hope you two passed the test?"

Even Duke half laughed. "Oliver, I'll catch up with you later."

"Okay, see you lunchtime."

Callum shut the door. If anyone had looked very closely, they would have seen the beads of sweat on his forehead.

Oliver was pleased he had got the result he wanted and Duke called Paul again to discuss what they were going to do about the latest attack on the Bluebird Club.

CHAPTER 18

George stepped through the double doors into Heathrow Terminal 5 at midday. The BA flight had landed on time and it had been a good flight. He had enjoyed his three days in Dublin, enjoying a few pints of the black stuff; but he was pleased to be back as he felt his family needed all the support it could get. The two bodyguards sent to pick him up were nowhere to be seen so he decided to take a taxi. He went out to the taxi-rank and joined the small queue. He didn't have to wait long, a gleaming black cab pulled up in front of him and he jumped in the back.

"Kingly Street Soho, please."

"Sure gov. Good trip?"

George knew how to shut taxi drivers up, he didn't reply and just smiled.

The taxi pulled away from the kerb and George leaned back into the seat and closed his eyes.

The crash woke him from his slumber and at first he couldn't work out what was happening. The taxi had been hit by a car and had crashed onto and over the kerb and smashed into a low brick wall. He was jolted first forwards and then snapped backwards in his seat; he thought about the money he would claim for the whiplash injury. The taxi came to a stop and George pulled himself together; he stretched out his hand and pulled the door handle up and pushed, the door opened and he took a step out. Hands grabbed him by the arms and pulled him out, he was surprised but thankful that help had arrived so quickly.

He stood straight up and expected the men to let go. "Thanks I'm fine,"

But the men didn't let go, instead they dragged him towards a shiny new black Mercedes sprinter van parked twenty yards away. He was still slightly groggy but he looked at the men and understood immediately; he was being taken. He tried to move his arms but they were held in vice like grips by the two men. Before he could say anything, the sliding door of the van opened and he was shoved in and unceremoniously dumped onto the floor. New powerful arms took control of him and he felt his legs being tied, and then his arms were painfully pulled behind his back and tied as well. He closed his eyes and started to sob. The van pulled away at speed, heading for Essex.

"I've got your boy here and he's going to suffer, he's going to suffer for all the shit you've given me. I want you to hear him, listen."

Graham took the razor sharp knife and lifted it towards George's face. George turned away and Graham smiled as he held his head tightly with his huge left hand. He cut quickly and firmly; half the ear fell to the ground as blood shot from the wound. George screamed in pain.

"Did you hear that Bolton? This is only the beginning. I'm going to send you the ear as a memento and then

Return to Bermondsey

tomorrow, it will be another part of his anatomy, maybe his cock and balls?"

George heard and tried to move the chair away in case he changed his mind and wanted to do it now.

Paul, Duke and Oliver were in Paul's office.

The phone was on loudspeaker because Paul wanted Duke and Oliver to hear exactly what was going on and understand why the Philips brothers had to die.

"If you stop now, I give you a guarantee that there will be no retribution, it will be over. I just want my son back."

Kevin screamed down the phone, "I want my fucking gear back, my fucking money and not forgetting you killed two of my best boys! You're such a cunt, Bolton!"

"If it's all about money, I'll pay you! How much do you want?" asked Paul.

"To return your boy," he wiped the froth from the sides of his mouth, "twenty million, I've got enough money Bolton what I want is to be left alone to get on with my business"

"You're no saint, burning down three of my clubs! Do you have any idea what that's cost me? You'll fucking well pay for that and the old boy dying!"

"I have no idea what you're talking about, I haven't been anywhere near your shit clubs, but good luck to whoever is setting fire to them and may he continue till you haven't got any left."

"You lying bastard Philips! When I get hold of you..."

"Yea Yea and the rest, I'm bored! Fuck you!" and the phone went dead.

There was silence in the office.

Paul looked across at the three men with all their wire-tapping and communications equipment. The head man Phil Richards, was turning dials and studying one of the three laptops.

"He's in the Basildon area," said Phil.

"I could have told you that, fucking hell," Duke said with irritation.

Oliver could barely breathe, having heard his brother screaming in agony.

"Let's get every person we can lay our hands on and get down to Basildon, it's better than doing nothing."

Paul rubbed his face, "I have a feeling those bastards are not responsible for the fires, that means we have someone else to worry about." Paul had not recovered from his mini stroke and was feeling like shit. He felt like everything was unravelling. All the years of hard work and sacrifices were dissolving before his eyes and he seemed powerless to do anything about it; there was so much bad news he was feeling swamped, and couldn't think clearly.

"You two need to take over otherwise I'm going to be very ill, I've got to rest; I'll be at home with Lexi. Lexi was the only good news, she had got a lot better and had stopped blaming Paul for Katie's death. They still had a long way to go but he knew they would make it. Paul limped out of the office and met his bodyguards on the way to his car for the journey back to Virginia Water.

As soon as Paul left the office, Oliver turned to Duke, "You hold the fort here, and I'll go to Basildon with a small team and see what we can find out."

"You realise you are going into enemy territory? The Philips have been in Essex all their lives, they own it."

"That bastard Philips will phone again tomorrow just to wind us up, tell him Paul has had another stroke and that you are running the show and want a meeting to agree to peace; it can be in Basildon and we would already be there."

"If he agrees to a meeting, how will we let you know where it's being held?"

"No idea, but one step at a time eh? I'll be leaving early in the morning."

It was difficult for Oliver to function at all, he had to shut off all thoughts of George or he would have had a breakdown, which wouldn't help anyone.

Callum had been given control of security at half the London clubs. It was a big job and he spent hours on the tube travelling around the eight clubs he was responsible for. He was told that the business could not afford to lose anymore clubs to the arsonist. He told Oliver and Duke he would not let them down.

George was dragged back to the basement room where he was again shackled to a pipe. He hadn't eaten or had as much as a cup of water in twenty four hours. He felt very weak and now he had to contend with the terrible pain on the side of his face where they had cut half his ear off. He slumped against the wall, he thought his position was hopeless. There was no possibility of escape, and they would torture him every day until he died. He thought of his mum who he loved so much, he prayed they had not told her what was happening. He wondered if he could find a way to finish it early and take his own life. He looked around for a weapon of any sorts, there was nothing. He closed his eyes and started praying again, something he had been doing a lot of recently.

***

Paul arrived home and Lexi came out to greet him as he got out of the car. They hugged and she took his arm to help guide him to the front door. Paul didn't know but Oliver had called her and told her Paul was not well. They strolled slowly through the entrance hall to the family lounge and plonked themselves down in a couple of comfy armchairs.

"What's happening Paul?"

Paul took a deep breath. "It's bad, so bad I don't think I can cope," he shuddered and rubbed his eyes. "So much bad news, it's overwhelming me."

"You've always coped before, Paul." She felt sorry for him.

"It's the stroke, I can't explain but I don't feel well; it's like I could keel over any minute."

"I'll get doc to call in as soon as possible, I'm sure he'll give you something. Now tell me, what's going on?"

"Three clubs burnt to the ground, a night watchman dead, we missed the Philips brothers, no fucking progress in the..." he couldn't say Katie's name. "It's all bad news." Then he thought about George and tears ran down his face.

Lexi wiped the tears with her hand. "What happened to my big tough man?"

"He got old, and tired and worn out."

Lexi thought for a second then said firmly, "It's not all bad news, you're alive, I am, Oliver and George are fine, and Callum's working out okay."

Paul hid his face and didn't answer. Lexi knew there was something else.

"I want the whole truth Paul, is there anything else? I'll never forgive you if you keep something from me."

Paul sat upright and wiped his face with his hands. "The Philips brothers took George on his way home from Heathrow, they have him somewhere in Basildon, they're..."

"What! George taken! They're what Paul?"

"Hurting him Lexi," he paused, looked at her sadly and said, "Hurting him badly."

Lexi didn't say anything for what seemed an eternity, and when she finally spoke, it was a new Lexi who spoke with a voice of steel and fire of vengeance in her eyes.

"We chose our life Paul, it wasn't just you, we are both responsible but I can't lose another child, I won't lose another child, so we have to sort it and sort the Philips brothers. They need to die and if needs be, I'll be the one that rips their intestines out of their bodies with a blunt knife. Now let's relax, we'll have an early night, we have a lot of thinking and planning to do tomorrow."

Paul looked at Lexi and knew she was stronger than him at the moment. He was full of admiration for her.

"Lexi, I love you so much, always have. I'll be strong again soon."

Lexi kissed him. "I know, you are still my hero in life and my man. Don't worry, together, we'll sort it."

***

The next morning, Oliver and three of his most trusted team jumped in his grey BMW six series and drove down to Basildon. They left at nine thirty from the Den club and took a leisurely drive; there was no rush and Oliver needed time to think. It was a vague and hopeful plan, Duke was to convince Kevin Philips that Paul had had another stroke and that he was now in charge; he would press for a meeting to discuss peace terms but on the condition that George was not hurt anymore. Once agreement had been reached, George would be handed back to Duke and Oliver.

***

They followed the M25 and eventually passed under the river Thames through the Dartford tunnel. Another ten minutes and they turned off the M25 onto the A127, it was a straight road down into Basildon, and about thirty minutes' drive away. The silver Range Rover pulled into the Hotel Campanile on the Southend Arterial Road. They chose it because it was outside Basildon and was not the sort of Hotel the Philips brothers would be seen dead in, which caused some laughter as one of the boys said it. They all booked in to single rooms and met immediately afterwards in the Bistro for a light lunch.

***

Duke was sitting in Paul's office, he couldn't concentrate as he was waiting for a phone call from Kevin Philips. The tech guys were all setup and ready to go. Duke was tired, everybody was tired but one thing he knew for sure was that Kevin and Graham Philips were dead men walking. It got to three O'clock and Duke Thought he may not call. The office was tense, the tech guys were sitting around drinking coffee and Duke had foolishly said they could smoke, so the office was in constant smog. The phone rang at three fifteen.

George had been dragged upstairs and tied to the chair in a small unused smelly office. He was getting weaker by the hour and could now barely stand. The wound was still terribly painful and he was dreading what they had in store for him.

"It's Duke."

"I don't want to speak to the hired help, put Bolton on."

"Not possible I'm afraid, Mr. Bolton had a further stroke last night and is back in hospital in intensive care."

"Really! What a fucking shame!" The phone went quiet for a few seconds; Duke was sure he could hear someone talking to Philips in a whisper. "So what hospital is he in?"

Duke hesitated for a second, "Frimley Park in Camberley. Why do you ask?"

The phone went dead. Duke put the phone back in the cradle.

Kevin Philips phoned directory enquiries and asked for the phone number for Frimley Park Hospital. He was given it and was asked if he wanted to be put through, he said yes and heard the buzzing of the numbers.

"Frimley Park Hospital. How can I help you?"

"Good afternoon, my name's Gary Bolton. I understand my brother Paul Bolton is back in having suffered another stroke. I'm abroad at the moment and was desperate to speak to him even just for a second."

"Hold on a moment please, sir."

Philips waited and waited then the voice returned. "I'm putting you through to Mr. Bolton's Consultant."

"Thank you so much."

"Doctor Patel. What can I do for you?"

"This is Gary Bolton. I really wanted an update on how my brother is and if possible just to speak to him for a second."

"You're his brother, I understand?"

"That's correct."

"Well Mr. Bolton has suffered a further stroke and it's a very serious situation, he's hardly able to speak but you might cheer him up a bit so yes I think that would be okay." Five seconds later Paul muttered into the phone.

"Hello," the voice was barely audible and croaky but unmistakably Paul Bolton's.

"This is Kevin Philips I hope you fucking die," and Paul heard him laugh as he put the phone down.

"Thanks Doc, I owe you one."

Paul turned, "Come on Lexi, we've got work to do" and they smiled at each other.

Duke picked the phone up again. "Duke."

"So who's in Charge now?"

"I am, we need to meet, we should be working together not trying to kill each other for God's sake."

There was silence for a few seconds then Kevin said, "Yes I agree now that Bolton is out of the picture. Yes, it's a good idea."

"Before we go any further, there is one condition."

"What's that?"

"George, no more beatings. Give him some food and look after his wounds."

Silence again, then, "In the interests of us starting a new relationship, I agree but the meeting has to be on my turf."

Duke didn't want to give in too quickly. "Yea okay. How do you want to play it?"

"I'll let you know." The phone went dead.

Duke took a deep breath and rubbed his eyes. He picked up his mobile and rang speed dial two.

Paul Bolton answered.

"He's agreed to a meeting and George is okay for the time being."

"Brilliant, Duke! where is Oliver?"

"In a hotel just outside Basildon."

"Good, see you shortly."

Paul turned to Lexi and smiled happily for the first time since Katie's murder, "I love it when a plan comes together."

CHAPTER 19

Detective Inspector Karen Foster had said goodbye to Jeff and packed up early on Friday afternoon. She left Rotherhithe nick looking forward to a night out and a good drink. It was four thirty and the weather was grey as usual. Everything in Rotherhithe and Bermondsey looked grey, cold, tired and worn out; some would say that this was what gave the town its unique flavour of life while some would say that was complete bollocks and the area was a pile of shit. She was back to the safe house within ten minutes and relaxed in the lounge with a glass of red wine two minutes later. She had no real friends in the area, it would have to be another solo night out. She looked at the glass of Australian Cabernet Sauvignon and thought she'd better go easy or she would end up in some unexpected bed somewhere, having been fucked by a complete stranger, man or woman.

Her thoughts drifted to times spent with Chau and Esme, probably the happiest times in her life. She regretted leaving both but it could not be undone and it was all in the past. She drained her glass and decided to have a long soak in a hot bath. She made her way upstairs to her bedroom and undressed. She looked in the full length mirror, her tits were still good, firm and a good size, her eyes went south and she cringed at the slight belly that was appearing. Bloody wine, she said to herself, can't be helped; she wasn't giving it up. Her legs were long and still looked attractive She looked at her pussy, she would have to rub it with soap and shave again to get it really smooth. She wrapped a towel around herself and went through to the bathroom. The bath was extra-long and Karen luxuriated in the hot water. She scrubbed herself and felt weak especially from the heat. She lifted her left leg over the side of the bath and touched herself, it felt good. Then she leaned forward and grabbed the bar of soap...

It was still early, Karen had dressed in her evening gear: sexy matching red knickers and bra, a cream short skirt that really showed off her legs and a see through cream blouse. She was happy and knew she could still turn heads in the right place. She messed about with her hair for ages and decided to tie it really short. As she finished, she thought of Alison Carter, the blonde haired sexy new policewoman. Karen thought it was funny that she had never been out with a policewoman. She of course had had a passionate relationship with Esme Delon but she had been with the French Police Nationale.

Karen called a cab and left the house at seven thirty. It was early and she had already finished one bottle of red. She got the cab to drop her at the Tentaziarno Restaurant in Tooley Street, not far from Tower Bridge. It was one of her favourite Italian restaurants and was in a former Dock Warehouse. It had plenty of atmosphere and the most beautiful red brick walls. She knew most of the staff and was led to her usual table which was in a corner, with a good view of the door. Karen liked to see who was coming in, or more to the point, what talent was entering the restaurant. She loved the white tablecloths, the strong thick napkins and the beautiful heavy cutlery. She started with a light tomato and basil salad, which was refreshing and delicious; she was hungry and soon polished that off. She then went for the Tortellini with Ricotta and pine nuts. She could never sit in a restaurant without a bottle of wine, and had ordered a classic Italian red Barbaresco.

The waiters were attentive and she knew she could have one if she wanted; they were all dribbling over her, telling her how beautiful she was and that they should meet after the restaurant closed. She always laughed to herself, *why is it Italian men all think they are God's gift to women?* She blamed the mothers for spoiling them too much. The restaurant was getting busier and it was mostly couples. She ordered another bottle of red and felt so comfortable, she thought she might just sit there all night drinking and then get a cab home.

Four women suddenly entered and they were all in there thirties and scantily but well dressed. It looked like an executives' night out or just very well off housewives on a night out. Behind the four women came in two women and Karen had to do a double take; one of them was Alison Carter. She looked fabulous in a black mini skirt and white blouse. Her friend was tall and statuesque, like a roman goddess, long blonde hair and a figure to die for, all wrapped up in a dramatic multi-coloured designer dress. Karen couldn't believe her eyes, were they friends? Lovers? Karen licked her lips in anticipation of finding out.

Alison and her friend were shown to a seat on the other side of the restaurant, Karen could just see them through the rapidly filling tables. Karen wondered what to do, she could leave quietly and go home, she could go over to their table and say hello. But Alison might think she was a bit or even very sad, being out on her own. Or, she could stick to the original plan, sit still and get very drunk. She decided to wait. She knocked back a few more glasses of red and was beginning to feel tipsy and then it happened. The tall long haired blonde strode through the tables, obviously in a huff about something and left, just like that. Karen glanced over to where Alison was, she was sitting there calm as you like, sipping a glass of white wine. Karen signaled to the waiter.

Alison's friend Emma had stormed out because in her opinion, the relationship was going nowhere and she'd had enough. Alison took another sip of her wine knowing full well that everybody in the restaurant had seen Emma storm out. She decided quickly she would never speak to her again as long as she lived. Alison looked up to see a waiter approaching, holding a bottle of something; she hoped it wasn't Emma back already. The waiter placed the bottle of champagne on the table and handed Alison a note. She was excited, this hadn't happened for a very long time, and then she changed that to ever. She opened the note.

'I'm on the other side of the restaurant bring the bottle.'

Alison slowly closed the note and put it in her small clutch bag. She looked across the restaurant, trying to see who it could be. The restaurant was so busy now it was impossible to see whoever the note was from. There was only one thing for it, she had to be brave. She scooped up the bottle of champagne, stood and started to walk slowly, meandering around tables. She got half way across the room, scanning from left to right; then she saw her. She couldn't believe her eyes at first, it was the boss, the legend; their eyes met as Karen stood and smiled when Alison got to her table.

"Alison how are you?"

"Eh... I..."

"Call me Karen, we're off duty."

"Yea, well I've had better evenings," Alison said, still looking a bit confused.

Karen smiled sympathetically, "I saw your friend leave."

"Are you on your own?" asked Alison.

"It's what happens when you get seconded from Surrey Police back to Bermondsey, I don't know anybody now and all the ones I do know are married."

"We better open this, you shouldn't have, and it's so expensive."

"We better sit down then," and they both laughed.

Karen gave Alison chapter and verse on her life, and the more she drank, the more stories and details unfolded. Alison, for her part, listened intently to someone who she regarded as a legend in the police force. Then it was Alison's turn to give up her secrets; if Karen could have remembered anything from the whole night she would have known Alison had packed a lot into a relatively short time.

What Karen did know for certain though was that she had slept in the same bed as Alison, because when she opened her eyes Saturday morning at ten o'clock, she was staring at the naked form of the young woman, and very nice form it was. Karen didn't remember getting the cab home and didn't remember undressing and collapsing onto the double bed. She crawled out of bed and just about made it to the kitchen where she filled the old fashioned silver kettle and switched it on. Every time she moved, her head throbbed. She opened the drugs cupboard, for some reason she was always shocked at the huge number of packets and bottles of pills and medicine. She searched for some paracetamol, found a packet, took three out and swallowed them with a swig of cold water. The kettle boiled just as the very naked form of Alison appeared in the doorway. Karen stared at the gorgeous body, wishing she felt in better condition to take advantage of the goods on offer.

"Come back to bed, I need a cuddle," cooed Alison.

"I'll come back to bed as soon as I've finished my coffee and brushed my teeth, and then I'm going to do a lot more than give you a cuddle."

CHAPTER 20

Paul was playing with a blue Barclays bank biro, twisting it between his fingers but he kept dropping it onto his impressive desk top. You could have cut the atmosphere in the office with a knife.

"I don't want to sound too bloody dramatic but George's life depends on how we handle this situation."

Duke, Lexi and Callum were present in Paul's office, it was ten am, coffees were being sipped, and everybody was tense and very alert.

"So Duke drives down to Basildon and waits at the designated place, he's then told where to go, he calls Oliver who arrives later and kills the two bastards, simple."

Duke spoke up, "It's more likely they'll pick me up and drive to the meet, and that means that Oliver will have to follow, and a one-car tail is never a good idea, too easy to spot."

"Okay, so we send as many fucking cars as needed." Paul was breathing laboriously, he was feeling the pressure.

"The number is not an issue, Paul," said Duke. "But we need drivers with brains and some common sense. Not so easy to find nowadays."

Lexi spoke for the first time, "Paul, you go with Lenny, Callum's number two, three cars should be enough, shouldn't it?"

Paul looked thoughtful. "What do you think, Duke?"

"Yes, I agree. We get George and take care of the Philips brothers at the same time. I'll get the cars organised pronto. Callum can go down and meet up with Oliver at the hotel. Paul it's up to you whether you go early or follow me down."

"As soon as you hear when and where you're going I'll leave, and remember, those bastards could be watching us now, so we take all precautions."

Two hours later Callum went to the back entrance of the club to be given his car. He tried to keep calm but was so excited he couldn't wait to get in and feel the luxury of the new Audi A4 grey Saloon. Audis were without question some of his favourite cars. He loved the superb style and just as importantly, the power and precision of the engineering under the bonnet. Duke told him to take care of it and if he so much as put a small dent in it, not to bother coming back. Callum left thirty minutes later and felt like a million dollars as he put the Audi through its paces. It was a straight forward journey around the M25, through the Dartford tunnel and down the A127. Two hours after leaving the Den Club, he was sitting in the Campanile hotel bar, having a coffee with Oliver.

Duke had never felt so pressured, he didn't like speaking on the phone and would always choose a face to face chat if he could. He had almost moved permanently into Paul's office and the tech guys were still there cluttering up the place with all their communications equipment.

The call came in at midday from Kevin Philips.

"Duke how are you?"

Duke wanted to puke and call him a cunt but he knew what he had to do.

"Good, you?"

"Fine. I've been thinking about things, you in charge gives us the opportunity to work more closely together. With your presence in London, we could be making millions moving gear. We have the suppliers and logistics, you have the clubs; it's a marriage made in heaven."

Duke had nothing but contempt for Philips; he would never push drugs in the clubs and anybody found doing so was quickly evicted and banned for life.

"It's certainly something we can talk about, I'm open to new ideas and who doesn't like making shed loads of cash? "

"Duke, you'll be a very rich man and I mean very rich. Good, so I want you to come down to Basildon, you drive, and on your own, capiche?"

"Okay."

"Once you get close I will tell you where to go, no bodyguards, no fucking around, any funny business and the first to go will be George, you understand?"

Duke got in quick, "Yes, How is George?"

"Ask him yourself."

Two seconds later, "Duke, it's George"

Duke looked across at Paul and Lexi and smiled.

"George, are you Okay?"

"Yes, still in one piece, looking forward to coming home."

Kevin came back on. "Alright, cut the shit! Jesus! You'll have me in fucking tears in a minute! Aim to get to Basildon at seven pm." And the line went dead.

Lexi was crying after hearing George's voice. "Thank God he's alright," and tears rolled down her cheeks.

Return to Bermondsey

Paul put his arm round her and gave her a hug. "He'll be home soon." He turned to Duke. "Duke, I'll leave in an hour's time and meet up with the boys at the hotel; put some extra weapons in the boot. Just in case, take two mobiles and don't forget the tracker on the car, we need to be prepared for any eventuality."

"I wish I was coming," said Lexi

Paul smiled at her. "You're better off here, I'll call you as soon as we have George safe."

Paul was happy, it was good to be busy, and he was happy that Lenny was driving him. Lenny had been on numerous jobs with Paul, and as well as being a brilliant driver, he was able to act calmly under intense pressure. Machine guns and pistols were secreted in the hidden boot boxes and everything was ready. Paul said goodbye to Lexi and told Duke he would see him later. They pulled out of the club in a sleek Jaguar XE S in Italian racing red, with luxurious cream leather interior; it was Paul's pride and joy.

"Just take it nice and steady eh? No rush," Paul told Lenny as he picked up the on-board phone and called Oliver to tell him he was on his way.

Lexi stayed at the club for two main reasons, one she felt safe their and two it was where all the news would arrive, and she wanted to be there when it did.

Duke was nervous but he liked that it made him function better when the shit hit the fan. He had more weapons in his car than the SAS had and he hoped to use them on the Philips brothers and their bodyguards. He mooched around the club making sure everybody were on their toes. Then he sat with Lexi for ten minutes before he decided at last to leave. It was three thirty when Duke pulled out of the club in his black Range Rover Sport. He rang and told Paul he was on his way and sat back for the relaxing journey to Basildon.

***

Kevin sneered as he looked at George who was tied to an old worn out office chair. He still looked like death and the wound where his ear had been was still red raw and weeping, but he had been given a cheese sandwich and some water, hardly a meal but still enough to keep him alive and give him a little strength.

"You might be going home tonight but then again, I don't trust this Duke character as far as I could throw him." He turned to Graham. "Is everything ready?"

"Yea, boys will arrive at five. If Duke plays by the rules, then it's all good, if not..."

His words trailed away then continued, "If not, Graham, I want him dead." Then he turned and smiled evilly at George. "And this one as well, make sure there are no mistakes."

The brothers were in a unit on an old disused industrial estate on the outskirts of Basildon. It was perfect for them, off the main beat and track, so no traffic and no unwanted visitors. Guards were placed at various locations ensuring no one could approach without being seen.

The crew at the hotel was growing in numbers. Paul and Lenny had arrived and had met with Oliver and Callum. Paul went through the plan of multiple-car following and thought that Callum and Oliver picked it up quickly. The golden rule was to never stay behind the target for too long, and never get too close. If the three cars kept changing and kept in good communication, then they would be alright. They just had to pray that they got the first contact when Duke was picked up.

Duke had stopped for some food at one of the cheap burger vans in one of the many lay-bys all the way down the A127. He was relaxed as he ordered a cup of strong tea, no sugar and a pork sausage sandwich with brown sauce. He sat in his car thinking about all the different scenarios that could take place. He decided that whatever happened, he would kill the two Philips brothers. Whatever they had said or promised, at some point in time, they would want to take over, so the best thing was to nip it in the bud and sort it. In fact, he was quite looking forward to it. Tea and sausage had gone down well and he felt more alive now. He started up the range rover and pulled out, driving past the burger wagon; he put a hand up as he passed and the woman nodded at him. He pulled back onto the A127 and pressed the accelerator, he was prepared. It was now six pm and was getting a little dark. Duke kept driving at a steady thirty five on the inside lane, he was in no hurry. The car phone buzzed, Duke let it ring three times before he answered it automatically from the steering column.

"Duke."

"Why don't you answer your fucking phone when it rings?"

"I was blowing my fucking nose, is that alright?"

"Yea, keep your hair on. Keep coming down the 127, when you get to junction A130, turn left and pull straight into the lay by, sit there and wait." The line went dead. Duke checked the phone and the conference call button which was set at on. Fifteen minutes later, Duke turned left onto the A130, he looked around and instantly didn't like the location. The lay by was on top of him before he knew it, and he pulled in and sat tight, waiting. Every second was like an hour, his heart pounded but he was calm. After five minutes a black Ford Mondeo pulled up alongside him and two men got out, they both held machine guns and Duke knew instantly he was a dead man. They opened fire spraying the range rover with hundreds of high velocity shells. Duke took multiple hits in the head and chest, and his whole body shook as bullet after bullet thudded into him. The two men stopped firing, walked back to their car and drove off.

There was smoke and the smell of cordite all around the bullet riddled Range Rover. First on the scene four minutes later was Oliver; he parked behind Duke's car and could see it was hopeless. He sat there thinking Duke couldn't die, it must be a mistake. He got out his BMW and took the few steps to the driver's door, he grabbed the handle and pulled and Duke's bullet riddled body fell half out the car. Oliver jumped back and he heard a car pull up behind him, it was Paul. Paul didn't get out the car, he saw Duke's body and turned away. It had all gone wrong, they had been played like fools, the Philips brothers were more ruthless than he had thought and Duke had paid for it. Paul sat quietly thinking, there was one more conversation to have with Kevin Philips and then he would kill them all, the two brothers, children, wives, aunties and anybody else who got in the way. Oliver, Paul and Callum, who arrived a few minutes later, sped away from the scene and headed back to London; it had been an exceptionally bad day.

Callum went straight back to the apartment in Chelsea Harbour. He parked in the underground car park and strolled up to the front door. He let himself in and went to the kitchen, he took a bottle of whisky out of one of the cupboards and poured himself a generous measure, tossed it down his throat and shook his head at the burning sensation. He poured another huge measure and took the drink to the lounge. He sat down in one of the leather seats and relaxed, he lifted the glass in the air and smiled.

"To Duke and George!" and he started laughing out loud, and once he started, he couldn't stop.

Paul and Oliver went back to the Den club, it was late but Paul wanted to pick Lexi up and Oliver was saying there. Paul had not only lost a valued advisor but a friend who had been with him for years. Lexi was equally very upset but she was now more concerned than ever for the safety of George.

They didn't know it but as they spoke George was being buried in an old churchyard in a derelict church in South Benfleet. As soon as Kevin Philips had got the phone call, he had decided to kill Duke and George. Graham had done the killing, slashing George's throat with a razor that was sharper than a meat cleaver.

The next morning, Callum got a call from Paul asking him to join him and Oliver at the club as soon as possible. Callum was intrigued so set off to find out what was going on. It was better than he had dreamt of. Callum was now operations Director for all the clubs, only Oliver was senior to him and with the new job came a massive pay rise.

CHAPTER 21

"Someone knows where the bastards are, I don't care how much it costs, do you understand? Paul looked at Oliver and Callum. "Any amount of money is worth it to get a result."

Paul, Lexi, Oliver and Callum were at the house in Virginia Water. It was the morning after the Duke killing and Paul and Lexi were still coming to terms with it. Paul felt like his world was collapsing, Katie and now Duke, and no word on George; it was a pile of shit. He grabbed the phone on his desk, "Needs must," he said to no one in particular and punched some numbers into the phone.

"Karen, Its Paul. How are you?"

"You've got some front calling me after all that shit in Essex. Yea, I'm okay and you?"

"Like shit. Did you hear about the killing in Basildon yesterday?"

"No, why?"

"It was Duke killed in his car, shot to pieces, literally."

"Oh no, it wasn't that long ago he was sitting in here with me, a nice man, well unless he didn't like you of cause. So, who do you think did it?"

"I know exactly who did it, the Philips brothers and they have George."

It went silent for a few seconds the Karen exclaimed, "Shit! It's all bad news then! What can I do to help?"

"Anything you can, I know your intelligence people must be watching them, I need a location, and I'm sure they're holding George in Basildon or nearby."

"Paul, do you realise what you're asking me? If we have that information and I get it and then tell you, I could not only lose my job, I would more than likely end up in prison; can you imagine that, Paul?"

Paul didn't know what to say. "He's our son, I wish I could swap places with him, I'll give you a million pounds." It was his last throw of the dice.

Paul heard the phone click off.

"You tried," said Lexi despairingly.

"Yea." Paul turned to Oliver, "Get some more boys in, we don't know what those bastards are going to do next."

"Dad, we'll have more guards than punters soon."

"I don't give a fuck! Haven't we lost too much already?"

Paul's mobile rang.

"Yes," he listened, picked up a pen and wrote something on a scrap of paper.

He looked at his contacts and scrolled down to chopper, he pressed the green button.

"It's Paul Bolton. I want Max Long and a chopper at my address in Virginia Water yesterday. How long?" he looked at Lexi. "Basildon. Okay, make it quicker and there will be a bonus." Max had worked for Paul before and knew how he operated.

Paul rubbed his eyes, "Oliver, get machine guns and bullet proof jackets from the safe room in the basement," he held up the piece of paper. "We owe Karen big time." Oliver sped off and Callum followed him. Lexi got up and hugged Paul, "Let's hope we're in time and if possible, kill the two brothers very slowly."

"I'm looking forward to it, don't worry they'll suffer."

It was eleven o'clock when they heard the rota blades of the helicopter approaching. Paul had a raised landing site marked in white and yellow paint at the bottom of the huge garden; he had used choppers from a charter company at Redhill Aerodrome a couple of times before for getting somewhere quickly. Paul, Oliver and Callum ran down the garden path as the Eurocopter EC120 single engine chopper landed. They ducked under the still moving rotor blades and jumped into the already opened door. Callum had never been in a chopper and immediately fell in love with the cream executive leather seats, but what he found unnerving and taken aback by was the level of noise. As soon as they sat down, they were handed ear guards which reduced the noise considerably and even further when the door was slid shut.

Soon, they were hurtling at the top speed of one hundred and seventy five miles per hour towards Basildon, it would take fifteen minutes. Paul handed Max a piece of paper and he keyed the post code into his on board Satellite Navigation system. It was an old disused industrial estate and Paul was hoping there would be a near-by practical place for them to land safely. The chopper ride was over in no time and Max kept back from the location, trying to find somewhere he could put down. He eventually saw the perfect site, a field ringed with massive oak trees which would shield them from the industrial estate.

Graham Philips was inside what used to be the main office and it was where he had killed George Bolton. He was putting together a number of drug shipments and had two men helping him. Kevin Philips had left that morning and was up in Chelmsford, negotiating with a new distributor.

Max expertly put the chopper down as the rota blades whipped up a storm of grass, leaves and small stones. He turned the engine off and the blades came to a slow stop and only then did Paul, Oliver and Callum jump down and move to the line of trees. They stopped behind the trees and had a perfect view of the estate. Two men were loading a van with white bags which Paul said looked like drugs. The men were going up and down a set of small metal fire escape steps to the first floor of a dilapidated old building which had definitely seen much better days.

"There could be more of them in the office," whispered Paul. "Callum and I will deal with the two men while they are loading the van. Oliver, you go up the steps and be prepared to shoot whoever is in the office; be careful, George could be in there."

Paul wanted to go up the steps himself but Oliver was stronger, fitter and could take care of himself more than Paul could. They made their way very quietly to the edge of the estate, working their way around to the building next to where the van was being loaded. Paul shook hands with Oliver and Callum, they took the safeties off their weapons as Paul took a swift look and saw the two men coming down the steps; they would have their backs to them in five seconds. He nodded to the boys and started to count down in a whisper, "Five, four, three, two, one, go!" The three of them sprinted across the ground, Oliver made for the steps and hit them taking them two at a time, holding his weapon ready to kill anything that moved.

Callum was ahead of Paul, the two men turned as they heard running over the concrete ground. It was too late, Callum hit the first man full on the head with his machine gun handle, and the man fell heavily to the floor with a smashed skull. Paul knocked the second man over and Callum was on him, caving his forehead in with his gun butt. They took a breather and looked at the steps; Callum was first to move, taking the steps two at a time. He burst into the office to see Oliver holding his weapon aimed at an enormous man who looked as though he could be one of the bosses. Paul was a second behind as he entered the office.

He looked at Callum, "Watch outside, I don't want any surprises."

Paul turned to the huge man, "Well, well, if it isn't one of the ugly sisters!"

"Fuck you cunt!"

Paul couldn't believe his luck. "Sit down, I have one or two questions for you."

The man sat on the same chair where George had bled to death.

"Where's my son?"

"Who's that?"

Paul knew straight away it was more than likely going to get messy, "George Bolton, where is he?"

"Never heard of him."

"You must be Graham Philips, we met at Pat O'Connor's funeral. Where's your brother?"

"What brother?"

Paul had heard enough he shouted, "Callum, find some rope and tie this piece of shit up!"

Callum came back in five minutes later with some rope and some plastic ties. He secured Philips hands behind his back with the rope and his legs at the ankles with the plastic ties.

When Callum had finished, he went back to the door to keep watch.

Paul got closer to Philips. "Where is my son?"

Philips spat on the floor in front of his seat.

"This is the LAST time I am going to ask you politely, "Where is my son?"

Philips smiled at Paul and said nothing.

Paul took one step forward and smashed his fist into Philips face, hitting him just below the left eye. Philips rocked back on the chair which just managed to stay upright.

Paul turned and whispered something to Callum. Callum left and went down the steps. He came back seven minutes later with a heavy hold-all. Paul took it off him and placed it on an old table near to where Philips was sitting. He opened the bag and started taking out tools one by one, screw drivers, pincers, pliers, scissors, hammers, hacksaws, a Stanley knife and wrenches, and all sorts of other odd looking tools, specifically for helicopters.

He looked at Philips again. "Now I want to know where my son is?"

Nobody could have watched someone take tools out of a bag knowing full well they were to be used on themselves to inflict severe pain and not look worried. Philips was no different. The tough exterior had gone but he wasn't going to give in easily, they were going to kill him and he knew that.

"You Boltons are all the same, winging wankers," and he spat on the floor again.

Paul looked at the tools for a few seconds and then picked up the pliers, he made sure Philips saw them as he moved behind the chair. Paul opened the pliers and closed them around the small finger on Philips right hand and squeezed with all his strength. He felt the tiny bones and muscle tissue being crushed and ripped apart as he moved the pliers to and fro. Philips was close to screaming. Paul then moved the pliers to the big middle finger and closed over it and squeezed again and this time, Graham screamed in agony, "Bastard! Bastard!" He was choking with the pain as Paul ripped his finger almost to shreds.

"Where is my son?"

Graham Philips could barely talk, he was in so much pain but he managed to spit out again, "Fuck you cunt!"

Paul worked his way through the fingers on both hands and Graham had fainted with pain twice but still, would not say where George was.

Paul took Philips shoes off and pulled his socks off.

"Your hands are fucked so now we'll start on your feet!"

Paul didn't bother with the pliers but instead he grabbed the claw hammer and brought it down hard on Philips left foot several times. Philips was screaming as bones were smashed and skin, muscle and tissue were being beaten to a pulp.

Paul was shouting in Philips ear, "Where is my son! You fucking cunt!"

"Dead!" Philips laughed cruelly. "Dead, you cunt! And I killed him, slit his throat on this very chair, he squealed like a baby, crying for his mummy!"

Paul nearly fell. "Where is he, you bastard? I want to bury him properly!"

Philips laughed again, "Fuck off!" and he kept laughing.

He had thought the worst but to hear it like that, he grabbed the hammer and swung it hitting Philips on the left knee, Philips jumped and the chair fell back. Paul was on him in a flash the hammer flying through the air and landing repeatedly on bones muscle and fat. Oliver pulled Paul back, shouting, "Wait! We need to make it last longer!" Philips was now just moaning, his body had been beaten almost to a pulp but he was nowhere near death. Oliver wanted his turn and pulled the chair back upright, although Paul had struck him repeatedly with the hammer, Philips face was relatively unscathed. Oliver decided that should change.

He put his mouth close to Philips ear, "I'm George's brother Oliver, and I know you can hear me. You enjoyed killing my brother, so I'm going to enjoy this very much."

Oliver looked down at the tools and picked up the Stanley knife. He let the safety bar off and the blade slid out. He grabbed the top of Philips head and held it firm, he gripped the Stanley knife and cut down the nose from top to bottom. The knife went through it like butter and the nose fell off. Philips screamed in pain, but Oliver had only just started. Next were the ears, then Oliver stopped and spoke again loudly.

"You're making far too much noise Philips, you need to learn to be quiet," and he grabbed Philips tongue and whipped the Stanley knife across as far in as he could, the tongue came away as he withdrew his hand; he threw the piece of pinky red meat onto the dirty wooden floor.

Oliver was beginning to enjoy himself but Paul wanted to finish the job.

"Take his trousers off."

Oliver cut the plastic ankle ties, undid his belt and trousers and pulled them down, it was so difficult in the end he cut them off with the Stanley knife. The man looked so beaten and damaged that Oliver wondered what more Paul could possibly do to hurt him.

"Lie him on the floor."

Oliver pushed him down.

"I hope you can hear me Philips, this is your time. Death is close but one final act before you go, I'm going to cut your penis and balls off and stuff them in your mouth." Paul saw a flash of recognition in what was left of Philips face and smiled. He took the Stanley knife off Oliver and hacked at the penis and balls as copious amount of blood squirted in every direction. It all came away easily and Paul collected the bloody mess into a ball in his hand, he dropped the knife, he prised open Philips mouth and stuffed the penis and balls in as far as he could. Paul stepped back, Philips still wasn't dead but he wouldn't last long, he was bleeding to death from so many dismembered parts, particularly from between his legs.

Paul just stood and watched him die and he enjoyed every second of it, a small bit of payback for George and Duke. Paul also enjoyed the thought of the brother finding him, it was a beautiful message. Kevin Philips was next and Paul was looking forward to it.

Paul cleaned up as best he could but was still a bloody mess when he got back in the chopper. Max took one look at him and Paul could tell he was unhappy. Paul took a large brown envelope out of the hold-all and passed it to Max.

"Fifty k Max, thank you."

Max smiled and hoped Paul would call again soon as he lifted the chopper and swung her north back towards Virginia Water.

Lexi was crying brokenly again, she was thinking of Katie, and now George.

Paul and Lexi were sitting at the breakfast bar in their kitchen drinking piping hot coffees.

"I hope that bastard suffered, Paul?"

"Believe me, it was a bad death for him but a joy for me," he paused and continued, "If you live by the sword then you must be prepared to die by it."

Lexi was so scared she found it hard to get the words out, "Paul," she took a deep breath, "Oliver if..." she stopped again, then blurted it out loudly and quickly, "If anything were to happen to him, I don't think I could live."

Paul jumped off his stool and wrapped his arms around Lexi, "I think I would be the same Lexi, so we have to make sure nothing happens to him."

Lexi pulled away from him and looked him in the eye, "Send him away Paul, somewhere a long way away, just till it's all over, please do that for me, Paul," floods of tears gushed out afresh, sobbing her heart out.

Paul didn't want to but said reassuringly, "I agree, and I know exactly where to send him."

"Where?"

"Las Vegas, he can learn about casinos from the experts."

"That sounds wonderful. Do we know someone there who can keep an eye on him?"

"Yes my darling, we do. Oliver will be very safe and as soon as we sort that bastard Kevin Philips, he can come straight back. Are you happy with that?"

"Yes," and Lexi burst into tears again. "Very happy," and she smiled through the tears.

***

Kevin Philips got a phone call and rushed back to Basildon late that night. His brother had been found by two members of the gang who could not get anybody at the estate to answer their mobiles. The two hard men had seen some sights but the body of Graham Philips lying naked on the dirty office floor was the worst they had ever seen. The floor was covered in blood, Philips legs and arms were at funny angles to the body and they noticed immediately his genitals had been cut off. There was a strange fascination looking at a dead body and neither of the thugs could look away. Then suddenly, there was a rush of stinking air that escaped from his bowel which made them jump and hurry to the door.

Kevin had arrived back and was standing at the bottom of the steps. The two gang members had told him not to go up because it was a terrible sight. Kevin hesitated but then marched up the steps, determined to see his brother. He pushed open the door and took a step in. The smell was so disgusting he could hardly breathe and he couldn't take his eyes off his brother's dismembered body. He saw the penis hanging out of his mouth and turned away. He now knew exactly what would happen to himself if he was taken. He said goodbye to his brother, turned and walked briskly back out the door and down the steps. He got straight on the phone and told his right hand man Tony to send six bodyguards to his house. He got back in his car and left the two men to dispose of the body.

***

Paul had called a meeting at the house, Lexi, Oliver and Callum were present.

"Good news Oliver, you're going away on a visit."

Oliver couldn't believe what he just heard.

"Business doesn't stop, you're going to Vegas to learn the casino business."

"Las Vegas? Now? When we have clubs being burnt down, Kevin Philips on the loose? For Christ's sake, dad! I need to be here, supporting my family."

Lexi had to concentrate hard to stop herself from bursting into tears, it was all she seemed to do these days.

"I can handle it Oliver, and Callum's here to help and as much muscle as we need; you'll be gone for only a month, two at the most."

"Darling, it's for a month, go and enjoy yourself and learn the casino business, please." Lexi was trying to sound as normal and as relaxed as possible.

And then Oliver got it, he was the last child, and his mum and dad were protecting him. He looked at them both and knew what he had to do.

"Well I'm not happy but I'll go on one condition."

Paul quickly said, "What's that?"

"If there's bad trouble like an emergency, you must call me and I'll be back here by private jet in a few hours."

"Agreed," Paul said with a smile.

Lexi embraced Oliver, she was relieved and pleased and it showed.

"So, when do I go?"

"Tomorrow, first class with BA, all taken care of."

Callum had kept quiet and now stepped forward to shake hands with Oliver. "Don't worry, I'll be here taking care of the old man." They both laughed.

"You better do as well," Oliver said.

Callum once again took a backseat and spent the next ten minutes admiring Lexis' arse and tits; he wanted her, and he thought once his plans had come to fruition he would have her so many different ways. He smiled to himself, yes and he might make Paul watch, that was if he was still alive.

Oliver left the next morning for terminal five and a non-stop first class BA flight to Las Vegas. He was glad to be going to Vegas but was sick with worry for his Mum and Dad.

CHAPTER 22

Karen was back firing on all cylinders. She had been out buying new clothes and spent ages in Marks and Spencer, selecting the sexiest new underwear she could find. The relationship with Alison Carter had given her a new lease of life. The sex was incredible, Alison was young, gorgeous and insatiable in the bedroom and in fact, all over the house.

It was autumn, the leaves were falling off the trees and there were kaleidoscopes of colour all around the nick which Karen found comforting. She was in her usual comfortable dark trouser suit and as usual early in the morning, was sitting at her desk with a mountain of paperwork in front of her. She couldn't concentrate and wished she hadn't given the Basildon address to Paul Bolton. For some reason, she was worried and prayed that it wouldn't come back to haunt her.

The investigation into the murder of Pat O'Connor was once again at a standstill and Richard Martin had confirmed they were making no progress with the Katie Bolton case. The only good news was that Paul had insisted on continuing the testing of all staff at the clubs. The Polygraph program had ended and they were about to start DNA testing. Karen was still hopeful that it could produce a result, she still thought it could not possibly have been a stranger who killed Pat and Katie.

By ten thirty, Karen had had enough of the paperwork and needed a break. She left her office and strolled down the stairs towards the canteen. She would have a coffee and see what Jeff was up to in CID. Five minutes later, coffee in hand, she pushed open the door to CID.

"Hey Jeff, what's happening?"

He held his hand up pointing to the phone at his ear.

Karen sat down and sipped her coffee, listening to the conversation.

"I've got to go, the boss is here."

"Yes, we can talk later."

Jeff put the phone down. "Sorry, that was the wife."

"Everything alright?"

Jeff didn't speak for a moment or two, he looked serious then said slowly, "Not really, marriage is on the rocks, it's a fucking mess."

Karen was speechless for a few seconds then said, "I always thought you were solid, that it was a good marriage."

"Karen, what copper do you know with a good marriage? It's a mess Anyway, less of that. What's happening?"

Karen felt sad for Jeff. It was true, she didn't know any coppers with good marriages. She suddenly snapped out of it.

"Look, we'll go for a drink soon and talk, okay?"

"Yes, now, let's get back to work."

"Well, there's not much…" she never finished the sentence as the door burst open and one of the reception constables came in, looking a bit flustered.

Karen and Jeff both looked straight at him, waiting for him to speak.

Karen finally gave up. "Well, what is it?" Then he said the few words that she had not expected and really didn't want to hear.

"Internal affairs to see YOU, boss." The officer whispered, as if he was afraid someone else might be listening,

Karen was apprehensive that they had found out about the Basildon address. She was sure she must have gone a white as she felt the life drain out of her, then she thought perhaps they were here for somebody else, she quickly discounted that idea they were here for her she was sure of it.

"Stop whispering, how many of them are there and where have you put them?"

"Two officers in dark suits, surprised they're not wearing sun glasses; there sitting in reception."

"Thank you, tell them I'll be out in a minute. On second thoughts, I'll be back in my office in five, then I'll buzz down and you can bring them up. See if they want coffee."

The constable retreated back out the door.

"What the fuck have you done now?"

"Something so stupid Jeff, I... I'm going to lose my job, I think."

"Is it that bad?"

"Worse, believe me."

"I'll be in the office with you."

"That's not procedure Jeff, they'll want to talk to me on my own."

"I'm guessing Paul Bolton is involved in this?"

Karen nodded, "No point getting all emotional, I better face the music. I, eh, I'm not sure what will happen, so if I have to leave, see you sometime."

Jeff jumped up and grabbed and hugged Karen, "It'll work out, I'm here for you, always will be; remember that."

"Thanks Jeff." Karen got the feeling there was more to Jeff's comment than what he said, but that was for another time. She left CID and rushed upstairs to her office.

Karen tidied her desk, rang down and asked for the officers to be shown up. She sat ramrod straight looking at the door. There was a tap and the constable opened the door and announced, "Internal affairs Ma'am." She smiled to herself, he had used the correct terminology and she thought maybe it would be the last time she would hear it. She stood and went round the desk.

"Shall we sit at the meeting table? It's more comfortable."

Karen looked at the two officers, mid-forties, been around, hard cases. Why did internal affairs officers always look like nightclub bouncers? She wondered.

"So, what can I do for you?" She wanted it over and done with as quickly as possible.

One of the officers slowly opened his briefcase and placed a file in front of himself on the table. Karen's eyes moved to the file, it looked pretty harmless but the contents, that was the question. She snapped out of her trance, one of the men was speaking.

"I am DI Jack Robinson, this is Sargent Phil Casey, you are DI Karen Foster seconded from Surrey Police, is that correct?"

"Yes correct, what can I do for you?"

Jack Robinson cleared his throat, "We are here to talk to you about possible Lawbreaking, Criminal behavior and Officer Misconduct. At this meeting, we will ask you various questions and dependent on the answers, will inform you of the next step. A serious complaint has been made against you and therefore has to be investigated. Do you know of any reason why a complaint might have been made against you?"

Not very subtle, thought Karen. She considered her options for a second, she could come clean but why make it easy for them.

"I have no idea what you are talking about, I think perhaps I ought to have some representation here from Unison."

"If we decide to progress action against you, then you can certainly have any legal, or otherwise, representation you wish; but that may not be necessary."

"Sargent."

Phil Casey picked up a piece of paper and read for a second.

"DI Foster, you had three new recruits from Hendon join Rotherhithe Police Station recently, is that correct?"

Karen was taken aback, it was nothing to do with the Basildon address and Paul Bolton, but it could still be very serious.

"Yes, we had three new recruits join us recently."

The Sargent looked at the paper again. "One of those recruits goes by the name of Alison Carter, is that correct?"

"Yes, I believe so." Karen was thinking ahead, they wouldn't sack her for sleeping with a new recruit, or would they?"

The questions continued.

"DI Foster, you are the senior serving officer at Rotherhithe Police station?"

"Yes, I am."

"A complaint has been made that you and Constable Alison Carter are involved in a sexual relationship, is that true?"

Karen thought for a second and said firmly, "What I do in my private life is my business, and I will not answer questions that clearly intrude into my private life."

"We are talking about a new recruit that has joined a police station for the first time. The ranking officer has a duty of care to new young officers, it is alleged that you have used your rank to seduce and corrupt a naïve virgin who is in your care."

Karen couldn't stop herself from chuckling. "I'm not being funny but is this how you spend your time? This is a wind up, isn't it? Oh God! You're not strippers?"

Jack Robinson spoke next, "Karen, we have to investigate everything that lands on our desks; you know the drill, it's the system, we don't pick and choose what to investigate. Following this interview, we have to write a report and recommend what course of action, if any, should be taken."

"I'm sorry Jack, you're quite right, my answer to all this is that it is none of the Mets business what I do in my spare time. I suggest you interview Alison Carter and ask her some questions."

Jack looked at his watch, Alison Carter is actually being questioned right now. Are you a lesbian?"

Karen stood up angrily. "How fucking dare you ask me such a personal question! If I find out LESBIAN," she pronounced it loudly, "is on my record, I will go public and sue the arse off the Met for thousands; make sure you put that in your fucking report."

Jack was very calm. "Have you finished?"

"Yes, now isn't it about time you fucked off?"

Jack turned to Phil, "I think we're done here Sargent."

They both stood and turned to leave, but Jack stopped and turned, "We may be back in touch. Thank you for the coffee."

Karen said nothing; she just stared at them as they opened the door and left. She moved back to her desk and sat down. Her first thought was, where they were interviewing Alison, and secondly, who the hell made the complaint.

It was so tempting to call Alison but she didn't want to interrupt any interview which would not look good at all. She waited at her desk, looking at her mobile and willing it to ring. Five minutes passed and she couldn't take it anymore, she rang Alison's number and let it ring once, it was a message that she was available to talk. The mobile rang three seconds later, it was Alison.

 Karen didn't give her time to say anything.

"Alison, you alright?"

"Yes, and you?"

"I told them to fuck off and mind their own business."

"I was scared at first but pulled myself together and told them the same, but in a very nice and friendly way."

"We're going to have to be very careful, that is if you want to..."

"Yes, I really want to. Shall I come over to you tonight?"

Karen wasn't sure, they could be following her and Alison, surely not, but...

"These internal affairs people are like the gestapo, I just don't know how serious this is..."

"They told me I could get kicked out the force, but if I co-operated and said you had seduced me at the station, then I'd be alright."

"Bastards! Let's meet at a hotel. I want to see you and get my hands on you..."

"Don't, I'm feeling horny already."

"I'll call you at about six, okay?"

"Look forward to it, see you later."

"Yes, bye Alison." Karen was in unchartered waters, could internal affairs be monitoring their phone calls? Surely not, they must have much more important things to do, she thought.

There was a knock on the door and Jeff stuck his head in. "Alright boss?"

"Come in, yes it was not what I thought it was, so should be okay."

Jeff didn't look particularly happy with the good news. "Was it about Alison Carter?"

Karen was shocked, "How did you know about Alison?"

"Come on Boss, everybody in the station knows."

Suddenly, Karen had a thought that Jeff could have...

"Well it was and I told them it was none of their fucking business."

"Coffee, boss?"

"Yes, I'll come down in five."

Jeff smiled and left.

Karen couldn't get the thought out of her mind, Jeff? No, surely not.

Karen sat and calmed herself and then left her office and made her way down to CID. She pushed the squeaky old door open and went in, coffee was on Jeff's desk waiting for her; she picked it up.

"Why Jeff?"

He didn't reply straight away, just looked sick and forlorn.

"You know why."

"I have an idea, but this, it could cost me my job."

"No it won't. Internal affairs weren't even interested there, just going through the routine, you won't hear from them again."

"Jeff, we've known each other..."

"Yes, Karen, and I've been in love with you all that time, couldn't you see?" he sipped his coffee and then planted his face in his hands. "I've been a complete fool, I'll have to resign, I'm sorry."

"What you need to do is take a week off sick and sort your marriage out, Jeff. I've always liked and respected you so much but not anymore, after that."

"I have to get out of here, I'm sorry, Karen." Jeff looked as if he was going to start crying. He stood and took a step towards the door. Karen stopped him with a hand on his shoulder.

"Listen, you have your career here, take a few days off. We will never mention this again, I mean it. Nothing changes."

Jeff smiled, "Thanks Karen, you're a remarkable person as well as a legendary copper. See you in a few days then." He walked to the door and was gone.

Karen shook her head, sipped her coffee and thought of Alison's fabulous firm breasts.

CHAPTER 23

Oliver checked his gold omega watch, it was eight am. He got out of the black cab at the terminal five passenger drop off point. The cabbie took his small brown leather case out of the boot and handed it to him. Oliver gave him sixty quid and said keep the change. It was Oliver's first visit to terminal five and he was impressed, just looking at the majestic modern glass building rising skywards. He pulled the handle up out of the expensive case and walked towards the entrance. He entered through the double glass doors and was wowed, the cavernous interior seemed to go on forever. He looked up and saw the beautifully constructed roof, he smiled and wondered how much it had cost to build. Suitably impressed, he was soon standing in departures, looking up at the flight information display, his flight BA3502 direct to Las Vegas was scheduled to leave at ten fifteen, so he had plenty of time for some breakfast.

BA staff seemed to be everywhere, almost outnumbering the passengers. He said good morning to a very attractive passing uniformed BA lady who stopped.

"Good morning sir, can I help you?" Oliver smiled, he thought about a chat up line and decided against it.

"I want to check in."

"How are you travelling sir?"

"First class."

"In that case sir, if you look over there," and she pointed in the direction of a row of check-in desks, "You will see the first class check in desk. Staff there will be very happy to assist you further. Is there anything else I can help you with this morning?"

Oliver was smitten, "I, eh, God I'm so scruffy today." He was wearing denim jeans and a plain crisp designer white shirt with a light blue cotton jacket.

"You look perfect sir, for comfortable travelling. May I ask where you are travelling to?"

"Las Vegas, for a month or two, work."

Oliver just stood there, he couldn't ask for her phone number and then he had an idea.

"What is your name please, miss?"

"Rebecca but my friends call me Becca."

"Well, Becca, you have been most helpful," he whispered and added, "And I hope to hear from you soon." Oliver turned and as he did, he dropped a business card and it fluttered to the floor.

Oliver strolled over to the check in desk.

The two staff were smiling and were well trained.

"Good morning sir, are you checking in?"

"Yes."

Oliver passed over his passport and ticket. His case was taken, paperwork done in seconds and he was finished.

"Can I get some breakfast?"

"Of course sir, the first class lounge is open and complimentary champagne breakfast is being served."

"Hmm, that sounds good. I'm just going to buy a book to read and then I'll be back."

Oliver walked back towards WH Smiths to look at some books. He strode across the massive shiny tiled floor and thought of Becca, the beautiful BA lady. He was half way towards Smiths when something alerted his senses, a man dressed in a black suit carrying a hold-all was matching his step twenty yards away to his left. Oliver didn't know why he was concerned, the man was walking perfectly normally and seemed to also be heading towards Smiths. Oliver slowed and the man slowed, he didn't want to look at the man directly but could hear him as his shoes scraped on the floor. Oliver thought that his father might have sent a bodyguard to watch over him. He continued walking, he sped up, and the man matched him; they both arrived at the entrance to Smiths.

Oliver entered the front of the store and picked up a cookery book from a pile on a table, he flicked the pages open and listened, very alert. The man was to the side of him and had picked up a magazine, Oliver could see him through the mirrored pillar in front of him, the man was tall and broad shouldered and looked like he could handle himself. Oliver continued to flick the pages of the book, he saw the man put the magazine down and look towards him, he placed his hand in the hold-all and strode towards Oliver, he had two seconds he turned quickly as the man brought a large knife out of the bag and lifted it in the air to strike. Oliver raised his hand and caught the man's wrist, Oliver took the strain and pushed, the man was strong and was pushing down which made it easier, the knife was getting closer to Oliver's face and he thought for a second he was about to die, he gathered all his strength and pushed up, at the same time he kicked and connected with the man's knee, the man crumpled and lost his balance. Oliver heard screaming in the background as he lunged for the man as he hit the floor, the man rolled and was up quickly, knife held in front, he started swinging it and moving towards Oliver. Oliver started backing away, he grabbed a hardback book and held it in front of himself for protection. The man attacked and Oliver jabbed with the book, feeling the knife hit it hard.

Oliver backed away and then disaster, he slipped on the floor and fell, he hit the floor and was disorientated, the man was on him in a flash and Oliver saw the knife plunging towards his chest, Oliver put his hands up to try and deflect the knife and then he heard a loud bang, the man dropped the knife and fell on top of him, there was a hole in the man's forehead and blood and brains were dripping out onto Oliver's white shirt. Oliver was in shock, the man was a dead weight and he couldn't move him. Suddenly, strong hands grabbed the body and pulled him off. Oliver took a deep breath as he looked gratefully at a police officer who was speaking to him.

"Are you alright sir? Are you injured?"

Oliver tried to pull himself together; he was still shaken.

"I'm not injured just need to rest for a second, I'm alright."

He looked up and was surprised to see the BA lady Becca, leaning over him anxiously.

"Mr. Bolton, are you okay?"

Oliver nodded, "We can't keep meeting like this you know, people will talk."

Becca smiled and pushed the hair back from his forehead and tenderly touched his cheek.

"Call me Oliver."

"I will do when we meet next time, I have your card, take care."

Becca had seen the medical team arriving and moved to the side.

Oliver sat up and took deep breaths, another minute and he would be ready to go.

The medical team pronounced the assailant dead and police officers took Oliver to one side. They took his name, address and asked him if he knew the man who had attacked him. Oliver replied that he had no idea who the man was and that he was some sort of madman who must have escaped from a nuthouse. Oliver explained he had a plane to catch, and although the police were loath to let him go, they eventually did. Oliver was soon in the First Class lounge, tucking into a full English breakfast with a very delicious and much needed glass of champagne. Oliver finished his breakfast and did one more thing before his flight was due to leave, and that was to make one phone call.

CHAPTER 24

It was Friday afternoon, Paul had been thinking about it all week and finally decided to do something about it.

"Karen, I'm serious give up all that police shit, come and work for me."

DI Karen Foster was sitting at her bog standard old fashioned CID desk at Rotherhithe Police Station.

"Doing what exactly?"

"Head of security, in charge of everything, you report to me and I leave you alone to get on with the job. What could be more perfect than that? Oh, and a salary; well, I don't know, how much do you want?"

Without thinking, Karen said, "It would have to be at least 70k a year."

Paul laughed, "Jesus! You're so badly paid! I'll give you a hundred and fifty thousand a year, car of your choice, pension, private health insurance plus a Christmas bonus."

Karen couldn't believe her ears! "Are you sure?"

"I don't mess about with money Karen, you'll earn it, weekend and night work, hundreds of staff, it's a big job and vital to the future of the clubs. What do you say?"

"Paul I have to think about it, my pension, my career it would be a huge move for me." Then she thought of something else, "There is something else, I would like to bring some people with me, that is assuming they would want to come and the money was right."

"No problem, well hold on! We can't take the whole Metropolitan Police force!"

"No, no, Paul, one or two."

"Of course, if they're good people we can use them."

"There's really just one more stumbling block."

"Spit it out."

"Nothing illegal, no let me rephrase that, nothing terribly illegal," she laughed.

"I've got this business ninety five per cent legit, it wouldn't take much to move the other five per cent. You're seriously interested then?"

"Yes Paul, it would be a new start, a new challenge; I like the sound of it."

"I want you to start straight away."

"I would have to give a minimum of three months' notice and they won't like that much either, but hey ho, on a serious note, I've given my all to the Met, including my blood, literally."

"Karen, nobody could question your commitment over the years. So look, think about it and come and have lunch on, how about Wednesday?" Paul was giving her two days to think it over.

Paul liked Karen, he knew she was a very professional police officer and had been through the mill. She was tough and had killed in the line of duty, she would fit in really well; and it was a bonus that Lexi got on with her so well. She could also prove to be very useful, her contacts within the Met would be an added bonus.

"You're very persuasive Paul, I'll come for lunch."

"It's a once in a lifetime offer Karen, see you Wednesday."

Karen knew he was telling her this was the one and only offer, he would not go back to her in the future. She was tempted, so bloody tempted the money alone was over double what she was getting, it was an incredible offer.

It was strange if they could have seen each other they probably would have burst out laughing. Paul was sitting at his desk twiddling his biro and wondering how his offering of the job had gone, while Karen was sitting at her desk wondering what the hell to do, the two of them in deep thought.

***

"What do you think Paul, will she come?"

"I honestly don't know, we have to remember she's been at the Met and Surrey police for years, it's hard to leave when you have been somewhere for such a long time."

"Yes but on the other side, a new challenge and not forgetting a huge pay increase."

"I can tell when talking to her she's interested so we'll see what she says on Wednesday. You better come as well Lexi, use your considerable charm." He laughed.

"I think that went out the window a long time ago," she laughed too.

Paul turned to Callum, "What do you think?"

He spoke slowly, "I think she may or may not come, firstly for all the reasons you said and also because she's a woman, a man in the same circumstances would move in an instant."

"That's interesting, why do you say that?"

"Women are like birds, they build nests and they keep going back to them, men don't give a fuck where they sleep."

"There's some truth in that for sure, you know I'm going to be relying on you while Oliver is in America."

"Yes, and I'm ready, we need to find and kill that bastard Kevin Philips and sort it once and for all."

"I couldn't agree more, but he seems to have disappeared, seeing his brother's body might have shaken him."

"Yes, short term, but he'll be itching for revenge, it needs to be finished or you'll be forever looking over your shoulder."

***

Callum was now closer to Paul and Lexi than ever, Paul seemed to trust him and certainly didn't keep anything from him. Callum had been spreading money all round London and Essex trying to find a location for Kevin Philips. Nothing had come in yet but money talked, eventually a call would come in from some greedy grass who would cough up the address; it was just a case of remaining vigilant at all times and waiting. The weekend was pretty much the same as usual, working till the early hours of Sunday morning, shagging Mandy, drinking and recuperating on Sunday.

CHAPTER 25

Monday morning was windy and cold, the beginning of September had been miserable and this particular morning was no different. Callum had arrived early at the Den club at eleven am. He strolled in the back entrance noticing a very clean white van parked in one of the visitor's bays. He made a mental note to find out who was visiting. He got to security and asked the guard who was the visitor with the white van. The reply shook him for a second, the DNA testing had already started upstairs and staff were given their time for testing when they clocked in for work. The guard had heard that apparently, it was far simpler than the polygraph testing, a cotton bud swab was rubbed on the inside of the mouth and that was it. Callum continued into the club saying good morning to various people he met on the way to his small first floor office. As always, he knocked on Paul's office door opened it and said, "Good morning! I'm in."

"Morning Callum, come in for a second." Callum went in and shut the door.

"You may have noticed DNA sampling has started, let's hope we get lucky." Callum's mouth had gone dry and he could feel his breathing become slightly laboured.

"Be a good idea if you get tested, makes the staff happy if we're all seen to be taking part. I've already done mine, only takes a second, it's in Duke's old office. Once they're finished, Karen will put them through the Met system, looking for a match to what they got in the Nadler hotel and at the Blue Anchor. Exciting isn't it?"

"Certainly is that, let's keep our fingers crossed, anything else?"

"No, see you about two for something to eat?"

"Yea, good, see you then."

He shut the door and whispered "Fuck!" He strode down to his office, went in and shut the door. He had to think, he was beginning to sweat and his heart was pounding.

Ten minutes later, he left his office and went downstairs to the staff rest room come canteen. There was nobody in; he opened one of the cupboards and pulled out the green plastic first aid kit. He quickly opened the box and saw what he was after, he took out a cotton bud, and he grabbed one of the dirty used coffee cups off a table and wiped the bud around where the person's mouth had been. It was now lunch time, Reg Fielding and Matt Fisher, the two testers, had left the club to get some fresh air and grab a sandwich. Callum entered Duke's old office and looked around, there was a box full of plastic bags under the desk. On closer inspection, he could see they had cotton buds in them. He looked closer again and breathed a sigh of relief, they were the same as the one he had, and the bags were named 'marked'. On the table was a box of empty new plastic bags and next to that, a box of new cotton buds. On the side was a clipboard with an attached list of something. Callum picked it up and saw it was a list of everybody who worked at the Den club and his name

Return to Bermondsey

was on it. Some of the names had ticks next to them and it was obvious they were the ones who had been tested.

The biro was next to the clipboard, he ticked his own name, and placed his cotton bud in one of the plastic bags, wrote his name on it and put it in the finished samples box. He stood for a second and glanced at the list and the box, he was sure that was all he needed to do, turned and left. He skipped down the corridor congratulating himself yet again for being so damn clever. It was a long process testing all the staff as so many came in late in the afternoon and early evening. At seven pm, Reg and Matt packed up and left the Den club, the samples would be delivered to the Metropolitan Police and matched against what they had in their system.

Callum joined Paul for lunch in the upstairs VIP restaurant. Paul always had the same, a small tuna salad with a couple of boiled charlotte potatoes. Callum ordered a toasted ham and cheese sandwich.

They discussed the testing, Callum told him he had done it, and then general chit chat about the clubs. Paul's mobile rang and judging by what he said it was good news.

"Hi Karen!"

"Tell me more."

"Yes, I know the name, he was a manger of one of our pubs."

"Brilliant news! That's a weight off my mind."

"Yes, anytime you like, do it on Wednesday when you come for lunch."

"Thanks for letting me know."

Paul pressed red to end the call and turned to Callum, "Fantastic news, the Metropolitan Police, God bless them," he laughed. "Have got there finger out and arrested someone for the arson attacks. Philip Brown used to be manager of the Frog and Whistle, he was on the take and Duke sacked him. They visited his house and found jerry cans of petrol, balaclavas and even one or two items he'd nicked from the clubs before setting them on fire, that's a real result; things are starting to look up."

Callum agreed, "Yea, really good news, one less thing to worry about."

CHAPTER 26

It was Wednesday, Paul and Lexi were expecting Karen for lunch in about ten minutes. Karen was driving down to Virginia Water in Surrey and the closer she got, the more she thought about one day moving to the country. She loved the abundance of trees, fields of crops, and the greens and yellows of the countryside. The views across open fields and beautiful countryside were new to her, she could just see herself with someone living in a little cottage and making love on the rug in front of the log fire. She came back to reality as she saw the sign for Virginia Water, six miles to go, she would be there shortly.

Karen had told Jeff she was out on operational duties and he would let her know if anything happened or someone was chasing her. She was dressed more casually than usual in Jeans and a new light blue blouse.

Lexi had cooked something simple but delicious, a fish pie with broccoli and fresh peas. Paul was nervous, he was desperate to get Karen on board and not just because she would be very good as head of security, but he really liked her and knew she would fit in really well.

There was a phone call from the security gate, she had arrived. Paul told them to let her through.

Lexi had dressed smart casual in her well-worn red jeans with a see through blouse and black bra. Although Lexi was quite conservative, she knew Paul liked her to dress like that.

Paul and Lexi had planned to do everything possible to get Karen on board and that started with the simple act of being outside the front door when she arrived. Karen pulled into the drive and was soon in front of the house, she parked right next to Paul's gleaming Red Jaguar XE S. She got out the car and smiled and waved as she saw Paul and Lexi coming towards her.

"Karen! Good to see you! How was your journey?"

"Fine, thanks Paul. Hello Lexi." They all kissed cheeks.

Paul was looking at the Ford Focus, he didn't want to be rude but he did want to make a point.

"Please excuse my language Karen, but what the fuck is that?"

Karen laughed, "That's Sally, my beautiful car."

Lexi stepped in "I know how you feel Karen we love our little cars so much"

Paul continued, "Look, let's start as we mean to carry on," he looked at the Ford Focus disdainfully, "We can sell that for scrap, and then Karen you can go to an Audi, BMW or Mercedes dealer and get yourself a real car, whatever model you want," he laughed. "Well, within reason, that is." They all laughed.

"Come on in Karen, Lexi has cooked THE most amazing lunch!"

"Good, because I had no breakfast and I'm starving."

Lexi took Karen's arm, she didn't mean to but she touched her breast, it was like an electric shock for Karen. Karen looked at Lexi and thought, yes she would, any time, any place; she definitely would.

They went through to the dining room where Paul opened a bottle of Moet champagne. Karen looked through the multiple glass sliding doors at the view.

"Lexi, I'm thinking of moving to the country. God! It's so different to Bermondsey! I love it!"

"We used to live in an apartment in Chelsea Harbour; don't get me wrong, it was beautiful, but I'm so happy we moved. We still own the Chelsea Harbour place, Callum is living there with a... what shall I call her? Young lady I suppose, but from what I've heard, she's hopeless in the kitchen but a whore in the bedroom, the lounge and the kitchen, you get the picture..."

Karen laughed, "No wonder he likes her then." All this talk of sex was getting Karen hot.

"Sex isn't everything you know; when times are hard, you want to know your partner is standing right next to you," Lexi said seriously.

"Strange, Callum turning up like that?"

"Paul will answer that, I'm going to the kitchen."

"Yea, really strange, he's a good lad doing a good job, honestly can't complain," said Paul.

"Does he know...?"

Return to Bermondsey

"I don't think so, he's too busy working or shagging Mandy to think about anything else."

Karen hoped he was right if he found out how his father died, it could be a different story.

Lexi returned and announced, "Lunch is ready!"

Karen enjoyed the food and the chilled white Cotes du Rhone.

After the meal, Paul took Karen to his office for some serious chat.

"Did you enjoy lunch?" Paul asked as they sat at the long meeting table sipping their coffees.

"It was lovely Paul, thank you very much."

"Good, I..."

"Sorry to interrupt Paul, but I've already made my decision regarding your offer."

Paul was downcast and pissed off, he had hardly spoken and she was already telling him she didn't want the job.

"I think you should reconsider, after all, I..."

"Paul, I accept your offer, I want to join the business."

Paul was surprised but elated. "Oh, I thought you were turning me down."

"I want you to offer employment to two of my colleagues, Jeff Swan, who you know and an Alison Carter a new copper; whether they'll come over is another question but those are my terms, not forgetting the salary, car, expenses…"

Paul was beaming, "Let's go and tell Lexi and open another bottle of champagne! Fantastic! You won't regret it Karen, believe me. Shit! I am so delighted!"

Lexi was also very pleased and the three of them settled down in the lounge, celebrating with more bottles of expensive champagne and Chateauneuf du pape. Soon, all three were happily drunk and slurring their words. Eventually, Paul excused himself and went to lie down. Lexi and Karen were doing girlie talk when Lexi shocked Karen beyond belief.

"Karen."

"Yes, Lexi?" she slurred.

"Do you eh, do you like… emm… girls? There I said it, I've been wanting to say it for ages, so…"

"I've had plenty of both, big cocks, small cocks young girls, older women, you name it, I've had it. At the moment, I'm with a young lady, wonderful body. Yea, been there, done it, got the tee shirt." She took another swig of red wine. "What about you?"

Lexi laughed, "Only men, and preferably with big cocks," she laughed again.

"Have you ever wondered? You know…"

"Of cause; us women are gorgeous. I often look at women and think, yea, I'd like to touch her," she slurred and giggled.

"You should try it then; trouble is, you might like it too much."

Lexi laughed, "Not going to happen. I like men to much, and particularly Paul."

"I can see the attraction, I've always liked him, not fancied but liked."

Lexi and Karen chatted for a couple of hours and sobered up with coffee in the process. Paul reappeared and Lexi went to make some sandwiches.

"There's something I need from you," Paul said.

"Paul, don't ask me for anything else, I want to leave the force not get sacked from it."

"I tell you what Karen, let's come to an agreement now, I'll give you a hundred grand as a welcome to the company, AND for that, I want one more piece of information from you."

"I can guess what it is."

"I want Kevin Philips, he's put a contract out on me and Oliver, Oliver was attacked at Heathrow."

"Is he Okay?"

"Yes he's now in Las Vegas out of harm's way, Lexi insisted."

"I can understand you couldn't lose... anyway, what's he doing in Vegas?"

"Learning the Casino business, exciting eh?"

248

"Yes I guess so, look I'm no saint but this will be the last favour I do before I come on board, and I'm not even sure we'll know where he is this time. You think he could have gone abroad?"

"His drug business is still running but he doesn't have to be here, God knows where he is."

"I'll see what I can find out."

"Thanks Karen, I knew I could rely on you."

Lexi appeared with a tray of delicious looking sandwiches which they all tucked into. An hour later, Karen left Virginia Water in her old banger. She drove back with a lot to think about, she wondered if Intelligence at Sutton would have any information on the whereabouts of Kevin Philips? Also, whether if she got Lexi on her own one day, could she seduce her? Did she want a Mercedes, BMW or an Audi? And lastly, she had a big signing-on fee, which could go towards a new property in the country.

Karen had a big smile on her face as she pulled onto the M3 heading back to central London.

CHAPTER 27

Kevin Philips was holed up in a small house he owned in Beverly Avenue in Canvey Island, Essex. It was a two bedroom terraced house and had been used as a safe house for drug distributors and friends. The paper was hanging off the walls, the carpets were threadbare and the toilet was blocked. He was well pissed off, he knew Paul Bolton had put the word out to find him. He was safe where he was and his only concern was the relationship between Bolton and the woman police officer. Would she help Bolton find him? He had to think the worst, so the answer was yes, and that was why he was staying put in the house with hardly anybody knowing where he was.

He hadn't heard from the mystery person who was giving him information for some time. He had given him George Bolton on a plate and then the other brother but that had been well cocked up at Heathrow and he had got away to America. Kevin was desperate to sort Paul Bolton but the trouble was, he had so much protection that even if he took him out, he himself would probably not be able to escape. There was nothing on the planet that would stop him getting revenge for the death of Graham his brother. Every time he thought of Paul Bolton, he got into a terrible rage and started chucking cups or whatever else lay within easy reach, smashing them into pieces on the floor or wall.

He had been in the house two weeks and it felt like six months. He had started using gear which he knew was

Return to Bermondsey

bad news, but now he couldn't do without it. Cocaine was addictive and Kevin had always dabbled but now, he was snorting three or four times a day, his habit was getting worse and it was costing him a fortune. He had stopped eating so much and had lost weight, which was the only good thing to come of being a drug addict, and that didn't last long, as he knew his health would deteriorate. He used his mobile as little as possible, he suspected, or he thought the Met, possibly in league with GCHQ, could monitor where he was through picking up chatter of him talking on the phone.

***

Karen had gone straight home from Paul's; there was nothing happening at the station and she was in the mood to celebrate all her good news. She decided to call Allison.

"Ali, you must come over, there is so much good news, and guess what, some of it involves you."

Alison was very excited, "Come on! Tell me then!"

"No, No, No! You have to come over, and trust me, it is well worth hearing."

Alison was quiet for a few seconds then said teasingly, "Is this just a trick to get me over there and get my knickers off?"

Karen laughed loudly, "That does sound very appealing but no, there is real news, come on! Champagne's on ice."

There wasn't any champagne but there were a few bottles of Cotes du Rhone Karen had picked up from Majestic the weekend before.

"Okay, I'm on my way, BUT if you're scamming me, I warn you, I will not be happy. I just need to have a quick shower and put some very sexy undies on."

"Hmm, that sounds good; be as quick as you can and drive carefully."

Karen had a shower herself and dabbed perfume into all the right places, she wore a black embroidered lace kaftan with no underwear, and then poured herself a large glass of red. It wasn't long before the door-bell rang and she opened the front door to see Alison wearing a full length dark green trench coat done up with a beautiful belt.

"Come in, Come in!"

Alison sashayed in and Karen closed the door.

"Let me take your coat."

"No, let's go in the lounge," Alison said as she walked past Karen into the lounge and stood at the far end, smiling at Karen.

Karen followed her in. "I love the kaftan, what's underneath?"

Karen held the two sides and pulled it up very slowly till it was very obvious she had nothing on underneath.

Alison was loving the show and then she slowly undid the belt on her coat and slipped it off. She was wearing a stunning green matching bra and pantie set with sexy hold up black lace stockings.

Karen's jaw dropped. "Wow!" was all she could say.

"Well, how about the champagne?"

Karen made a face, "I forgot; I drank the last one, but the day is saved with a very nice Cotes du Rhone."

Alison smiled, "Okay that will do nicely."

Karen went to the kitchen and soon returned with two large glasses of red.

"You look gorgeous enough to eat!" Karen said as she eyed her up and down appreciatively

Alison smiled, "Well, before you eat me, which by the way, sounds delightful, I want to hear all the news."

Karen was really excited. "Wait till you hear this, Paul Bolton has offered me a job which I have accepted; the pay is incredible, a top of the range car and perks. It's a fantastic opportunity."

There was silence and then, "Sounds wonderful, I'm very happy for you, and what about the connection to me?"

"I've asked him to give you a job as well and he said yes." Karen was almost wetting herself with the expectation of Alison's happiness.

The smile disappeared off Alison's face.

Karen became anxious, "What's wrong?"

"Karen, are you insane? You want me to leave the Met and go and work as a lackey for some night club owning gangster?" She was shaking her head. "I think you've lost the plot, I've sweated buckets to get this job; I'm not leaving! I just started for God's sake!"

"I thought that we..."

"You thought wrong darling. Jesus! I can't believe this! I'm in bloody shock!"

Karen put the glasses of wine on a side table nearest to her and went towards Alison but Alison put out her hand in the classic don't come any closer stance.

"The moments gone," she shook her head again. "Leave the Metropolitan Police, the best police force in the world to go and work for a two bit gangster! You're unbelievable!"

"I just thought..."

"No, Karen, that's the trouble, you haven't thought at all. I hope you didn't tell him I'd take the job?"

"No, I didn't even mention your name, I..."

"Thank God for that! And don't you dare ever mention my name to him."

"Well, I'm sorry, I thought we could get a flat together and..."

"I can't believe I'm hearing this!" Alison grabbed her coat put it on and tightened the belt and strode past Karen angrily.

"We're finished! It was fun, don't speak to me at work unless you have to. Goodbye!" She let herself out the front door, slamming it loudly.

Karen couldn't move, she was still standing in the middle of the lounge. She couldn't physically move, and the tears started. She was back on her own again. She hadn't meant anything by it, she was only trying... Then she crumpled to the floor, sobbing; she bunched her hand into a fist and started hitting the floor. She went on blubbing until she was an emotional wreck. She cried for what seemed an eternity and then she managed to pull herself together. She stumbled up and looked for the glass of red. She drank the first one straight down and then started on the second; she needed to drink, she needed to forget, she knew she was again on her way to oblivion.

CHAPTER 28

Callum had taken the call at ten in the morning. Kevin Philips told him everything, where it happened, who was there, what time it was, he held nothing back, knowing full well that Callum would go totally berserk, and he wasn't wrong. Callum was crying as he hurled plates, cups, pans and anything that came to hand at the kitchen wall. He had found out, the truth was out and his rage was unquenchable, his father had been murdered, stabbed to death by his own brother and a gang of thugs. He had closed his eyes, felt the sharp steel entering all over his body, he imagined the blood in his throat and the pain, his own brother had murdered him, just as Caesar had been stabbed to death on the steps of Pompey's Theatre by Brutus and his own gang of thugs. He eventually tired and couldn't even lift a cup, he sank to the floor swearing revenge; he would start with the most evil one of them all, his father's brother, his uncle Paul.

It was that call that was intercepted and logged by the Met intelligence team, Philips' location was known and Karen was informed at three pm that same day. She was sat in her office contemplating life, booze, Alison and again, as to whether she should leave the Met or not. Now that she had Philips' address, she just sat and looked at it. She knew what would happen if she gave it to Paul; not long afterwards Philips would be found dead, after probably having been tortured. Live by the sword, die by the sword, she said to herself. She was signing some ones death warrant; what about his wife, his children? She sat there for an hour, wondering what to do. She wanted the hundred grand but money for a life? What the hell had she turned into? She decided it was time to leave the Met and start a new chapter in her life. She hadn't mentioned to Jeff yet about the job offer but after the Alison situation, she'd have to give that a bit more thought. It was decision time and she picked up her mobile.

***

Callum got the call just before he left for work at five pm. Paul told him that they had the address for Kevin Philips and that he would be picked up by one of the team to head down to Essex.

Callum was in a quandary, if he warned Philips Paul could guess there was a mole and it wouldn't take too much working out to know it was Callum. He then thought it might possibly be the perfect opportunity for Kevin and him to turn the tables and kill Paul. The only problem was, Paul would be taking a sizable team and anybody could end up getting shot. He quickly forgot that idea, he wanted to deal with Paul on his own, his way.

The car turned up at Chelsea Harbour and Callum was on his way to Essex. Toby the driver told him he'd been instructed to take him to the meeting place at Castle Point Golf Club which was a couple of miles from Canvey Island.

The drive to Essex was as boring as hell. Toby said he'd heard there would be at least six shooters. Callum didn't give a shit about Philips, in fact, he had to die at some time, so why not now? The drive took two hours and soon they were pulling into a lay-by in Canvey Road, very close to the Golf Club. It was dark with no lighting and the team were all milling around chatting and burning cigarettes; the wisps of smoke caused the whole scene to look extremely menacing. He laughed to himself, why was it they all wore long dark coats and looked like club bouncers. He got out the car and waved as he walked towards Paul.

"You made it then?"

"Yea, it's an army," said Callum, looking around.

"We don't know how many goons he may have with him, better to be safe than sorry."

"Of course."

Paul handed him a loaded glock pistol.

"Do you know how to use one of these?"

"Point and pull the trigger?"

"Hell, we need to get you some training. Keep at the back and only get involved in an emergency."

"Okay."

"We go in ten minutes."

Callum looked at his watch, it was seven thirty.

***

Kevin Philips was sitting at the two seater cheap dining table in the lounge, eating his dinner, a ready meal

Return to Bermondsey

cottage pie from the microwave. It was a single portion and in his opinion, enough to feed a fly and not a grown man with a healthy appetite. He had decided he was fed up with hiding and had to take some other course of action to remain sane. He spooned the cottage pie into his mouth and hated the glutinous sticky feel of the tasteless meal, he spat the food onto his plate and pushed the chair back so hard it fell onto the cheaply carpeted floor.

"Fuck it!" he shouted. He went into the tiny hallway, opened the cupboard under the stairs and took out a machine gun and an automatic pistol. He put the pistol in his side pocket and carried the machine gun. He then lifted his short black coat off the bannister, put it on and opened the front door and shut it behind him, making sure it was locked. He strode to the end of the terrace and turned to the back where there was a row of old council garages. He opened one of the ancient worn doors with a key, and pulled it up. Inside was a gleaming grey Range Rover Sport, he looked at it and felt better already. He squeezed down the rather tight space between the car and the wall, pressed his key and the lights flashed and he heard the comforting click as the doors opened. He climbed in, put the machine gun under his seat and sat back and immediately, the luxury and smell of leather cheered him up no end. He inserted the key and started her up, then he pulled out the garage, on his way to the Labworth, a contemporary modern eating restaurant ten minutes away with beautiful sea views; he was going to have a decent meal and couldn't care less about any consequences.

***

Paul, Callum and two minders were in the lead silver coloured Ford Mondeo car, following them was a dirty blue coloured Vauxall Astra with three other shooters. They were two minutes from Beverly Road and everybody was getting ready. They drove past the house which was in darkness. They turned at the end of the terrace into the garage space, they could see the back of the house and again it was pitch black. Paul could feel there was no one home, it was early, and he wouldn't have gone to bed unless he'd been drinking.

"We're in the open, not good news, what do you want to do?" asked Lenny the driver.

Paul saw the opened garage and looked at his watch, it was ten past eight.

"He's gone out for dinner, he's a big bloke, needs a lot of grub. Yea, he'll be at a local restaurant. Callum, go and knock on the end terrace house, ask them for a good local restaurant. Oh, and make sure it's English, yea, no foreign muck anyway."

Callum jumped out the car and ten seconds later was knocking on number twenty four, Beverly Avenue.

"Oh hi, sorry to bother you, we're meeting someone in a local restaurant but can't remember the name of it, any ideas?"

The bloke who answered the door scratched his chin.

"There's the Spice Lounge Indian five minutes away."

Callum spoke quickly "No it's not Indian, more like English food."

"Oh well, in that case, it must be the Labworth. Funny name but good basic food, down on the coast, only a few minutes away."

"I'm sure that's it, where exactly do we go?"

He had the directions and trotted back to the car and got in.

"The Labworth Restaurant, go to the end of the road and turn left, its five minutes away."

Paul rubbed his hands together gleefully, "Fucking lovely!"

***

Kevin Philips spotted the restaurant and looked at the parking available, back and front, then drove slowly following the drive round to the rear of the building. He parked his car as close to the back door as possible. He was a cautious man and had always done this in case he had to make a quick exit. He entered the restaurant and looked around, a few couples and not that busy, he chose the table right at the back, one step away from the door to the kitchen. One of his mottos was, always prepare for the worst because you just never knew what was around the corner. He had a perfect view of the glass front entrance door and no one would be able to see him as they came in because it was quite dark. He ordered a pint of lager, and then his food, a filet steak, cooked medium rare with French fries and a side salad. Now he was feeling happy at the prospect of eating good sizable food.

He sipped his lager and anticipated the succulent filet steak to come.

***

The silver Mondeo drove slowly past the restaurant followed by the blue Astra. They were in communication by mobile phone. Paul told the men in the Astra to park at the back of the restaurant, keeping hidden as best as possible. Lenny drove the Mondeo back to the restaurant and entered the drive, heading for the front of the restaurant and parked in the furthest space, which could not be seen from the small restaurant windows. Callum was chosen because he was the only one who didn't look like a gangster. He got out the car, it was a pleasant warm evening he pulled the zip down on his short black leather jacket and strolled to the front door. He pushed the handle on the glass door and it swung open easily, he took one step in and stopped. He scanned the seating, noting the couples; his first thought was that they were in the wrong place. He took a couple of steps and then caught sight of someone at the back, sitting in a less lighted area. His heart started pumping, he was sure it was Kevin Philips. His thoughts were interrupted by a waiter asking if it was a table for one, he said no, that he was looking for a friend and walked slowly towards the table by the kitchen door.

***

Philips had finished half of his pint and expected the steak to arrive any second. He was casually looking around the restaurant when suddenly the front door opened. He stopped and focused his attention on whoever was going to enter. A young man casually smartly dressed entered; he was well built and looked strong and hard, someone who could handle himself. The young man looked all around the restaurant, Philips' hackles rose on his neck; something about this young man wasn't right, and where was his date? Why was he here on his own? Who was he looking for? Philips saw the waiter approach the man and spoke with him. Philips strained to hear what was being said, the man didn't want a table, he was looking for someone, and then he started walking straight towards his table. Philips drew the pistol from his belt and slipped the safety off. The young man was nearly upon him, he watched his hands; there were no weapons. The young man then sat at the next table in the seat nearest to Philips.

"I gave you George and Oliver, Bolton is outside front and back, six shooters. Good luck."

Philips watched as the young man stood to leave. Phillips said "Thanks," and stood up himself. He walked to the kitchen door and pushed it open. He nearly knocked over a waiter who was carrying a tray of food into the restaurant.

"Can I help you sir, you're not..."

Philips kept on walking, calm, thinking, he had his pistol in his right hand ready, he wanted to get away, get to the car, get the machine gun, be ready and drive out casually. In the kitchen, he picked up a box of vegetables off one of the many stainless steel tables. He was sweating, a chef made to grab his arm, he lifted the gun and hit the man across the head, it worked; everybody else stopped and stood still, frightened. He could see the dirty stained white delivery door; he kept telling himself: keep calm, it'll be alright. He slowed down as he got to the back door, he took a deep breath and pushed it open. Holding the door open with his foot, he turned round and shouted, "Jim! Don't forget the table for six at eight o'clock!" He gave a thumbs up to the invisible Jim and waved. He then casually strolled the few paces to his car, he pressed open his key and the lights flashed as the doors opened.

He lifted the tail gate and placed the box of vegetables into the boot; he was in no hurry, he was the restaurant owner. He took a swift look around the car park and saw a car right in the corner with its lights off but he could make out bodies; it was them for sure. He stretched his arms and yawned as though he didn't have a care in the world. Then he opened the driver's door and slipped in. He placed the key in the ignition and started her up and she purred to life. As he switched the headlights on, and he glanced over at the car, no one had got out. He was the restaurant owner, he jumped out the car leaving the door open, he had forgotten to tell someone something, and he went back in the delivery door and stood still counting. One, two three... at twenty, he pushed the door open again and strode to the car, jumped in and put his seat belt on. He retrieved the machine gun from under the seat and let the safety off; he was ready.

***

Return to Bermondsey

Paul was watching the glass front door, it opened and Callum was on his way back.

"Everybody get ready." Paul heard guns' safety clicks being released.

Callum opened the back door and squeezed in, "From the description you gave me, he's in there and he's on his own."

"On his own? Are you sure? No minders?"

"Couldn't see any, could they be waiting for him?"

"It doesn't matter, as soon as he shows his face, he's a dead man."

The three men in the Astra parked in the dark corner of the rear car park were relaxed chatting about football, women and beer. The back door opened and all three went quiet. They watched as a man with a box of veg came out, they saw him turn and speak to someone in what they assumed was the kitchen.

One of the men whispered, "Hope he's paid for them veg."

There were giggles from the other two.

"Looks like the manager or even the owner, jammy bastard. Wouldn't mind owning a nice restaurant myself."

They watched as the man got in his car and then got out again and went back into the kitchen. Twenty seconds later the man reappeared, got back in the range rover and slowly pulled away. Philips pushed the window button and it slid quietly down till fully open, he took the machine gun and got ready. He slowed down as though he was being extra careful. One of the men in the car whispered.

"Nice car, always wanted a range rover." Just as he finished, his mobile rang.

"No, nothing's happening Paul, the managers leaving, that's about it…"

The hail of bullets shattered the windscreen killing the two in the front stone dead, the man in the back got hit in the shoulder and fell to the side, as the bullets continued to thud into the car, and he buried himself on the floor behind the front passenger seat and started praying.

Paul heard the glass shatter and the gun fire on his phone.

"He's out the back! Let's go!" All four doors opened and everyone was running towards the drive, they were twenty yards from it when the range rover careered around the corner heading for the exit. Paul, Lenny Callum and the other guys started firing. Paul could see and hear the thuds as bullets struck the car and then he was gone.

"Back to the car!" Paul ran like hell as they all rushed back to the Mondeo. Paul was beside himself with rage and frustration.

They piled into the car and Lenny put her in reverse and the car skidded backwards, creating a massive cloud of smoke, he slammed on the brakes and put it in first gear and roared away, kicking up a trail of flying stones and smoke.

"Don't let him get away Lenny!" shouted Paul.

The Mondeo screeched to a halt as Lenny got to the road junction.

"Right!" shouted Paul.

The Mondeo roared and hurtled down the Western Esplanade; the sea was on the left hand side and Callum thought it was a beautiful setting for a car chase.

"Keep your foot down Lenny! There! I can see him!" Paul shouted.

The range rover was half a mile ahead of them. Soon after he'd seen him, the range rover disappeared; the road turned to the right and Paul was hoping to see him again but he didn't. "Shit!" he swore angrily.

Lenny drove on, waiting for instructions. They passed some turnings on the right and left, any of which Philips could have taken. Callum was also desperate for them to find him. The only reason he had warned him was so that he might have killed Paul. As it was, he had already got two of Paul's boys and injured another. Lenny was driving at a hundred miles per hour and it was difficult to see anything as the car sped past road after road.

"Slow down!" ordered Paul.

They were in Thorney Bay Road and Paul had no idea whether Philips was still roaring away from them or had turned up a side road and was hiding, waiting for them to give up and leave.

"Stop the car!" ordered Paul.

Lenny pulled into the kerb. Two seconds later a police car lights flashing and siren screaming, hurtled past them in the other direction. Paul was more than gutted, he sat quietly, thinking what he would have done in Philips' shoes.

"Go back to the first turning on the right after we left the sea view."

Lenny swung the car in a tight turn and headed back the way they had come. Paul thought if it had been him, he would have doubled back. Philips had the advantage, he knew the area. The likelihood of finding him now was slight, plus the law would be all over the restaurant and surrounding area like a rash.

Lenny turned into Cleveland Road.

"Be alert, be bloody alert! He has a machine gun!"

Lenny stuck to twenty miles per hour as they made their way up the road, searching for the range rover. Philips had to give Bolton some credit but what he didn't know was that Philips had a spare car parked in Leigh Road which came off Cleveland Road. He was now sitting in a silver Audi coupe as he watched Bolton drive past; he smiled and chuckled to himself.

Paul told Lenny to drive back to Beverly Avenue.

"Park up at the end of the road."

Lenny turned the steering wheel and pulled in to the kerb and parked. Callum was wondering what the fuck was going on.

"Paul, what's happening? He's not going to come back to the house tonight."

Paul opened the front passenger door and stepped out.

"Everybody goes back to London, keep you're fucking mouths shut until I get back." nobody answered so Paul shouted, "Alright?"

"Yes alright," and then they shut up, not knowing what the fuck was going on, but trusting Paul's judgement.

He shut the door and walked off up the road.

Callum had no idea what Paul was up to, they all sat there in silence until Callum decided someone had to take action.

"Move Lenny, it's Paul's orders."

Lenny shook his head slightly and pulled away.

***

Paul walked quickly down Beverly Avenue and came to the house. He looked around, it was pitch black, the lamp light just to the right of the house was not working and the next one down cast shadows that produced a sinister feeling to the scene. He strode back to the end of the terrace and stopped, he was thinking what to do and then he decided.

Kevin Philips opened the boot of the Audi and took out two thick multi coloured blankets, he got in the back of the car wrapped himself up and fell asleep. He woke early at seven o'clock and had a stiff neck, he cursed and shook himself awake. He needed a hot cup of tea and knew just where to go. The angel café was five minutes away and he was soon sitting at the dirty plastic table, sipping a nice brew and scoffing down a full English breakfast, all for a fiver. He was sick of living like a nomad and decided things had to change. He ordered another mug of tea and sat thinking what he was going to do next. He was lucky to have escaped with his life. He thought about going abroad, he had enough money to retire to Spain or Portugal. He didn't want to live abroad, what he desperately wanted to do was to kill that bastard Bolton but at the moment, he seemed to have the upper hand. He wondered if someone was watching the house, they would assume he would not be so stupid as to return there so he doubted it. He was driving the Audi and didn't like leaving his treasured range rover just in the road. Eventually, someone would clock it and then it would be on its way to Africa in a container with other quality cars. So he knew what he was going to do.

He finished his tea and left the café. He got back in the Audi and headed back to where the range rover was parked. As soon as he arrived, he jumped out the Audi and got back in the range rover and pulled away, heading back towards Beverly Avenue. He reached over to the back of the car and picked up what he called his old man's hat; he put the flat cap on and pulled the front down. He drove down the Avenue, checking all the cars and looking at the house, everything seemed perfectly normal. He got to the end of the Avenue turned round and parked up and waited. He sat there for thirty minutes watching the road and the house, nothing seemed out of place, there were no strangers, it looked safe. He would pick up some money and gear he had stashed in the house and then be on his way. He wanted to be sure so he drove back down the road again, looking everywhere for anything unusual, again it seemed and looked safe.

He got to the end of the Avenue and turned back again, driving at thirty miles per hour, scanning, looking intently and watching. Then he pulled in behind the terrace, slowed right down and entered the garage, slowly edging the car forward until it was fully in and stopped. He took his cap off, opened the door and stepped out; it was tight as usual. He shut the door and pressed the lock button. He was about to turn when he heard something at the front of the car, he thought it was probably a rat and then he saw him. Paul Bolton was inching towards him from the darkness with a gun held out in front of him.

Philips knew he couldn't get away, he would have to talk his way out of it. "Paul, let's talk, we can…"

There was a flash as the gun went off. Philips didn't feel a thing as the bullet entered his head through his right eye socket and blew half his face off, blood and bits of flesh shot into the air and he crumpled to the floor. Paul took a few steps and stood over him.

"Now it's over."

He had to climb over the body in order to walk out through the garage and he pulled the big door shut behind him. He saw the padlock and snapped it into place, somebody would find him when the smell of the decomposing body became so awful it seeped out of the garage. Paul rubbed his arms, he had nearly died of cold in that garage but it was worth it. He took out his mobile and rang for a taxi, he needed a hot bath, hot food, and a hot drink.

CHAPTER 29

It was a typical Tuesday at the club, Paul had asked Callum to pop and see him.

"Callum, what's happening with the DNA test results?"

"Not sure, to be honest, police have had them for ages."

"Chase them up for me, I want to see the results as soon as possible."

"Presumably, they would shout if there was any connection."

"I'm sure they would, but give Karen Foster a call, she'll speed things up for us."

"Sure will do, anything else?"

"No, except I want you to go down to the Concubine club and see what's going on, profits are down, and somebody could be on the take."

"Okay, I'll catch up with you later."

Callum left the office and was sweating, any mention of the DNA tests and he immediately became anxious and concerned. One thing was for certain, he wasn't going to call Karen Foster to hurry things along. He was walking down the main staircase, thinking it might be time to kill Paul and make a hasty getaway. He would buy an open ticket back to Ontario, just in case. He got to the bottom of the stairs and had to sidestep Lexi, he hadn't been concentrating and hadn't seen her.

"Where are you off to in such a hurry?"

"Sorry Lexi, I was miles away. I'm off to the Concubine club, someone's on the take; need's sorting."

He took a good look at Lexi, she looked so sexy for her age, she was wearing designer jeans and a white tee shirt, and he could just make out her nipples which excited him tremendously. Very simple but absolutely stunning; and then it came to him, what did Paul value above everything, more than the clubs, even more than his own life? Yes, of course Lexi, he would have her for hours and then kill her, making sure Paul knew it was him. He watched her sashay up the stairs, knowing he was going to have his hands on that delicious arse in the very near future.

Lexi went in to see Paul and as arranged, they had lunch together before Lexi left to do some shopping with her gold cards. Paul was content, the Philips brothers were dead, Karen was coming to work for him, Callum was working out after all and everything seemed rosy. He still hadn't got over Katie or George or Duke, he missed Duke so much at work, and it just wasn't the same.

Callum sorted the problem at the Concubine club; he sacked the manager and promoted the deputy, problem solved. He still spoke to his mother every other day, telling her nothing but good news, so she was very happy. He was still shagging Mandy and if anything, she was getting better. Well, they say practice makes perfect. He had made his plans; he would be leaving England soon to return to Ontario.

It was the last Friday in September, he had taken the day off, saying he needed a rest. He knew Paul had meetings all day and it was time.

He woke up early and stretched his long legs and arms, it was nine thirty am, it was going to be a glorious day, a day when his father would have been very proud of him. He had three fried eggs on toast with strong coffee for breakfast. He showered, dressed in casual jeans and a blue shirt, threw on his black leather jacket and was ready to go. He thought of his father again as he shut the door of the Chelsea Harbour apartment behind him.

***

Paul Bolton had gotten up early and had a quick coffee. He had kissed Lexi goodbye and left Virginia Water at seven am. It was now eight thirty; he was now sitting behind his big impressive desk in his plush office at the Den Club as he looked forward to a full day of meetings.

***

Lexi had waved goodbye to Paul and went back to her room. She spent some time deciding what to wear for the day. She chose an old all in one yellow cat suit that was very comfy and practical. She had no plans except to relax, read some magazines and cook a lovely moussaka for dinner.

***

Detective Inspector Karen Foster had another hangover; she had been heavily drinking her favourite tipple, red wine at her temporary home and was feeling it as she woke up. She was used to it and knew two coffees would put her back together in one piece. She showered, dressed in a dark trouser suit and was on her way to Rotherhithe Police Station at eight forty five.

***

Mandy was naked and fast asleep in her own bed for a change. Callum had kicked her out of his apartment late the night before, saying he needed some serious sleep for a change. She had no plans for the day except that she had to be at work early at about two pm.

***

Callum loved the hustle and bustle of late morning London. It was fresh but not cold but he still did the zip up on his black leather jacket as he walked towards Fulham Broadway tube station. He passed the five star Chelsea Harbour hotel and strode on up Lots Road. He passed the Jam Tree, a gastropub he had spent many hours of enjoyment in. Five minutes later, he was there. Fulham Broadway tube station was busy, it was on the district line and people were still travelling into central London for work and leisure. He squeezed onto a train and was thankful he only had to go three stops. Soon, he got off at Notting Hill Gate and changed onto the central line towards Bond Street. He loved the tube, so easy to use and ideal for getting around London.

Four stops later, he changed again onto the jubilee line three stops and he was getting off the train at Waterloo. He stood on the right hand side of the escalators, looking at the advertising posters as they climbed up to the mainline station. He stepped out into the main thoroughfare and stopped. He looked for and saw the ticket office. He walked briskly, avoiding all the other fast moving people and arrived at the window. He bought a nine pounds eighty pence single ticket to Virginia Water. He strolled over to the giant timetable and noted the times; he waited thirty five minutes and then boarded the South West train which was leaving exactly at midday from platform twelve. He settled into a window seat and enjoyed the scenery as the train whizzed along, the journey would take forty minutes. The train pulled into the small four platform Virginia Water station exactly on time at ten twenty am. He stepped off the train, it was very quiet here, three other passengers were walking towards the exit and the noise of their shoes on the concrete was almost thunderous. He seemed to be in another world, everything seemed to be happening in slow motion; he felt light headed as he too made for the exit.

***

Paul had finished his first meeting. Harry Green had confirmed the casino project was going nowhere. The license application had failed due to the police report and he couldn't see a way round it. Paul had said to leave it with him, he would have a word with Karen Foster to see if anything could be done. He ordered a coffee and read some notes for his next meeting at ten with the wine supplier.

***

Lexi was lying on a huge green sofa with her feet up on the arm. She was flicking through the pages of the glossy HOME magazine, looking for ideas for the house. She wanted to change the décor in one of the entertaining rooms, from light purple to something more cream and beige. She was loving the tranquility and peace of a morning with nothing to do.

***

Karen was sitting at her desk, wishing she was back in Epsom. Her relationships with Jeff and Alison had both changed, making life at Rotherhithe slightly more difficult than it had been. She was fed up yet again with the drinking, with being alone and being a so-called legend. She decided to do what she always did when she was pissed off and that was to go for a walk around the station, see what was happening and to see if she could find anyone to have a meaningful conversation with.

***

Mandy lived in a tiny first floor one bedroom flat in a large old Victorian property in All Souls Avenue, Harlesden, West London. It suited her as she came and went as she pleased, was near central London and close enough to work. She crawled out of bed at eight am, her mouth was dry and she went straight to the kitchen and drank a glass of cold tap water. She then put on the kettle to make a strong coffee to help to get moving, not that she had anything planned for the morning. She loved to walk round the flat naked. As soon as the kettle boiled, she made a coffee and sat on one of the two brown easy chairs in the small lounge. She was sore as usual, Callum had been fucking her arse and it hurt; she would use some Vaseline which always helped. She sipped her coffee and thought about what she would do before going into work. She decided to do one of two things, either slouch around doing nothing or surprise Callum with a visit. He had just given her a key to the apartment in case of an emergency. She decided to get dressed up in some very sexy undies and pay him a visit on her way to work.

***

Callum breezed into the tiny local cab office next to the station, approached the ticket attendant sitting behind the glass partition and gave Paul Bolton's address to the fat man behind the counter. The man was absently munching on a huge baguette filled with egg and bacon. He said "five minutes" and a shower of egg shot from his mouth. Callum wanted to give him a slap but decided to leave it as he didn't want any trouble before he got to the Bolton house. He sat on the one available grotty old chair and waited. The fat man continued to chomp on his baguette and after a minute, Callum could stand it no longer and went outside. The fresh air was welcome, he reflected on how calm he was, considering what he was planning. He was really surprised, he thought his daddy would have been very proud of him.

He was woken from his day dreaming by a shout from a car across the road, it was his cab. He got in the front

Return to Bermondsey

passenger seat, the car smelt of stale sweat and body odour. He immediately pressed the window opened and it slid down and repeated the Bolton address. It was another Indian and he hoped he wasn't going to overcharge him. He'd enjoyed killing that other fucking idiot and he wondered if they'd found the body yet, he hadn't heard anything on the news or in the papers. He chuckled to himself as he reminded himself that he never watched the news and never ever read a paper. He sat back and relaxed.

"Very posh road you're going to, you know," the drive said, glancing at Callum through the overhead mirror.

Callum turned to the driver and said very quietly but in a menacing tone, "Shut the fuck up and drive." He turned back and stared out the window. The cabbie couldn't wait to get rid of his passenger, there was something about him; the way his eyes were shining so bright, he didn't like him at all.

**

Paul's meetings had gone well enough, he'd been given a case of champagne by the wine rep as a gift; even very wealthy people like a freebie. It was nearly midday and thought he should call Karen.

"Karen, how are you?"

"I've had better mornings, thanks Paul, but no, I'm okay. How are you?"

"I'm good. Quick call, we're trying to open a casino in Victoria and for whatever reason, your lot have strongly

Return to Bermondsey

recommended we don't get a license. Is there anything we can do about that?

"Well, you can always appeal through the proper channels."

Paul laughed, "Yea, well I know that, but you know a word in the right ear might help."

"Paul, honestly, I have no idea who says yes no or anything else about licenses," she paused, then added, "But I guess I can find out easily enough. I'll come back to you as soon as I have anything."

"Great, thanks Karen, looking forward to coming over?"

"Yes," Karen laughed. "But it's so tough deciding what car to have."

Paul laughed, "You have given your notice?"

"Yes," she lied

"So when are you leaving?"

"Three months, I know it's a fair time but a January start will be a great way to kick off the New Year."

"Good. Oh, before I go, did you speak with Callum?"

"No. What about?"

"He was meant to call you about the DNA testing." Paul thought it funny he hadn't called her.

"What about it?"

"The results Karen, where are the results?"

"I don't know, I thought the lab were sending them directly to you, I'll chase it up."

Paul was shaking his head in frustration, "Well let me know, speak soon, yea?"

The conversation was over. Karen picked up the phone. What the fuck had happened to the DNA test results, she wondered.

***

Mandy had a long soak in the bath, dried herself off, sprayed on some dove deodorant and dabbed some chanel perfume all over. She looked through her knicker drawer and picked out some new lovely white lace ones with the matching bra; she put them on and looked in the full length mirror propped against the wall next to her bed. She smiled, Callum would love them and would rip them off very quickly; she was looking forward to a good fuck before work. She put on a short blue pleated skirt and a blue jumper, grabbed her coat and she was ready to go. She closed and locked her cream coloured front door and descended the very steep tight stairs to the main house red front door.

It was a bit blustery; she pulled the collar up on her short blue coat and set off at a good pace for Kensal Green tube station. It was a five minute walk down to the end of the avenue and then two hundred yards up the west way, and she was there. It was an easy route, Bakerloo line train to Paddington, change onto the District line and straight to Fulham Broadway, followed by a ten minute walk to

Chelsea Harbour. She sat on the tube, cross legged, watching the people and imagining which of the men had the biggest dick and would be the best fuck.

***

"Drop me here," Callum said.

The cabbie pulled over. "Four pounds fifty please."

Callum decided that was a reasonable sum and gave him a fiver and said keep the change. He got out the car and the cabbie immediately slammed the accelerator down and screeched off up the road. Callum's heart was thumping, he was a hundred yards from the security gate and barrier leading into the private road. He studied the gate and couldn't see the security guard, he knew he was there but not exactly where. He decided to walk around the road and try to see where the back of the Boltons' house was. It had a massive garden backing onto fields so he would find it and break into the property from the back garden.

It took him fifteen minutes to find the main house; he had to climb a wall to reach the other side and then walk around the perimeter of a field to the back of the property. He was then faced with another wall that was about six feet high. He took a running jump and clambered on to the top and yelped as glass cut into his fingers. "Bastards!" he shouted as he looked down into the rear garden. This was it, payback time for daddy; his eyes shone and a tear trickled down his cheek. He jumped down as the red mist appeared and took over.

***

Paul was in another meeting, this time with six of the top performing club managers for September. He was handing out brown envelopes which had a grand in each, they would have a champagne lunch and they would leave very happy and very motivated. Paul still couldn't get rid of the nagging worry as to why Callum had not spoken to Karen about the DNA test results.

***

"Hello."

"I was just thinking about you, everything alright?" Paul had just had an impulse to give Lexi a call.

"Yes, why? Is there something I should know about?"

"No I was missing you, that's all."

"Ah, that's nice. What's happening at the club?"

"Nothing, just about to have a champagne lunch with some of the managers."

"Oh, it's a tough life, isn't it?"

They were both laughing.

"I've got meetings booked all day. Do you want to swap?"

"Oh my God, no! I'm planning some décor changes; you wouldn't have a clue."

They both chuckled again. "Well, I better go. Champagne awaits."

"See you later, Paul." Lexi was still very much in love with her husband and it was a nice feeling. She switched off her phone, yawned and went back to her pile of HOME magazines, looking for inspiration.

***

"You better send those results over to me pronto or sooner." Karen put the phone down and swore loudly, "Fucking incompetent prats!"

The DNA results had been kept in some office for two bloody weeks. Karen was furious, she had been promised them within the hour by email.

***

Mandy got off the tube at Fulham Broadway and jumped on the escalator and a few seconds later, she was pushing her ticket into the barrier and then she was back out in the fresh air. She positively skipped down Fulham Broadway and was soon striding down Lots Road in anticipation of giving Callum a wonderful surprise. It was a short walk and she couldn't wait to see him. Five minutes later, she arrived at the block of apartments. She wondered if they might even get married; if they did, she would insist they lived in the apartment, she loved it so much. She was in the lift and didn't feel as though it was moving; it soon stopped and the door opened. She stepped out and walked twenty feet to the front door of the apartment. She pressed the door bell and put on her best smile. She stood there and nothing happened, she rang the bell again; maybe he was in the shower she thought. But he still didn't answer the door, maybe he'd nipped out for something.

She wasn't sure what to do and then decided to call him. She hit speed dial one and on her mobile; it rang once and went dead, he had cut her off, or there was something wrong with the phone. She looked at her mobile, an antique; she needed to upgrade it as soon as possible. She began to fidget and then made a decision. She opened her handbag and searched through the lipsticks, tissues and coins until she found the key. She looked at it and thought about what Callum had said, "The key is for emergencies only, do not use it unless I know about it." Well, it was an emergency now and she was here and he wasn't in. She inserted the key, turned and pushed. She walked in and shut the door.

"Callum!" she called as she walked through to the lounge. "Callum! Are you in?" He obviously wasn't. She looked about, it was all clean and everything was in its place. She smiled as she thought it was the perfect opportunity to have a nose around without him knowing or finding out. She glanced around the lounge and decided there was nothing of interest. She made for the bedroom, if he had secrets, the bedroom would be where she might find them. She pushed open the door and hesitated, he did not have to know she had been in his room. She smiled to herself, what he didn't know couldn't hurt him or her and then she walked in. It was pretty tidy, she scanned the room, his red and white striped duvet was thrown across the bed. She went to the small chest of drawers next to the bedside. There were three drawers, she opened the top one and knew what she would find: condoms, her favourite eight inch black dildo and the slightly smaller but equally exciting rampant rabbit vibrator. She opened the second, pants and socks, and the third, tee shirts, all boring stuff. She was about to leave when she decided to look in the large clothes wardrobe. She opened the white Formica door and looked in, trousers and jackets mostly, on hangers and kept tidy. She was about to give up but then glanced up at the shelf above the hanging clothes where there were some shoe boxes; she decided to have a quick look. She reached up on tiptoe and grabbed hold of two of the boxes but she lost her balance. As she slipped to the side, three boxes hit the floor, the lids flying off in all directions. She righted herself and looked at the contents, a pair of shoes and a pair of trainers. She looked in the last box and her eyes lit up, it was just what she needed.

***

Callum had sneaked around the side of the garden, tiptoeing towards the back door. The garden was full of flower beds, hedges and trees which made perfect cover. He went from cover to cover and was soon very close. He stopped and listened, nothing but the odd bird noise. He prayed that Lexi hadn't decided to go out. His mind was wandering, he was thinking of Lexi naked, how he was going to enjoy fucking Uncle Paul Bolton's wife and the love of his life. He had plenty of time, he would take it slowly, savouring every moment and then in the end, he would kill her. He hadn't decided how yet, but it would be slow and painful, Paul would know she had suffered because of him. As he closed his eyes and felt the warmth, he suddenly heard a noise. He looked at the house, Lexi was in the kitchen at the back of the house; he could see her through the leaded window. He smiled and felt a stirring in his groin.

Lexi washed up a cup and then disappeared from view. He tip-toed quickly the last few feet to the back door; he was praying it would be open. He took hold of the old round handle and turned and pushed ever so gently. It moved and he was ecstatic as he pushed it very slowly, not wanting to make any noise. He stepped into the small doorway next to the kitchen, stood still and listened, nothing. She was either in the lounge or upstairs he thought and took one small step at a time towards the lounge. He was soon at the door, listening; then he heard the rustle of pages being turned in a paper or magazine. His heart was pounding, and he was almost shaking with the tension and excitement. She was sitting on one of the comfy chairs and had no idea he was five feet away from her. He quietly sniffed the air, sure that he could smell her perfume. His cock was hard and he was ready.

He took the step into the doorway, she turned and opened her mouth to speak, but he entered the room before she could say anything and said, "Hello Lexi, I've been looking forward to us being alone for such a very long time."

***

Detective Inspector Karen Foster had gone down to CID to see if anything exciting was happening. Jeff Swan was on his computer and stopped as Karen walked in.

"Hi Jeff, anything happening?"

"Sorry boss, nothing at all."

Karen shook her head, "I want to get back to Epsom, this place is driving me crazy."

"I thought you were going to work for Paul Bolton?"

Karen raised her eyebrows, "Yes, well, I haven't fully committed to that yet, although most people would say I'd be mad to turn it down. Truth is, I'm still thinking about it."

"What does Paul think?"

"Well, I did mention that I'd already given my notice in and was starting in January."

"Oh dear, but look, it's a massive decision; you have to be sure."

"That's right, Jeff, so…" Karen trailed off.

"Spit it out then."

Karen said quickly, "Paul wants to know if you would like to jump ship as well?"

Jeff was gob-smacked, "Leave the Met and work for a gangster? Are you serious?"

"Jeff, ninety nine per cent of his business is legitimate, the money on offer is incredible."

"Money's not everything."

"No, but this job could change your life. What's happening at home?"

"Not a lot. Come out with me tonight for a drink and I'll tell you all the gory details."

Karen wasn't sure but then decided it would be nice for a change. "Yes, let's do that, your treat," she laughed.

Jeff's face lit up like a Christmas Tree with flashing lights, "Good!"

***

Mandy walked into the staff entrance of the Den club at one forty five, she liked to be early so she could gossip with friends and take everything at a leisurely pace, instead of rushing like a mad person before starting work. She went to the ladies cloakroom, had a pee and changed into her work clothes. She still had twenty minutes, so went to the canteen for a coffee.

***

"What are you doing here Callum? Who invited you? In fact, how dare you come into my house without an invitation?" She stared at Callum, trying to work out what the hell was going on. "Has Paul sent you?" She didn't get a reply. "Does he know you're here, Callum?" Still no answer. Lexi got up from the seat and grabbed her mobile which was on a side table. She was just about to press speed dial for Paul when Callum launched himself at her and smashed the phone out of her hand.

"You bastard Callum! Stop now before you do something you will really regret!"

Callum was breathing heavily and his eyes were shining.

"I know exactly what I'm doing Lexi, and in a very short time you'll find out what. I know how my daddy died. Were you one of them Lexi? Were you one of the ten or was it twenty who stuck sharpened knives into his body killing him?" Tears were streaming down his eyes. "Or was it just your husband and some of his mates?" He was shouting.

Lexi stood her ground, "Your father got everything he deserved." she was getting annoyed and raised her voice, "He maimed, killed and tortured countless people and a lot of the time, it was just for fun. He was a madman and the *mates* you mentioned were relatives of those very same people he had cut up, disfigured, tortured and murdered!" She paused and spoke quietly, staring straight at him. "There is no hiding behind lies, Callum, he lived by the sword and died by it."

The red mist had descended and he was getting out of control, "His own brother Lexi, his own brother ramming a knife into his flesh, can you imagine that? What sort of brother is that, Lexi? A loving kind brother? A brother who looks out for his blood? Paul is going to pay and you are the first payment!"

Lexi rushed towards the door but he caught her before she reached it and threw her to the floor. She scrambled on all fours, still trying to get to the door. He grabbed her and held her, even as she struggled to get away, but he was too strong for her. He started slapping her body and face; she raised her hand, trying to protect herself. He sat astride her, holding her arms tight to the floor.

"Don't even think about it, you bastard! I would rather die!"

"That's after I've had my fill of you!" Then he leaned further down to kiss her and she was ready for him as she sunk her teeth into his lip and he hollered in pain. He slapped her round the face three or four times. He could taste the blood in his mouth.

"You fucking bitch!" He shouted angrily as he ripped at her yellow cat suit, pulling the zipper right down at the front. He was tearing and pulling and eventually, the suit came away in his hands. She was wearing pink knickers and pink bra; he could feel his huge erection. He let go of her and started undoing his shirt buttons; as he went to remove it, she attacked. She raked his face with her long sharp nails; he screamed as she dug her nails deep into his face and pulled with all her strength, tearing his face. The pain was unbearable as he tightened his fists and started pummeling her body and face. He reined blows down without mercy, after what seemed like minutes but in fact was more like ten seconds, her face was smashed beyond recognition. She managed to pull her legs up into the fetal position, moaning in agony through cut bleeding mouth and broken teeth. Both her eyes were swelling and closing. It had been her plan, would he really want to have sex with her now.

***

Paul had enjoyed his glass of champagne and the steak and salad lunch. He was sitting at his desk, enjoying a small coffee when his mobile rang.

"Paul, it's Karen. I'm sending the DNA results over in two minutes but wanted to run something by you before I do."

"So, shoot."

"The results for the Den club employees, it's probably nothing but something slightly strange…"

"Well, get to the point then."

"Two of the samples are identical; a man, name of Steven Jones, either he was tested twice, which doesn't seem likely, or someone has put in a false sample."

"Jeeze, Karen! If someone has put in a false DNA sample, they could be the killer, what's happening now?"

"They're checking to establish the name of the person whose sample is missing."

"And how long will that take?"

"I'm not moving from the phone, should be a matter of minutes. As soon as I have the name, I'll call you."

Paul was near to tears, he could soon have the name of the person who killed his special little girl. He held it together and called Callum's mobile, there was no answer. He rang through to the clubs security manager Phil Norris.

"Phil, what time is Callum coming in? I can't get him on his mobile."

"He's off today, not coming in."

"Nobody told me?"

"You'd have to take that up with him, sir."

"Yea sure, Phil, thanks." There was something happening, he could feel it.

Paul rang Phil back.

"Phil, is Callum's girlfriend in?"

"Yea, her name's Mandy. I saw her arrive, she's in the VIP suite. Why?"

"Send her to my office immediately," and he clicked off. He needed family round him, things were happening and he wanted people he could rely on, he needed Callum.

Five minutes later there was a knock at the door.

"Come in."

Mandy entered the office, looking very timid and apprehensive.

"Hello Mandy," he smiled; the young girl looked scared to death. "Don't worry you haven't done anything wrong. Do you know what Callum's doing today? I need to speak with him and he's not answering his phone."

"I don't know," Mandy stammered. "I went round to his apartment earlier and he wasn't in, sorry." Paul could think of no reason why she would lie.

"Okay, that's all." He looked at the new shiny silver phone Mandy had in her hand. "New mobile?"

Mandy smiled, "Yes just got it."

"Okay, you can go back to work now. Oh, if you hear from him, ask him to give me a call immediately."

"Yes, Mr. Bolton," and she quickly left the office.

Paul fiddled with his biro and wished Duke was about, then he welled up again. He sat back in his swivel chair, something was going to break very soon he could feel it, there was something else nagging at him, eating away at him.

His mobile rang; he hoped it was Karen and it was.

"Paul, you're not going to believe this; the missing DNA sample is…"

Time stood still for Paul, he felt as if he was in a trance, as if none of this was really happening.

"Is Callum's," Karen finished dramatically.

Paul registered the name Callum, but he couldn't quite grasp what it might mean. "Callum? Are you sure? I could have sworn he took the test. Could there have been a mix up?"

"I've asked them to double check, should hear soon."

"Call me back." Paul was confused. He pressed an extension on his office phone.

"Phil, Ralph somebody who organised the Polygraph tests, is he in today?"

"I think so. What's going on?"

"You find him and bring him to my office now and I'll need you to stay with me for the rest of the day."

"Sure, Paul," he could smell trouble brewing.

Phil and Ralph Black entered Paul's office a few minutes later.

"Sit down Ralph." Paul had placed a chair right in front of his desk. Phil stood to the side, wondering what the hell was going on.

"You organised the polygraph tests here a few weeks ago?"

"Yes Mr. Bolton." Ralph scratched his chin and loosened his collar.

"You look worried Ralph, is there anything you want to tell me?"

Ralph was turning white. "No, Mr. Bolton"

"The Polygraph, did everybody take the test?"

"As far as I know, yes, Mr. Bolton."

"You are a fucking liar Ralph, I want to know what happened!"

Ralph fell to pieces and started shaking. "He knew where my kids went to school, said he'd torture them, then cut their throats; what could I do? I had to protect my family."

Return to Bermondsey

He started crying, "I'm sorry, I should have come to see you."

"Who was it Ralph? The name!"

Ralph looked up and swallowed hard, "He'll kill me! He's a madman!"

Paul stood up and shouted! "The name Ralph! Now, or so help me, I'll have you killed myself right now!"

"It was Callum, Callum Bolton!"

Paul was flabbergasted. He looked down at the desk, trying to focus on his mobile as he thought, and then it came to him like a bolt of thunder from the sky. He turned and rushed to the door and pulled it open, "Phil come with me!" he ran along the thickly carpeted corridor towards the VIP suite, kicked open the door to the bar and rushed in. He saw her cleaning bottles.

He shouted, "Mandy come here!" She was terrified as she went to him, her eyes round with fright.

Paul was breathing hard, his heart was pounding and he thought he could explode at any moment.

"Give me your new phone!" Mandy took the silver Samsung out of her pocket and handed it to Paul. He flicked it over in his hands, studying it. Phil was more confused than ever. Paul gave Phil his own mobile, his hands were shaking.

"Go to contacts, Katie, call her."

Phil started to grasp what was happening, he got to Katie's name and pressed the green call.

Paul held the phone out looking at it, tears in his eyes. Suddenly, the phone burst into life and started ringing; he had to steady himself to stop himself from collapsing.

"Mandy where did you get this mobile from?"

Mandy was now putting two and two together, she knew it was Katie's phone.

"Mandy! Where did you get the phone from?"

She burst into tears and said between sniffles, "I told you, I went to Callum's apartment this morning. I found it in a box in his clothes cupboard; I thought it was a spare so I took it."

Paul was shaking so much Phil took his arm and led him to a seat. Duke was right all along, Callum, mad father, mad son! That cunt had killed my daughter! God! He would pay! Skinning him alive would be too good for him. Paul stood up and started walking back to his office. He needed to find him and then he stopped. He knew where he was, and the thought filled him with terror!

He looked at his mobile in his hands which had stopped shaking and he pressed speed dial two and it rang.

"I know who killed Katie, it was Callum!"

Paul listened for perhaps five seconds. "He's at the house with Lexi, we're leaving now! See you there!"

Paul's mobile rang, it was Karen, and he didn't bother answering it.

Paul pressed speed dial for Lexi, it rang and rang and rang….

Paul turned to Phil, "Two cars, you me and six shooters! We're leaving in two minutes! Move!"

***

Lexi was lying on the thickly carpeted floor, she was in terrible pain, her mouth hurt so much; she knew she had broken teeth as she had spat some bloodied pieces out of her mouth. Her eyes were closed, she had tried to open them but couldn't. She had heard her mobile ringing and she prayed it was Paul and that he would do something because she hadn't answered. She felt so alone, she felt like no one was going to help her. The maniac Callum, was free to do what he wanted with her. The final humiliation would be if he raped her. She said a silent prayer, hoping he wouldn't. If he started, there was one more thing she would do that might put him off. She closed her mind to everything and sent messages to Paul, *I am in trouble I need you, come and help me Paul, the man who killed our sweet daughter is here, come and kill him. I want to survive, Paul, come as soon as you can.*

***

Karen slowly put the grey phone down. Paul wasn't answering, why the hell was that, she wondered. She now knew it was without question Callum Bolton who had not done a polygraph test at the club. What really incriminated him was the fact that he had substituted DNA from someone called Steven Jones; he was hiding something. She wondered what to do next. Paul wasn't answering because he had other information, He knew Callum was the killer, but where was Callum? She picked up the phone and rang the Den club reception number.

"Paul Bolton please."

"Mr. Bolton has left the club and will not be contactable until tomorrow."

"This is Detective Inspector Karen Foster, who is that?"

"Sharon, Miss Foster, I've seen you at the club before."

"Well Sharon, listen carefully, I'm coming to work with Mr. Bolton in the New Year, we are very close, good friends. Trust me Sharon, I'm only trying to help, where has Mr. Bolton gone?"

There was no answer.

"Sharon please, where has he gone? I must know!"

"Well, I'm not too sure, but I heard he's going to Virginia Water."

"Sharon" the phone had gone dead.

Karen was thinking almost out loud, send an officer to the house to see what if anything was going on. She made an instant decision and picked the phone back up and pressed an extension number.

"Jeff, get tooled up, we're going down to Paul Bolton's house, meet me in the car park in one minute!" She dropped the phone, rushed around her desk, grabbed her coat off the stand, opened the door and rushed for the stairs two at a time.

The police car screeched out of the station, lights flashing and siren, blaring.

"Keep your foot to the floor Jeff, I need to know what the fuck is going on!"

***

Mandy was sitting in the bar, crying. She now knew Callum had almost certainly killed Katie Bolton and the pub landlord at the Blue Anchor. She desperately needed a shower, he had touched her intimately with his hands and his cock. She started to rub and scratch at her arms, she felt dirty. He was evil, pure evil, she hoped they killed him very slowly and very painfully. Half an hour later, one of the bar staff drove her home as she was not in the right state of mind to work.

***

Callum had searched for and found a bottle of whisky and had poured himself a wine glass full. He knocked back half of it, feeling the burning sensation as it hit his throat. He was standing over Lexi, looking down at the pathetic bloodied and smashed face. "Fuck you? I'd rather fuck a dog. I know you can hear me, you slut, you've ruined my fun!" he kicked her hard on the arse, and she moaned.

"What to do with you, that's the question, your face will heal you can get some beautiful new white gleaming teeth," he laughed. "In fact, you'll look better than ever."

His face turned to a sour look, "Uncle Paul will still have his lovely Lexi, unlike me who never even saw his daddy. I was growing in my mother's womb while my daddy was being carved up into pieces by Uncle Paul and his fucking mates." He lifted the glass and drank the remaining whisky.

"First thing we have to do is sit you up," he said as he grabbed her under the arms and lifted her, she was surprisingly heavy for a slim woman. He half threw her onto the sofa and then sat her as upright as he could.

He stood back and smiled, "That's better. Now, we can have a serious talk."

He picked the whisky bottle up from the small side table and refilled his glass and took a sip. She was in her pink knickers and bra and this gave him an idea. He bent down behind her and undid her bra and took it off. Then he pushed her down on the sofa, reached under her and pulled her knickers off. She felt what he was doing and tried to kick out but it was hopeless as she was too weak. She felt him turning her over, slapping and pushing her legs apart. Her arms were on the back of the sofa while she was on her knees her legs apart. She could hear his heavy breathing and smell the whisky on his breath. It was nearly time. She heard him pull his trousers down and then he grasped her tightly with his hands.

"Don't worry Lexi, you're going to love it." He moved forward to enter her and then she peed, it was like a dam bursting as a flood of stinking hot urine shot everywhere as she forced it out as fast as she could. He gasped and retreated back quickly.

"You fucking bitch!" he snarled as he viciously smacked her arse cheeks and worked his way up pummeling her torso with punch after punch; she collapsed sideways onto the soaking wet sofa.

He left her there and went to the kitchen, opened the cupboard under the sink and saw what he was after, extra strong thick bleach. He picked the yellow plastic container up and went back to the lounge.

He unscrewed the cap on the bleach, looked at the moaning figure lying on the sofa.

"And now my dear, we're going to make sure Paul remembers me and my daddy every time he looks at your ugly face." He then grabbed Lexi's face and turned it upwards; he laughed as he lifted the bleach.

***

Paul had tried Lexi's mobile and the house phone three times each, there was no answer to either. He was worried sick, all he could think about was what he would do to Callum. Lenny was driving at breakneck speed whenever he could; they had joined the M3 and were now only fifteen minutes away.

***

Lexi was still praying, the pain all over her body was terrible, she thought she had broken ribs as every time she drew in a breathed, the pain was terrible. She was thankful she was still alive and he hadn't raped her. She knew she would get over the wounds as long as he didn't hurt her any more. She was listening; she heard his footsteps and now he had left the room. She wondered where he had gone and why. She thought of Katie and tears filled her damaged swollen eyes. If only she could do something; she tried moving her legs and terrible pains shot through her body; it was hopeless, she couldn't move. Now, she could hear him coming back; she heard a swagger in his steps, almost like a skip. She turned her face so she could see him and noticed something in his hand. Then she shuddered when she saw a yellow bottle of strong bleach in his hand, which he must have taken from the kitchen cupboard; that's where he had been. She started crying; she knew he was going to pour bleach on her face and maybe even make her swallow some. She would have screamed if she was able to. She tried to push herself up to a sitting position, trying to get off the sofa.

"What the fuck are you doing, bitch?" He smashed his fist into her stomach. She doubled up in more agony and looked up at the bastard as he unscrewed the cap, lifted the bleach, and then she heard a voice, a different voice. She could have sworn she had heard a voice, a strong voice, a familiar voice in the room! She slowly turned her face to the door, and there he was! He was standing there! She was so happy but also very worried. She prayed for God to give him strength.

***

Karen Foster had a long way to travel across London to get to Virginia Water. The lights and siren made all the difference and they hit the M3; only a few miles to go and Jeff was driving at one hundred and twenty miles per hour.

***

"Don't do it Callum," the voice was calm but menacing.

Callum froze; he still had the bleach in his hand as he turned towards the door.

"You!" He was shocked, he turned fully and slowly put the bleach down on the small side table close to him.

"You're meant to be in Las Vegas?" Callum glanced around slowly, looking for some sort of weapon, there was nothing close by. He would have to rely on his karate.

"I didn't go in the end, your man at Heathrow failed," Oliver said, looking tensed and alert, ready to spring into action at any second.

Callum was slowly moving towards Oliver as he kept talking; he didn't know whether he had a weapon or not.

"Actually it was one of Kevin Philips men, shame he messed up but now you're here I can finish the job," said Callum and then he moved like lightning and attacked, his arms chopping blows at Oliver's face and torso. Oliver hadn't done martial arts and backed away trying to defend himself as best he could. Callum was quick; he shot a leg out and caught Oliver on the knee and as Oliver went down, Callum followed that up with a vicious right fist punch to the neck and another left to the jaw. Oliver knew he was losing and if he wasn't careful, the lunatic would get the better of him. He backed away down the hall, pushing away the punches and kicks raining down on him from every angle. He grabbed a vase on a stand and threw it at him, Callum ducked and hit the vase with his fist, shattering it into a million pieces.

"You're a fool Oliver! You think you could come here and take me! You were dreaming boy and I'm going to kill you and then finish your mother off!"

He attacked again a whirlwind of karate chops and kicks, Oliver tried to get in close but was beaten back. He was still backing away, gasping for breath, getting tired, a fist hit him in the kidney and pain shot up his body. Another kick landed on the side of his head, knocking him flying. His head bounced off the wall and he felt a little dizzy but was up quickly and back on his feet. He looked for an opening and launched himself forward at Callum and got him in a bear hug. He then brought his head back and head butted him viciously on the bridge of his nose. Blood flew in every direction and Callum stumbled backwards for the first time. Oliver seized the opportunity and rained in kicks and punches, but Callum, though floored, managed to push himself forward, reached over and hit Oliver full in the middle of his chest with all his strength. It was like being hit with a sledge hammer; Oliver reeled and he couldn't breathe and then he collapsed in a heap. Callum laughed and rubbed his hands together. He took hold of Oliver's collar and dragged him along the hall back to the lounge and through the doorway and dropped his head, it bounced on the carpet and he turned round. He saw the weapon in the hand of Paul Bolton and watched as it seemed to arc through the air and then there was blackness and nothing.

***

There was laughter and joking, Lexi was sitting up in the bed of her private room at Frimley Park Hospital in Camberley. Paul opened the champagne and the cork flew through the air. Detective Inspector Karen Foster and Detective Sargent Jeff Swan were on one side of the bed. On the other was Oliver who was holding his mum's hand. Paul filled the glasses and passed them round.

"Shhhh," Paul shushed and everybody stopped laughing. Paul held his glass up, "To life, and my wife coming home with me tomorrow!" Tears of joy and sadness rolled down his cheeks.

***

He woke up and opened his eyes, there was nothing but bright whiteness. Just for a second, he wondered if he was in heaven. He tried to move his arms but couldn't, then he looked down and could just see the leather straps around his wrists; he couldn't move his legs either. He turned his face, white walls, a white floor, then he looked up, white ceiling. Everything was so bright he shut his eyes and shook his head, then it came to him slowly, the blow on the head. He was in hospital for sure. He heard a noise, it was the door opening; he turned and saw what he assumed was an older male Chinese nurse.

"Where am I?"

"Don't worry sir, you'll be put on medication soon and then you can join the other patients."

Thank God for that, thought Callum.

"That's good but you haven't answered my question. Where am I?"

"You're Callum Bolton, aren't you?"

Callum was losing patience, "Yes, I am so…"

"I remember your father Tony."

Callum was shocked but pleased.

"A long time ago and he was in this room as well, on that same bed as you are now. Funny that, don't you think?"

Callum closed his eyes and smiled, what a wonderful feeling; daddy had been on this actual bed.

"So I'm in …"

"Yes Mr. Bolton, you're in Broadmoor high security psychiatric Hospital"

"What's your name please?"

"Kevin Bond, Mr. Bolton."

"Well Kevin, perhaps later you could show me where my daddy used to sit and maybe I could even have his old room?"

"I'm sure we can arrange something Mr. Bolton, after all you're going to be here a very, very long time."

THE END

OTHER TITLES AVAILABLE FROM AUTHOR CHRIS WARD @ amazon books

SERIAL KILLER: DI KAREN FOSTER BOOK 1

http://tinyurl.com/p5ld9dx

BLUE COVER UP: DI KAREN FOSTER BOOK 2

http://tinyurl.com/mzy5f2f

DRIVEN TO KILL: DI KAREN FOSTER BOOK 3

http://tinyurl.com/p8f9c4w

THE BERMONDSEY THRILLER TRILOGY

BERMONDSEY TRIFLE BOOK 1

http://amzn.to/1l3B3up

BERMONDSEY PROSECCO BOOK 2

http://tinyurl.com/nebwtys

BERMONDSEY THE FINAL ACT BOOK 3

http://tinyurl.com/nbuahoj

visit www.authorchrisward.com

18560045R00172

Printed in Great Britain
by Amazon